Sa

BRIAN K. VAUGHAN
WRITER

FIONA STAPLES
ARTIST

FONOGRAFIKS
LETTERING + DESIGN

IMAGE COMICS, INC.

ROBERT KIRKMAN CHIEF OPERATING OFFICER | **ERIK LARSEN** CHIEF FINANCIAL OFFICER | **TODD MCFARLANE** PRESIDENT
MARC SILVESTRI CHIEF EXECUTIVE OFFICER | **JIM VALENTINO** VICE-PRESIDENT | **ERIC STEPHENSON** PUBLISHER/CHIEF CREATIVE OFFICER
COREY HART DIRECTOR OF SALES | **JEFF BOISON** DIRECTOR OF PUBLISHING PLANNING & BOOK TRADE SALES
CHRIS ROSS DIRECTOR OF DIGITAL SALES | **JEFF STANG** DIRECTOR OF SPECIALTY SALES | **KAT SALAZAR** DIRECTOR OF PR & MARKETING
DREW GILL ART DIRECTOR | **HEATHER DOORNINK** PRODUCTION DIRECTOR | **NICOLE LAPALME** CONTROLLER

WWW.IMAGECOMICS.COM

BOOK THREE

ga™

CHAPTER THIRTY-SEVEN

Families are goddamn wildfires.

They may start out small, but brother, watch them grow.
God, I love her little snores.
I love the way she ***drools.***
Marko, we need to tell her.

Says who? I mean, **our** daughter is hardy as shit.
I'm beginning to think all that stuff we were taught about birth defects in *"hybrids"* was just more propaganda to keep our people apart.

I certainly hope so, love.
But Hazel's still processing how to be part of this family again...
All the more reason to give her time to prepare for the **next** big plot twist.

Five years old and she's already pulled off something I never did.
My little girl's going to be a big sister.

We are so fucking lucky.
No.
You're **spectacular**, and I'm just...

...orange?
My family and our newest house guests were in the middle of a long journey to our next potential safe harbor.

Whoever said "getting there is half the fun" was a complete asshole.

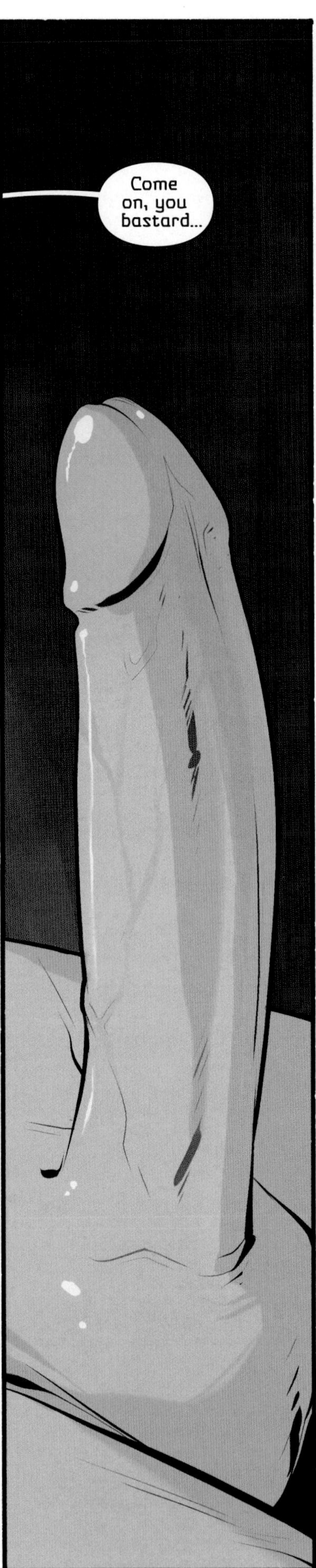
Come on, you bastard...

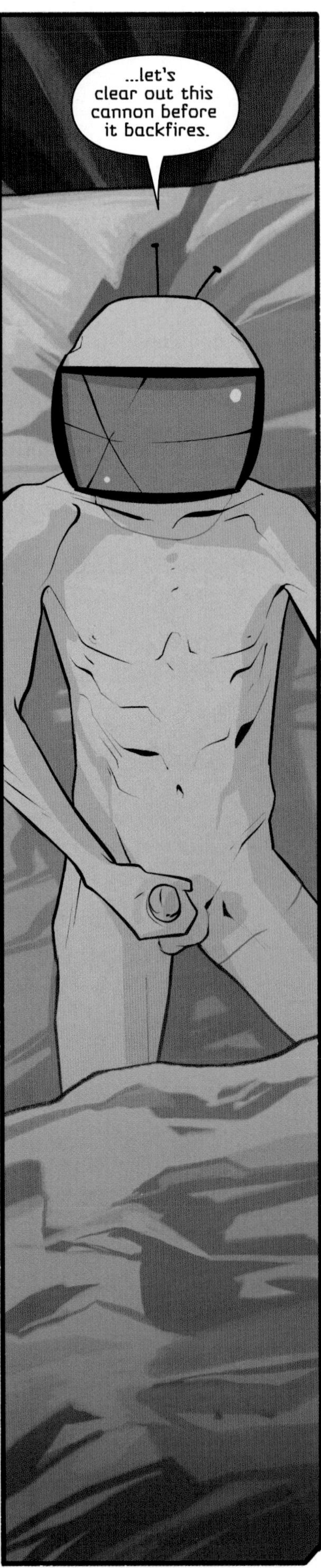
...let's clear out this cannon before it backfires.

That's the stuff...
nff
...sorry, dearest.
Mm, not today...
...almost...
...yes...
...fucking fuck yes...
...look me in the eye, you dirty...

GHH

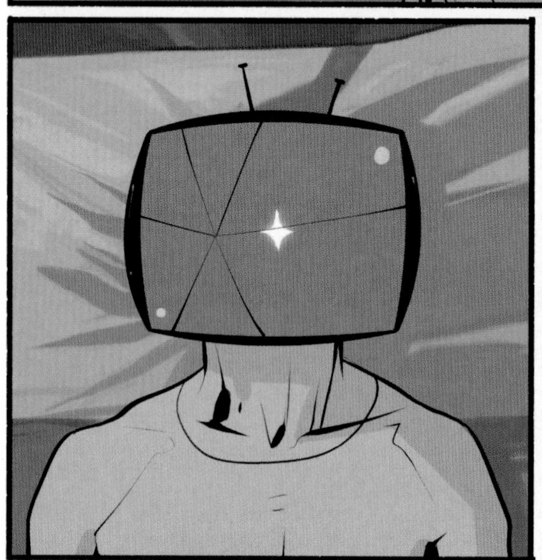

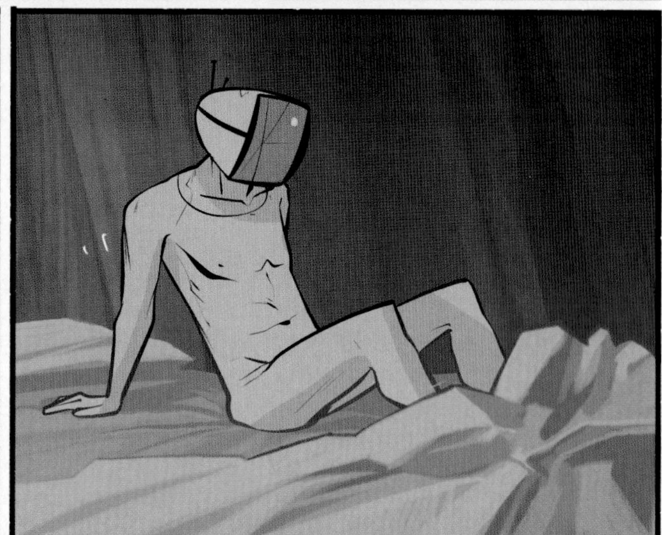

What is **wrong** with me?
There had been a time when Sir Robot had wanted nothing more than to kill both of my parents with his bare hands.

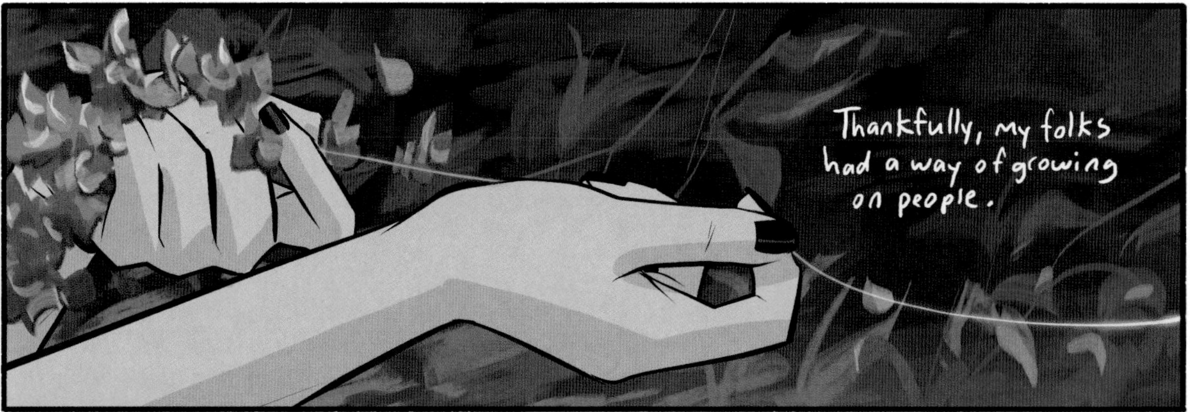
Thankfully, my folks had a way of growing on people.

Some of them, anyway.
Boo.
Get lost, Izabel.
I'm busy *"earning my keep"* for our new prison wardens.

Another romper for the kid?
How about some nice *maternity gear* for her mom, Petrichor?

I didn't study armory for five years so I could dress a filthy ***Landfallian***.
I'm grateful for the ride, but I hope Alana and that prissy ***drone*** of hers both get sucked out a hull breach.

Besides, everyone's first priority should be the **child**.
It's obvious she's still missing her grandmother... **all** her friends from the detention center.
And so am I, but little kids are way more adaptable than the rest of us. Trust me, I've been sitting for Hazel since she was a newborn. She'll be copacetic.

And do you think she's told the others of my... identity?
What, that you happen to be trans?
Who even cares, Petri?

You have no idea.

You'd be surprised what I know.
And Hazel's had to keep the truth about her **own** body a secret pretty much since she popped. The girl understands the value of privacy.
Do **you**, ghostie?

Lady, does it **look** like I give a shit what anybody's got going on below the waist?

Right.
Forgive me, but if your kind can shift into any shape you want, I struggle to understand why you choose... that.
Because, this is how I looked the last time I drew breath.

Plus, I got this sweet shirt at the final show before Pyrosis broke up.

You were alive to see Pyrosis?!

Ah, crappers.
Never good when this place goes all mood lighting.
You guys, come quick!

Sounds like something real bad is happening!

What have you sex criminals ruined this time?

One of those goddamn fuel arteries we plugged over Landfall must have sprung a *leak*. We're suddenly coasting on fumes.
But... my son.
We still have **light years** to go before we reach Squire. What the hell are we supposed to do?

If I toss our spent crash helm into the furnace, it should generate just enough thrust to get us into the next system.
Unfortunately, there's nothing there but a couple of sad little protostars.

True, there are no **planets** to land on.
But if we time things right, we may be able to hitch a ride on a **comet**.

No. No way I'm taking my child to that *meat grinder*.
Is she seriously suggesting we stop to refuel on...?
Phang.
Nothing in the universe was safe from the endless war between mom's planet and dad's moon...

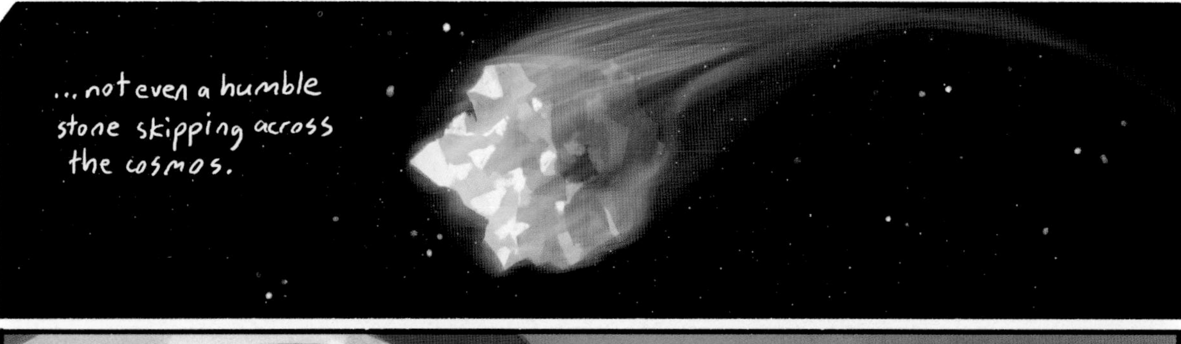
...not even a humble stone skipping across the cosmos.

PHANG, an exotic land of boundless diversity, home to thousands of different tribes, sects, and species...
...almost all of whom despised each other.

Their fractious world was brought to order by either a duly elected president or a strong-arm dictator, depending who you asked.

A violent insurrection inevitably rose up, and the interstellar community was forced to choose between a government and its people.

As always, the wings and the horns were happy to take sides.

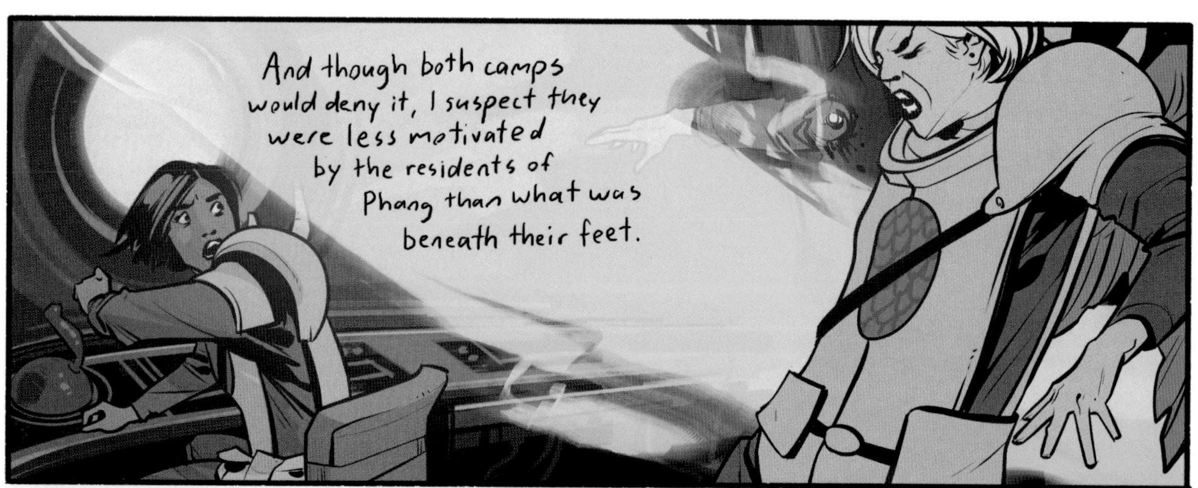
And though both camps would deny it, I suspect they were less motivated by the residents of Phang than what was beneath their feet.

Whether you rely on magic or science, your ass can't get anywhere without FUEL, which this old comet had in spades.

Over the years, wave after wave of young soldiers gave their lives to ensure that their enemies never seized control of this mother lode.

The locals had a pretty rough go of it, too.

Its infrastructure in shambles, Phang was left with only one real export...

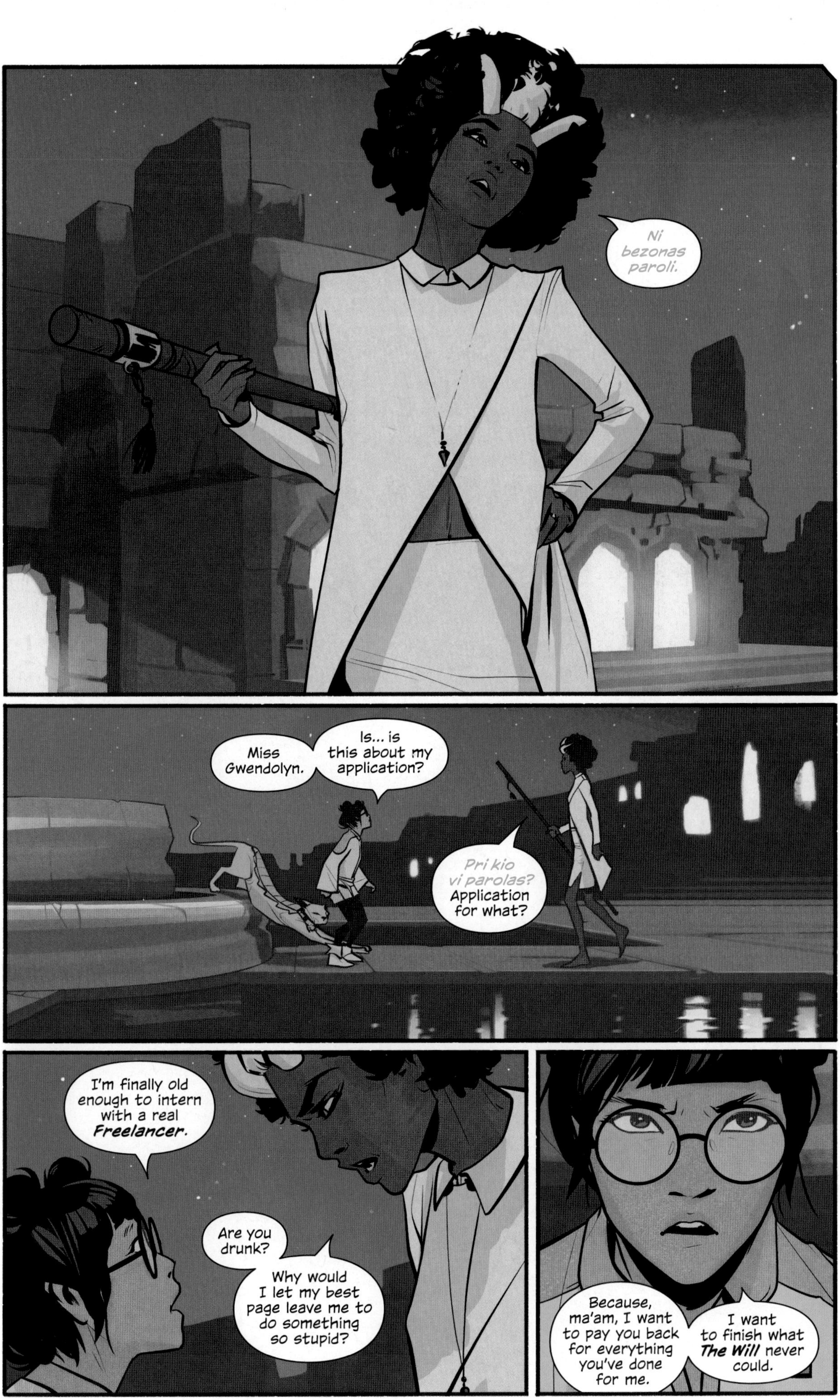

Ni bezonas paroli.

Soph, you're barely ten years old.

And I've already saved up enough to start paying my union dues.

If you let me learn from a professional, I know I could take care of your evil ex-boyfriend.

You're a sweet girl.

But I'm done thinking about Marko and whatever ***litter*** he's made with his dog.

But the rest of this moon isn't!

The whole reason you haven't gotten a better job in Wreath High Command yet is because of your past with that ***traitor***.

It's not that simple, Sophie.

LYIN--

--GHH?

Look, Vez assures me that the single best contract killer working today already picked up where The Will left off.
Then let me help!
Please, I know the way abusive creeps like Marko think, and I could --

Sophie, I'm not here about *my* past.
I need to ask you about your family.

But, they were all killed or... or abducted like me.
You're sure?
Because if you have so much as a distant cousin still left on that comet, you need to tell them to leave immediately.

Why now, Gwendolyn?
I mean, it's not like life could get any *worse* on Phang.

Gwendolyn...?

That's the last of the exotic matter.
It's now or never.
We should be able to break Phang's atmosphere on inertia, but the old girl's only got enough left in the tank to fire her landing thrusters.

Landing *where*, exactly?
This entire hellhole is an active theater of war!
Not the towns your cowardly *"Coalition"* already turned to rubble.

I beg your bloody pardon.
She's not wrong.
My unit fought in ***Rideout City***, and there's nothing left of that place but bombed-out old buildings and mass graves.

Are we moving somewhere new?
Just a quick pit stop, little goob.
Every new world we visited was an adventure.

And few adventures ended worse than this one.

Marko and I will make sure the ship's taken root.
The rest of you stay with Hazel.
Splendid, I'll be cheering for your demise right here.

Hold up, family man.
What are you --

No point in you being tip of this spear.

Goddammit, Petrichor!
Wait!

Relax, dye job.
There's nothing out here but ash and --
Hello?

Are... are you folks missionaries?

La malriĉa knabo.
Don't be scared, son.
What's your name, big guy?

I'm **Kurti**.
And I'm... I'm real hungry, please.
Oh, honey. Come with us, we've got some food inside.

Enough for all of us?
"Us?"

My family.

CHAPTER
THIRTY-EIGHT

TAAAAINTS.
WE'RE COMING... TO EAT... YOUR TAINTS.

What madness is this?!
The battle-fallen!
They've risen from their graves!

I'm not so sure, Uncle.
Kurti, get away from them!
These undead... I can't hear the **songs** their weapons usually sing.

I think it's just a ***trick***.

CRAP.
SORRY, BOSS.

No fooling the fine folks of Phang.

"Taints?"
What in the world are --
It was a good effort, Izabel.

Really?
Because it seems to me your immaterial queef of a pet continues to serve precisely zero purpose.

Says the dude who does nothing but jerk off in his room all day?
You... you dare to **spy** on my personal quarters?
Nope, but I'll consider that confirmation of my grossest suspicions.

I don't understand.
Wings and horns and ghosts and androids... working together?
Fucking *hardly*.

You people must be part of that death cult.
The Last Revolution?
We're not terrorists, sir. My wife and I are ***conscientious objectors***.

Like hell.
They're a couple of craven deserters masquerading as peacemongers.
Finally, something Rabbit Ears and I agree on.

I mean no disrespect, but we don't really care ***who*** you are.
Our homes were destroyed, and we've been wandering this land for ages.
Please, all we need is a little ***water***.

Oh, we got lots of sinks and potties and stuff in our tree!
Can I show them, Daddy?

Of course, my heart.

Marko--
These are innocent people displaced by an evil war. They're **us**.
You really want to turn them away in front of our daughter?

I really want Hazel to **survive**, which means getting out of this quagmire as soon as possible.
And we will.
But that doesn't mean we can't share what provisions we have while our rocket finishes refueling.

This comet's soil is rich with energy, so it shouldn't take long at all.
If there's one thing parents suck at, it's estimating how long any activity is going to take.

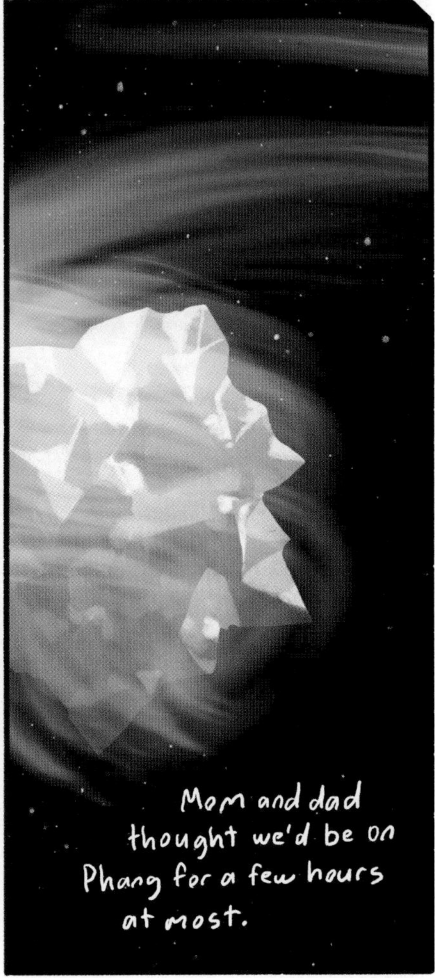
Mom and dad thought we'd be on Phang for a few hours at most.

We were there for six months.
Nizar! Ghada! Elif!
Finish your dinners or I will absolutely finish them for you!

Until everything went to shit, they were some of the best times my family and I ever spent together.
And I want to see you kids eat your veggies... especially because that's basically all we have.
Madam Alana!

A gift for you, my dear girl.
To celebrate the coming of your precious boy.

In my culture, this bracelet is to be worn until the day your son is born.
It's beautiful, Jabarah. But Marko and I actually don't *know* the sex of --
Trust me, I can tell by the way you carry him low in your belly.

Well, I'm pretty sure that's just all the jam cakes I've been shoveling into my fat face... but thank you.
Nonsense, it is we who owe you everything.

I know your treehouse would have been able to leave weeks ago had it not also been tasked with providing for my tribe.

Our tribe.

Any news from the front?
The nearest battle rages on... but still dozens of clicks from here.
Our position remains secure, at least for now.

Hazel isn't with you?
No, she's catching thunder beetles with one of her new playmates.
Why?

Because I'm more concerned with the enemies in our midst than the ones out there.

Look, I know Sir Robot can be a pain in the ass --
I don't give a good goddamn about the drone.
I'm talking about the clan of beasts you people have stupidly aligned with.

That's what my old platoon and I thought when we first encountered their kind out here.
Petrichor, those people are saints.
We couldn't have asked for a better group to be stuck with.
And then one of them blew themselves up at a checkpoint, killed three of my best men.

If my wife has taught me anything, it's that there's no such thing as *"their kind."*
You can't judge an entire race of people based on the actions of --
Yes, I'm well aware of your naïve beliefs.

I just hope I'm gone by the time you find out how wrong you've been.

Kill another!

Ha, okay, Kurti.
I'm just trying to remember how to spell this one. *Um...*

Eksplodis!

Whoa!
That fat one blew up real good!
Young lady!

What in the world are you doing?

Don't use your angry voice.
It doesn't scare me.

I'm not angry, I'm disappointed.
You're hurting innocent creatures? For laughs?
They're just bugs.

We... we can fix 'em, Miss Izabel.
You can't "*fix*" death, Kurti. It's --
God, just shut up!

Hey.
You're my baby-sitter, not my boss.
Why can't you ever leave me alone?
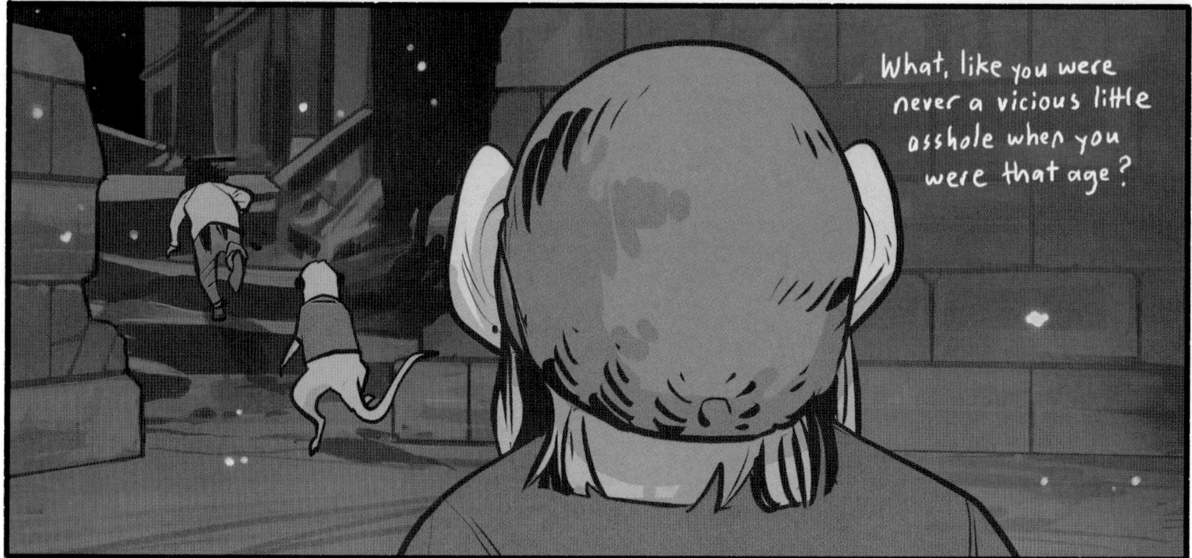
What, like you were never a vicious little asshole when you were that age?

As my mother used to say, "*Kids is a drag.*"

No offense, but Queen Robot sounds like a ***cunt***.
Mn.
A beheadable-yet-fair assessment.

What's with the getup?
Squire's birthday is in less than a week, and I have no intention of missing it. So I've decided to take matters into my own hands.
Thanks to your employers, my only son has been left in the care of a mentally deficient seal lad for far too long.

The Robot Kingdom has an old ***embassy*** on the other side of Phang.
It was abandoned as conditions here worsened, but if any fuel reserves were left behind, I may be able to pilfer enough to finally launch us out of this slough.

But, you'll have to cross like a trillion warzones to get there.
What choice do I have, phantom?

I could go.

I appreciate the gesture, but how the hell would you even be able to carry anything back?
I wouldn't, but at least let me act as your **advance team**.
No point risking your neck over stuff that might have already been looted from this joint.

You would do that for me?
No, I'd do it for Hazel.
For her parents.

I will never understand why you're so loyal to people who have essentially forced you into indentured servitude.
Dude, I'm the first person in my family who ever got to leave the rock where I was born.
As far as I'm concerned, Marko and Alana have wildly overpaid for my services. They've treated me like their flesh and blood.

They showed me the universe.

While my family enjoyed the world's longest pit stop, the various forces that wanted us dead were still hard at work.

Some harder than others.
BING BA DING

RRRRR
Knock it off, Sweet Boy.
I get she ain't your favorite cat, but --

Ĉu mi povas helpi vin?

Who are you?
Kiu mi estas?
You're the creep showing up on my doorstep speaking Language.

Apologies. Name's The Will.

A Freelancer? If this is about military garbage, you're probably looking for my mother.
Actually, I'm trying to get in touch with a gal named Gwendolyn. You know her?

Rather well.
She's my wife.

Huh.

Anyway, Missus...
Velour.
Missus Velour, I was hoping your, *uh*, better half could tell me where to find a girl named **Sophie**. I left an old Sidekick of mine with her and --

Gwen and her page are in Ĉefurbo for the week.
They're on High Command business.
What **kind** of business?

None of yours.

ARF ARF
Ahh, shut up.

THE
ROYAL EMBASSY
TRESPASSERS WILL
BE EXECUTED

Anybody home?
SNRRT

HRRNG

A grizzly boar?
What are you doing so far from home, little guy?
Funny.

Just about to ask you the same thing.

The hell are you two?
They call us ***The March***.
And Bootstraps here has got a knack for tracking down fellow creatures native to Cleave.

Oh. Is this about my unpaid student loans?
I'm not interested in ***you***, Horror.
I'm looking for a P.O.W. who escaped your home world, a Wreath foot soldier named ***Marko***.

Never heard of him.
Then how'd you end up on Phang? Your kind can only leave home if ***soul-bound*** to a beating heart...
...like one belonging to a newborn ***child***.

Sorry, fellas, I hitched a ride here with a nutty old spinster looking for company.
I'm headed back her way now, but if there's a ***reward*** for your guy, we'll definitely keep an eye out for --

NAHHH!

How...?
You ghouls aren't as untouchable as you like to think.
But quit your lying and tell us where Marko and his accomplices are hiding, and I swear we'll let you go.

And if I tell you I still don't know what the fuck you're talking about?

Then we run you through with ***this***.
And there's no coming back from our kind of killing, so choose your next words carefully.

Please, I... I don't want to die ***again***.
I'll tell you every-thing.

Should I address the ugly bitch or the uglier bitch?

Your loss.

Every night, Izabel would say the same thing as she tucked me in.
"Be a good girl tomorrow... but not TOO good."

No babysitter sticks around forever...

...but the best ones never really leave you, do they?

end chapter thirty-eight

CHAPTER THIRTY-NINE

Reach for the sky... or I'm gonna war-crime you in the *face*.

Whoa.
Where'd you get the rifle, Kurti?

I was picking berries out by the berm and found this in the grasses.
Is it real?
I think so, but I can't get the thing to shoot. Must be out of ammo.

Can I see it?
Pretty please?
Only if you give me a turn with the sky goggles you took off that dead soldier.

Deal.
No fair, I'm the one who told you about that moon lady's body!

Huh, it's a lot lighter than I thought it would --
bedeep

BRAKOOM

HEY!

What the fuck is ***wrong*** with you kids?!

Missus Alana said a cuss.

Sorry, ma'am!
A BL-48 is not a toy.
You could have killed yourselves... or worse, ***me.***

Have ***you*** shot one of those before?
Not in a long time.
But my jerk of a drill sergeant made me sleep with one in Basic.

Don't remember a thing I learned in twelve years of geography, but I can still field-strip one of these blindfolded.

Are... are you gonna tell our grand-mother what we did?
That depends. How are those little hands of yours at massaging swollen feet and --
HELP!

Hazel.

Somebody help me!

What's the matter, honey girl?
Don't tell me my bedtime stories gave her nightmares **again**.

It's Izabel.
I... I can't feel her anymore. I think she's **gone**.
I'm sure she's just helping your mom with the other kids.

Er.
D. OSWALD HEIST
LET'S DO LUST
LET'S DO LUST
HEIST

What the hell have you done, Robot?

What one of you indolent comet-lovers should have done ages ago.
I merely suggested that someone might check my embassy for reserves of **fuel**, and your specter offered to run reconnaissance.
You sent our babysitter on a suicide mission?

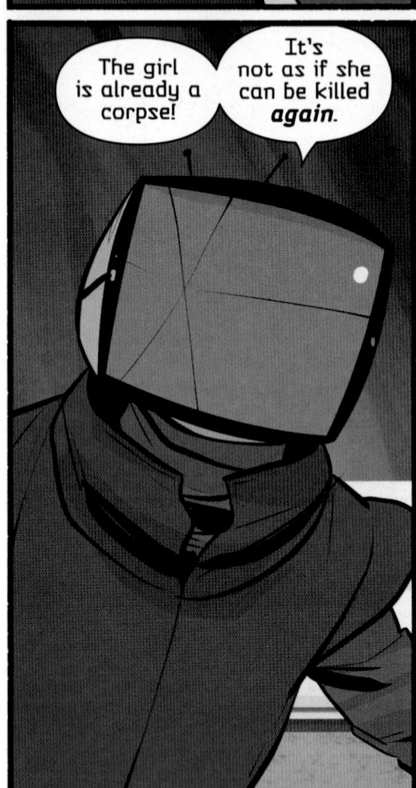
The girl is already a corpse!
It's not as if she can be killed ***again***.

Can she...?
Sooner or later, every last echo fades.
Even the loudest thunder in the deepest valley.

I was mean to her.
I was mean to her and now she's ***dead***.

Hazel, this isn't the first time we've... *misplaced* Izabel.
Daddy's already tracked her down once before, and if I could rescue her from that *egg-planet* before it hatched, I can certainly find her here.

Your family witnessed the birth of a *Timesuck*?
Phang nearly collided with one several winters ago, but the blessings from above protected --
You people are welcome to listen to another of Jabarah's endless sermons, but I'm off to find the ghost girl.

You're coming with?
No, Marko, I'm going *instead*.
You're a wanted man, and the ground between here and the drone's consulate is largely controlled by the same army you *deserted*.

Petrichor, you served just as many tours out here as I did.
What'll you say if you run into a soldier who recognizes you?

I don't think that will be an issue.

FUMO
DOMO

kbzzt
kbzzt

Who's this?
Your **agent**, The Will.
You remember what one of those is, right?

Erving. Listen, I'm still on **Wreath**, chasing down some personal stuff between gigs.
You haven't taken a "gig" in months. And don't think the union hasn't noticed.

As soon as I finish up here, I'll get back to that high-roller job, those enemy creeps with the ***baby***.
That target isn't even a baby anymore, you old fart.
And the moonies' High Command transferred that assignment to a "better-reviewed Freelancer."

Who, The Fluke? The Lights?
Not those psychopaths The March?!

And worse, our insurance guy says you failed your last drug test.
For a little Fadeaway? But, I kicked everything harder! I swear on my --
Sorry to have to break it to you like this, pal.

You're fired.
Hej, dikulo!

Via speco ne bonvena.

They **shitcanned** me? Erv, we gotta appeal!
You're welcome to try, but it'll have to be with a different rep. I decided to close up shop.
You're shutting down the whole agency?!

What can I say? It's a lousy time for our line of work.
Mi parolas al vi!

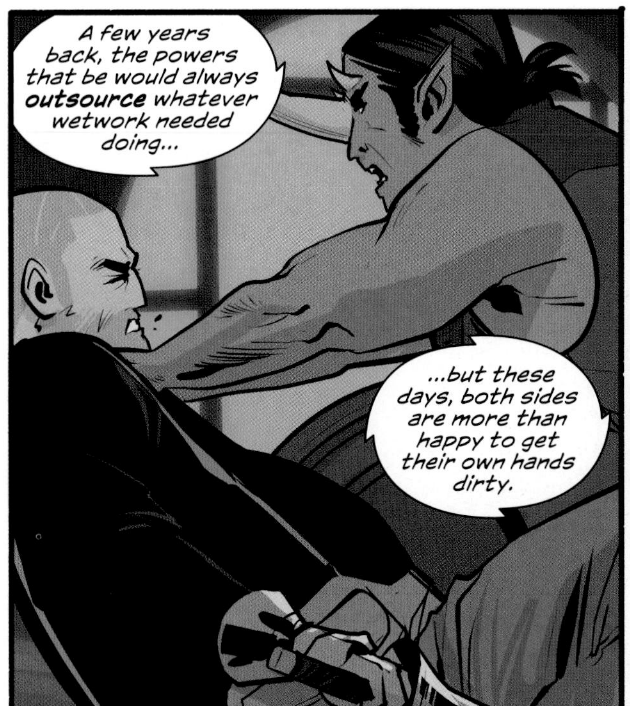
A few years back, the powers that be would always **outsource** whatever wetwork needed doing...
...but these days, both sides are more than happy to get their own hands dirty.

bzzzt
I mean, the average schmuck on the street doesn't care **what** nightmares his leaders are green-lighting anymore, right?

All he's thinking about is his next vacation, and frankly, so am I.
...my... fucking... *lance*...

Oh, and your weapon was ***deauthorized*** as soon as the union removed you from the database.
You're no longer cleared to legally terminate individuals...

...so careful what neighborhoods you end up in, okay?

hng
SSNAP!
GRAHH!
Mia brako!
...can't believe... I ever shared **ten percent**... with your worthless ass...
Gotta jet, but I wish you the best with your future, The Wi...
I mean, I wish you the best, **Billy**.

Hi, Hazel.
Um, I'm supposed to be at nighttime prayers now, but I wanted to say hi to you.
Okay.

I heard your sitter was, like, missing.
Do... do you think she's all right?

Uh-uh.

Oh.
Sorry about that.
Kurti, do you believe in Paradise?

Like, where we go after we die?
Sure, that's where my mom and dad and big sister are.
So what... what do you think it's like?

Dunno.
A lot like here, I guess... but you just get to never be dead.

Why, what do *you* think?
That it's all just a fakey story they tell. Like the Feather Fairy.
The heck is a Feather Fairy?

When I was real little, I got scared the first time one of my feathers fell out. Like, too scared to tell anyone but Izabel.
But she said it was *lucky*. She said that the Feather Fairy would trade me ***treasure*** for every feather I put under my pillow.

You got real treasure?
Not even.
The most I ever got was a few stupid marbles.

The Feather Fairy gave you marbles?!
Don't be dumb, Kurti.
Izabel put that stuff under my pillow. When I was asleep.
But --
There are no fairies. It's just like Paradise, another made-up lie they tell us so we won't be scared.
But we should be. We should be scared...
Yeah, but, how could Izabel put something under a pillow?
I mean, ghosts can't even touch stuff, right?
...sorry I called you dumb.
I'm gonna kiss you now, okay?
On the mouth?

In the beginning, love is mostly
about lying to each other.

It's like that in the end, too.
For the record, I hate this plan.
I promise you, I'll be fine out there.
At least let **me** accompany you. I could pretend to be your captor.

That fake prisoner gag never works. Who'd believe one of your kind would take someone ***alive***?
No, smartest to travel alone. If anyone stops me, I'll say I'm a widow looking for my husband's remains. Certainly wouldn't be the first.

If you're really going to do this for us, Petri, at least do it armed.
Please, I'd sooner die than be caught carrying one of your useless shit-sticks.
And knowing these savages, you might need it.

Remember, you have the future to think about.

And you've surrounded yourself with people who think only of the past.

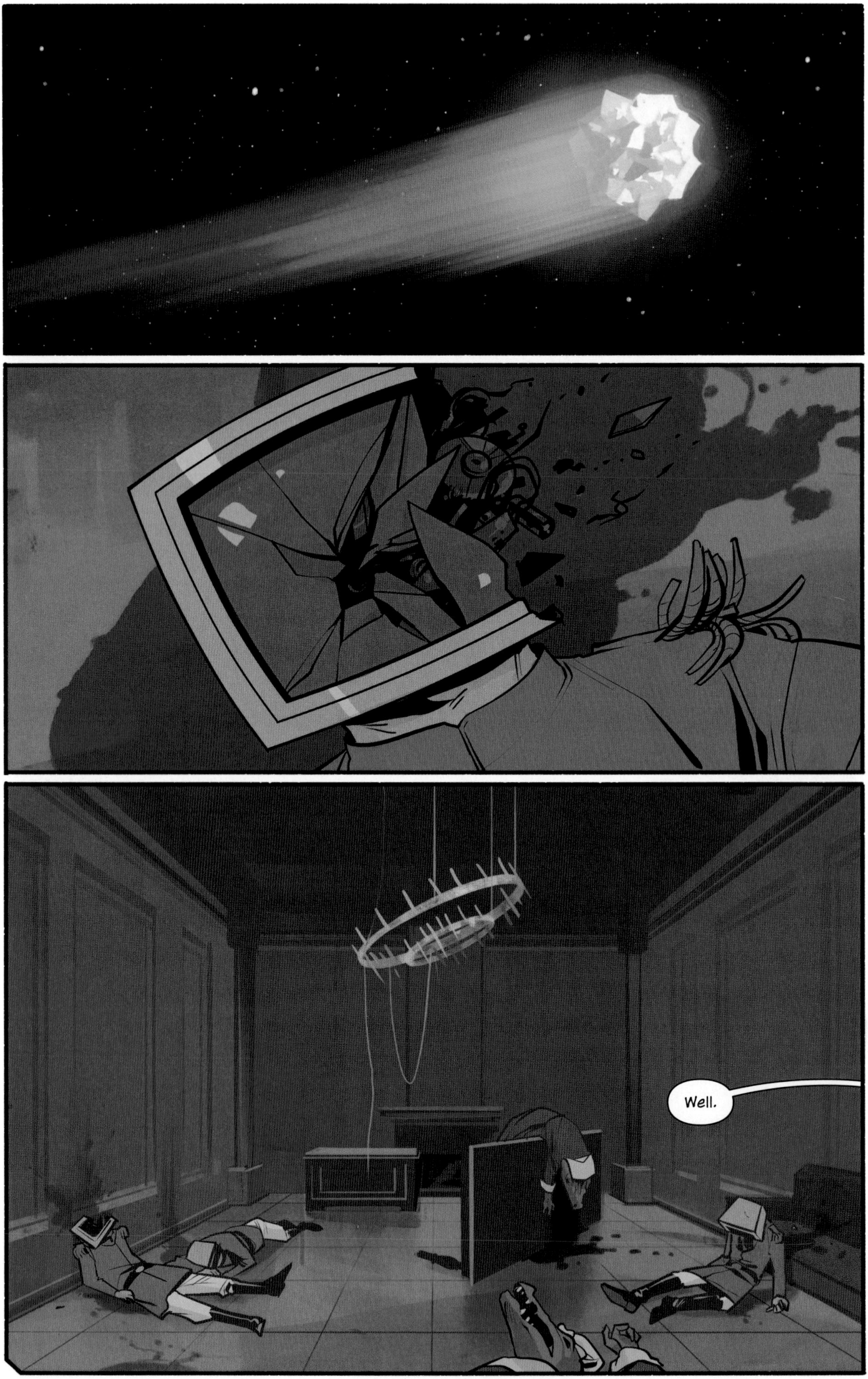

Well.

Doesn't look like a *magical* attack.
I'm not sure it was. These wounds were all caused by *android cannons*.
HRNGH

An inside job?
Who the fuck shoots up their own embassy?
Pardon me, my good man.

Would you be so kind as to find the bottle of *Juniperus* in my top drawer?
I'd prefer to taste something other than my own bile before I expire.

Ambassador Robot, I presume.
We'd be honored to pour your last round... as soon as you tell us exactly what happened here.
Hmf, always a bloody cost with you mercenary types, isn't there?

Wow, our grandfather used to drink this piss.
Sir, we're just curious if this bloodbath might have anything to do with our current targets.

Oh, this is much, **much** larger than whatever unlucky bastards you're after.

My staff and I recently uncovered some rather shocking news that we intended to share with our hosts here on Phang.
But there was a... ***disagreement*** with our colleagues in the Royal Guard over whether or not this was the most prudent course of action.
If you're looking to spill your guts about something, your body's way ahead of you.

I'm afraid it's far too late to do anything with what I learned.
The plan is already well underway.
What plan?

They intend to exterminate every living creature on this comet.

Who the hell is "they?"
Your people... or the wings?
Or are you talking about the horns?
"Or?"
HA HA HA HA HA HA!
hah
...Mother?
Apologies, a fatal exception has occurred.
Dammit.

I'd always wanted to see how these freaks drink.

end chapter thirty-nine

CHAPTER

FORTY

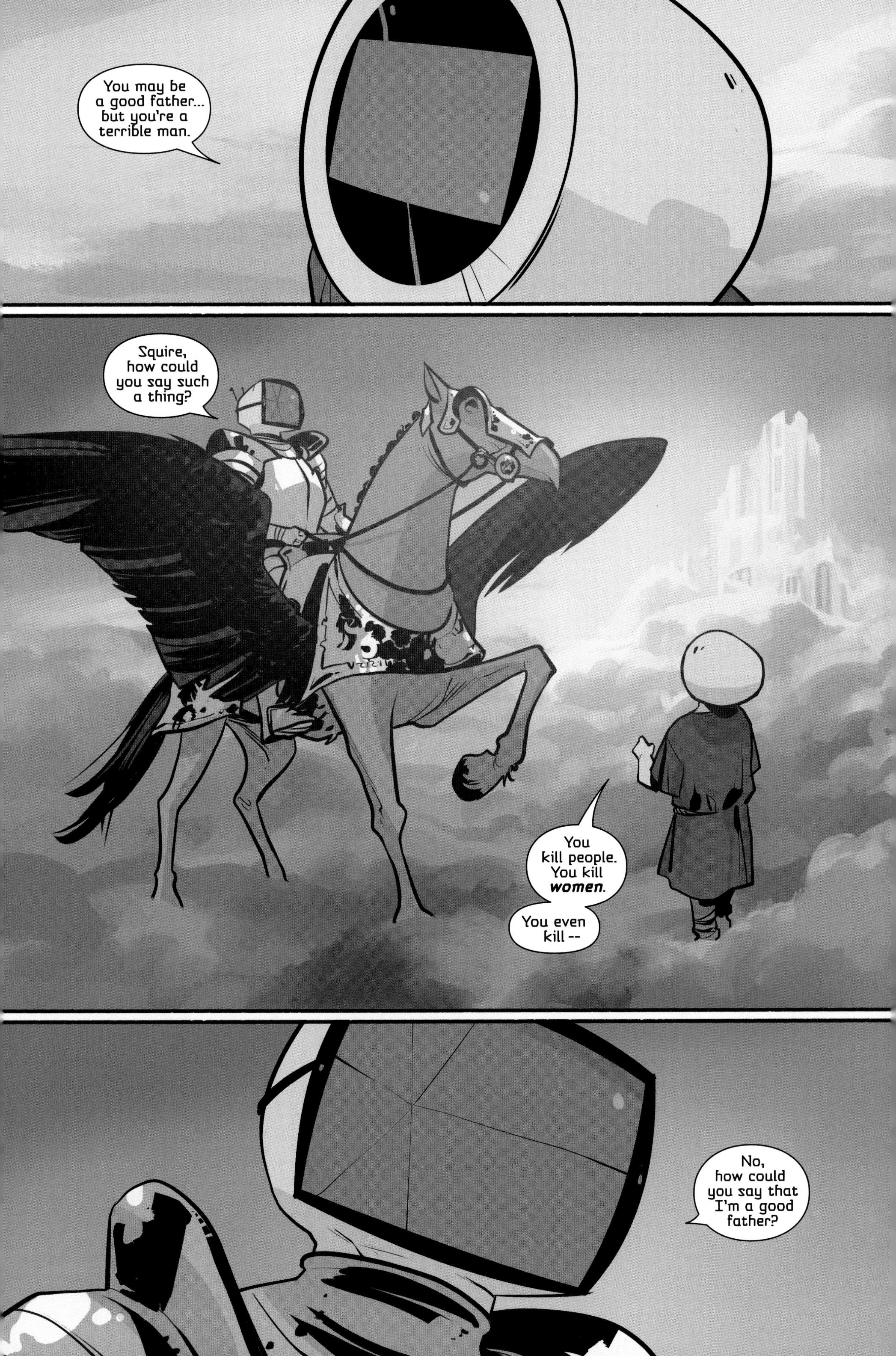
You may be a good father... but you're a terrible man.
Squire, how could you say such a thing?
You kill people. You kill *women*.
You even kill --
No, how could you say that I'm a good father?

Don't be self-effacing, Sir Robot.

It doesn't become you.
Izabel, thank the lord.
I was beginning to worry I'd inadvertently led your spirit to its doom.

You did, dummy.
But it's a far cry from the worst thing you've ever done.

Isn't that right?

This is a creepy one.
His dreams are ***always*** creepy, Kurti.

I s'pose. Least they're not as boring as reading sacred scrolls with my cousins.
Plus, we got to see Izabel again.

Hey, if Miss Petrichor can't find Izzy, I guess that makes you the sitter now.
Nuh-uh!
Wait, for reals?

After the baby that's inside your mom's tummy comes out?
In my family, the big kids always help take care of the littler kids.
But, I don't know how!
Um, I can help you. If you want. It's not too hard, Hazel.
Unless they get sick and stuff.
This is so not fair.
My uncle gets angry when we say that.
He says life is ***never*** fair.
But it should be! I just got a mom and dad again, and now I have to share them with a --
ehh?

You... you prepubescent perverts!
I told you to quit watching me sleep!

If a chain is only as strong as its weakest link, then a family is more like a ROPE.

We're lots of fragile little strands, and we survive by becoming hopelessly intertwined with each other.

Niaj sortoj ne mortu tie!
You heard her, boys!
Fall back to the ships!

Odd.
Marko.

You forgot something, my dear boy!

Jabarah, do you have any idea why the Wreath forces to our north are suddenly ***retreating***?
I'm afraid your deployments never made a lick of sense to me.

They must have the Landfallians outnumbered ten to one.
Since when do my people run from those odds?

All the more reason to be prepared.
In case those soldiers decide to run *here*.
I have all I need to defend our position... at least long enough for our families to *scatter*.

Phang may be just a *"position"* to you, but this world, this land, *is* my family. Her voice has been guiding us for generations.
Like you, I pray violence can be avoided, but if the worst should come to pass... we must be ready to protect *all* our loved ones.

I'm sorry, but I want nothing to do with instruments of death ever again.
When Hazel was kidnapped, I viewed weapons as a *necessary evil*. Now I'm beginning to remember that they're simply the latter.
Everyone born on this comet knows how wrong you are.

To our ears, a blade that's slain hundreds sings a melody no different from one that has never left its scabbard.
Any tool is only as *"good"* or *"evil"* as the person who wields it. You musn't be scared to --

I'M NOT FUCKING SCARED!

Forgive me.
It's difficult being back here. Phang is the first battleground where I... where I *killed* someone.

Ah. I see how hard it would be to take up arms again.
That's the thing. It wasn't hard at all.
Holding that sword was never anything less than *exhilarating*. I felt as alive as I did holding my daughter for the very first time.

More so, on my worst days.

So?
What do you see?
Financial independence...

I don't get it, ma'am.
Your meeting is in *there*?
They don't call it *"front-channel"* diplomacy, Sophie.

Malfermita sésamo.
Now stay out here, no matter what, and if I don't come out in fifteen minutes...

...tell my wife I died somewhere *exotic*.

Well, well, well.
You must be the mysterious Gwendolyn.

Obviously, this meeting never happened.

LYING

Oh, *hell* no.
I don't do business with those hairless sacks of piss.
Calm yourself, Gale. I only brought her to save you the trouble of opening this box for inspection, potentially *releasing* what's inside.

Instead, I solemnly swear that this is exactly what you assholes requested.
MRRR

Works for me.
You realize its contents are useless so long as the Robot Kingdom's satellites --
Don't worry about the bluebloods. They'll do whatever we say.
My concern is for the *rest* of Phang.
If this plan works, how can we guarantee that civilians won't be harmed?
You're joking, right?

Our bosses will spend as much political capital as they have to relocate as many locals as they can to whatever allies don't have the clout to tell them to ***fuck off***.
But this is first and fore-most about bringing a dignified close to a theater of war that's already cost both our sides way too much.

Is that all Phang is to you demons? *"Theater?"*

If you're so concerned about preventing needless deaths, maybe start with your own.
Anything goes wrong with this, Wreath High Command will have you quietly ***executed*** long before you can rat them out to the press.

Bet you never wanted that cat to open its disgusting mouth more, *huh?*

Most of us think we can hide our weaknesses from the world, and sometimes, we're right.

But only if we're very,
very strong.

Izabel!
Izabel, vi tie ekstere?
Lose something, dearie?

Tell me your story, and perhaps I can help.

What be you?
Merely an impartial observer.
We bluecaps are planted in places of conflict, to remember tales of battle for future --

I looking for friend.
You see *spirit* pass this way?

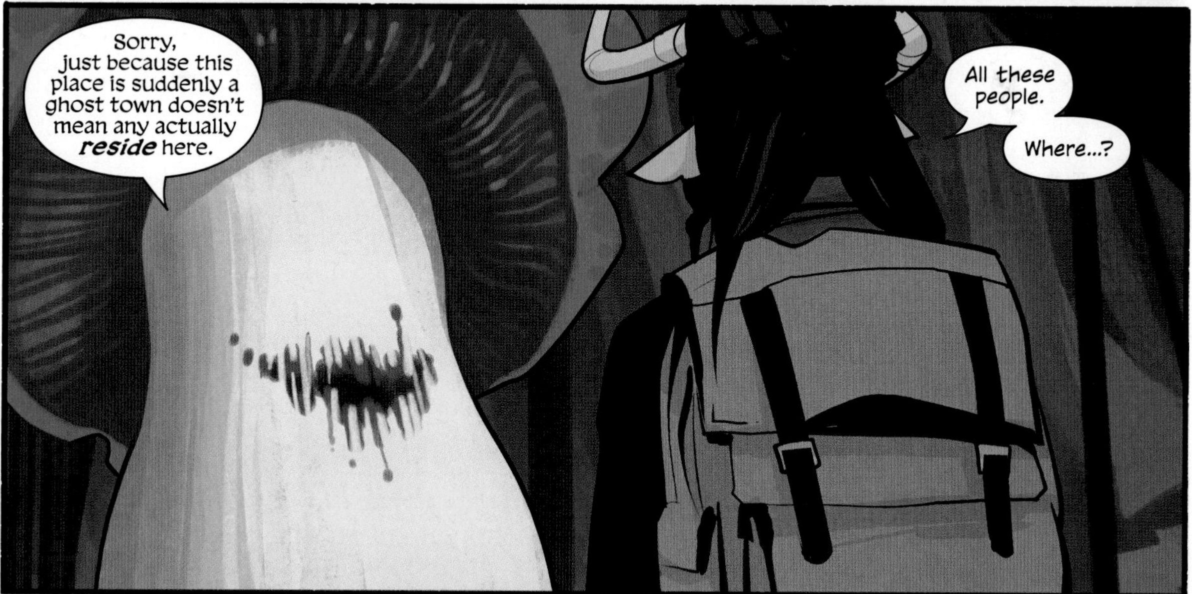
Sorry, just because this place is suddenly a ghost town doesn't mean any actually *reside* here.
All these people.
Where...?

Evacuated from Phang. Some of their own free will, most at gunpoint.
Why?
What is coming?

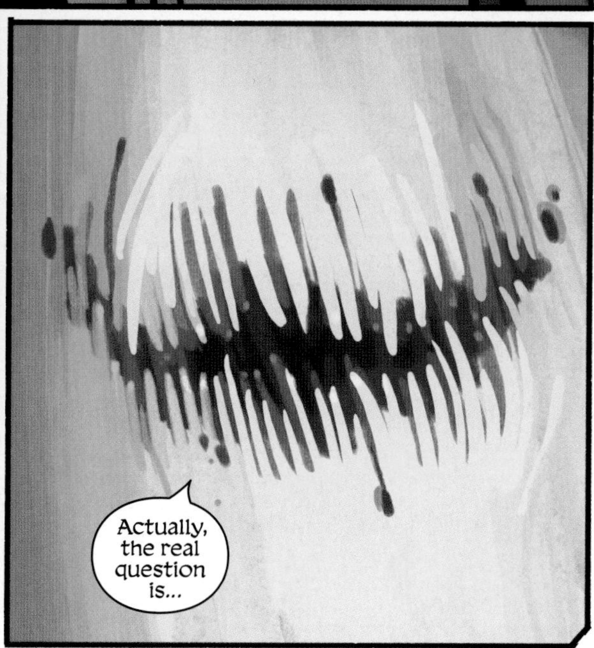
Actually, the real question is...

...where are we going?

So you're back.

My old nemesis **Weird Dark Belly Line**.
I thought you'd finally been vanquished, but it appears that --

Uhhn!
Alana.

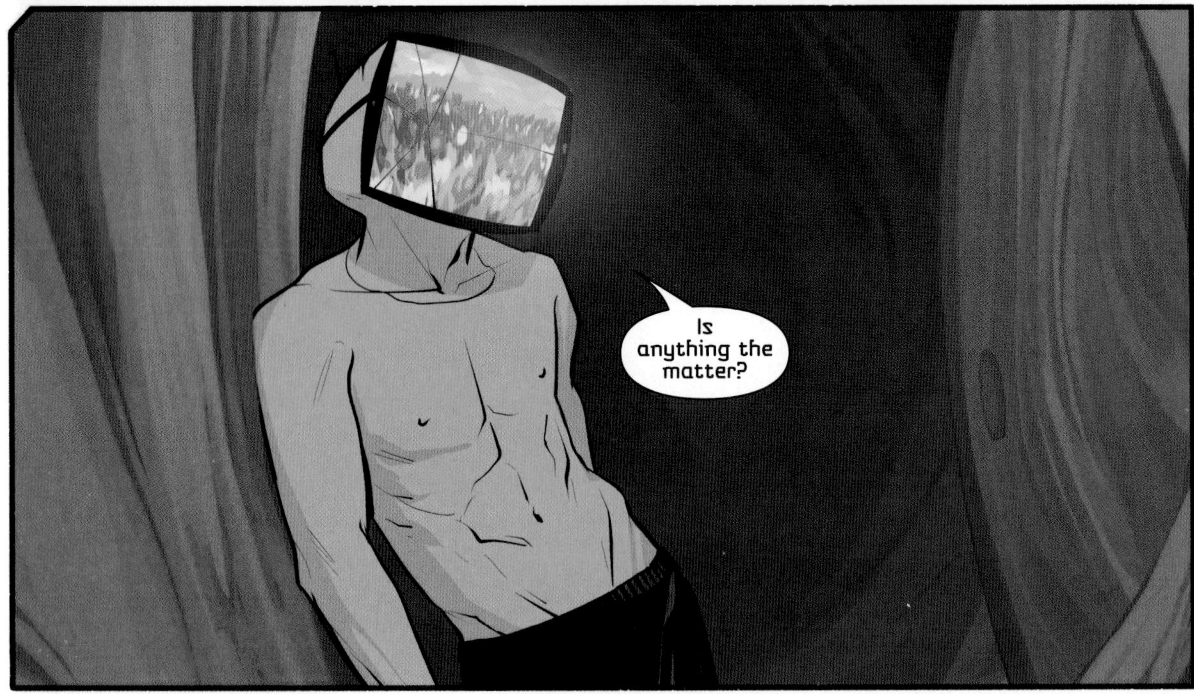
Is anything the matter?

Robot...?
Have you just been ***standing*** there?
You're not having contractions, are you?

No.
This kid just kicks like a son of a bitch.

I'm relieved to hear that.
I was hoping we could speak in private.
Yeah, I'm not really comfortable with the amount of shirts in here, so --

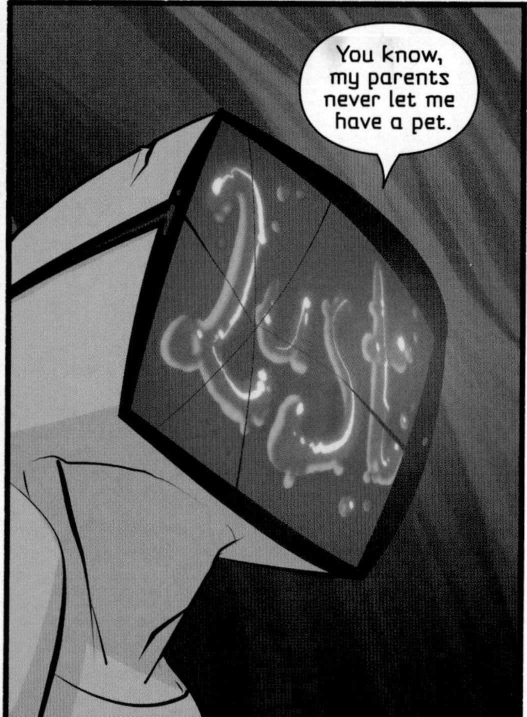
You know, my parents never let me have a pet.

Oh, no.
You're... you're ***high***, aren't you?

The opposite of war may be fucking, but that doesn't mean **peace** is a fiction.
As a matter of fact, I've just realized a surefire way to achieve it.
Where the hell did you get **Fadeaway**?!

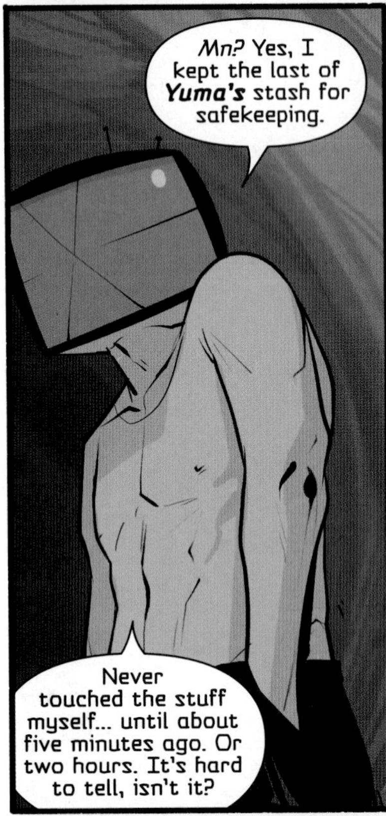
Mn? Yes, I kept the last of **Yuma's** stash for safekeeping.
Never touched the stuff myself... until about five minutes ago. Or two hours. It's hard to tell, isn't it?

I still have another square if you'd care to --
Listen to me.
I don't know what that crap does to brains like yours, but I promise that you're not thinking straight right now.

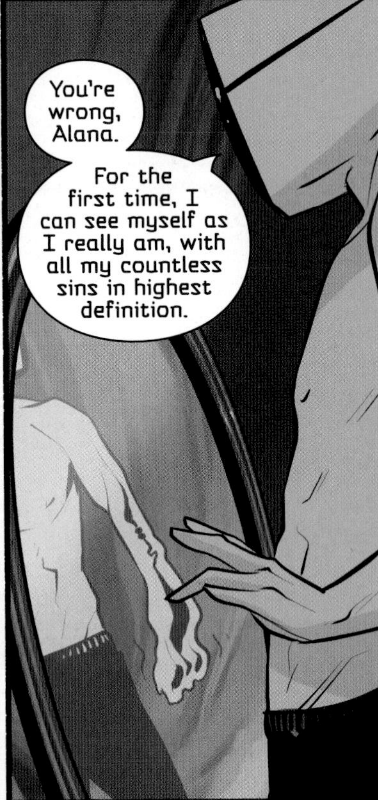
You're wrong, Alana.
For the first time, I can see myself as I really am, with all my countless sins in highest definition.

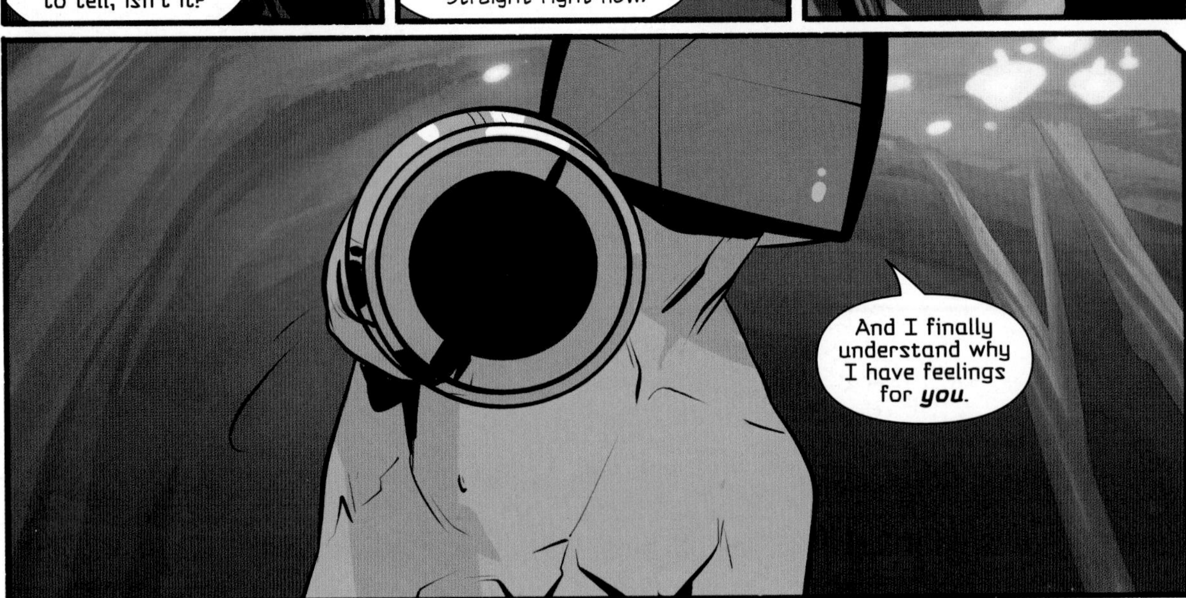
And I finally understand why I have feelings for **you**.

How *dare* you point that shit at us.

All I ask is that you be still.
Don't do this.
You're a goddamn *father*.

That's precisely why I *need* to do this. You see, my feelings for you aren't sexual, though I may have confused them as such at first.
Now I know that I fell for you because of what an excellent *mother* you would be to my son.

What an excellent mother you *will* be.

Please help him be a better man than I was.

end chapter forty

CHAPTER

FORTY-ONE

We're all gonna die.
And I don't mean, like, *eventually*.

Petrichor?
What **happened**, my good woman?
I found no sign of Izabel, but I did... **persuade** one of your local fungi to tell me why everyone is suddenly abandoning this pinball.

We're about to crash into a goddamn **Timesuck**.

Dearie, you can't believe everything you wrestle out of those bluecaps. They're as unreliable as they are aggressive.
I **saw** it, Jabarah, a real Timesuck... its hideous fucking face just cresting the horizon.
So unless you people have been sitting on enough fuel to get us off this comet, we'll be pulled into the giant's orbit within the hour.

That's what I feared the **last** time Phang approached such a heavenly body. But you must have faith that God will again keep our homeland safe.
God is a **joke**.
And this is her punchline.

Mind your tongue, Petri. I respect your secrets, but I won't tolerate **blasphemy** from --
Hold.

How long have you been on lookout?

I... I relieved Marko a quarter rotation ago, so he could finally round up Hazel and Kurti for bedtime.
Did I do something wrong?

It's subtle, but I swear I smell something *unfamiliar*... just a whiff of body wash, the expensive kind.

Or am I losing my mind?

Right.
Safe travels then.

Sir Robot, please!
If... if you hurt yourself, your son will be **haunted** for the rest of his life. You don't want to do this!
No, but perhaps it's time I finally do what's right...

...instead of merely pursuing what I **want**.

I implore you, look away!
What... what am I revealing?
Ew, is that supposed to be ***me***?!
Alana?

What is this?

Enemy contact!

Easy... no one's going to hurt you.
He's drugged out of his mind, Marko.
Grab the *ifle-ray* from the *oset-clay* before he does something stupid.

There's no need to bring more weapons into this, love.
Whatever's going on here can be resolved without --

SORRY
DIE, MOONIE CUNT!

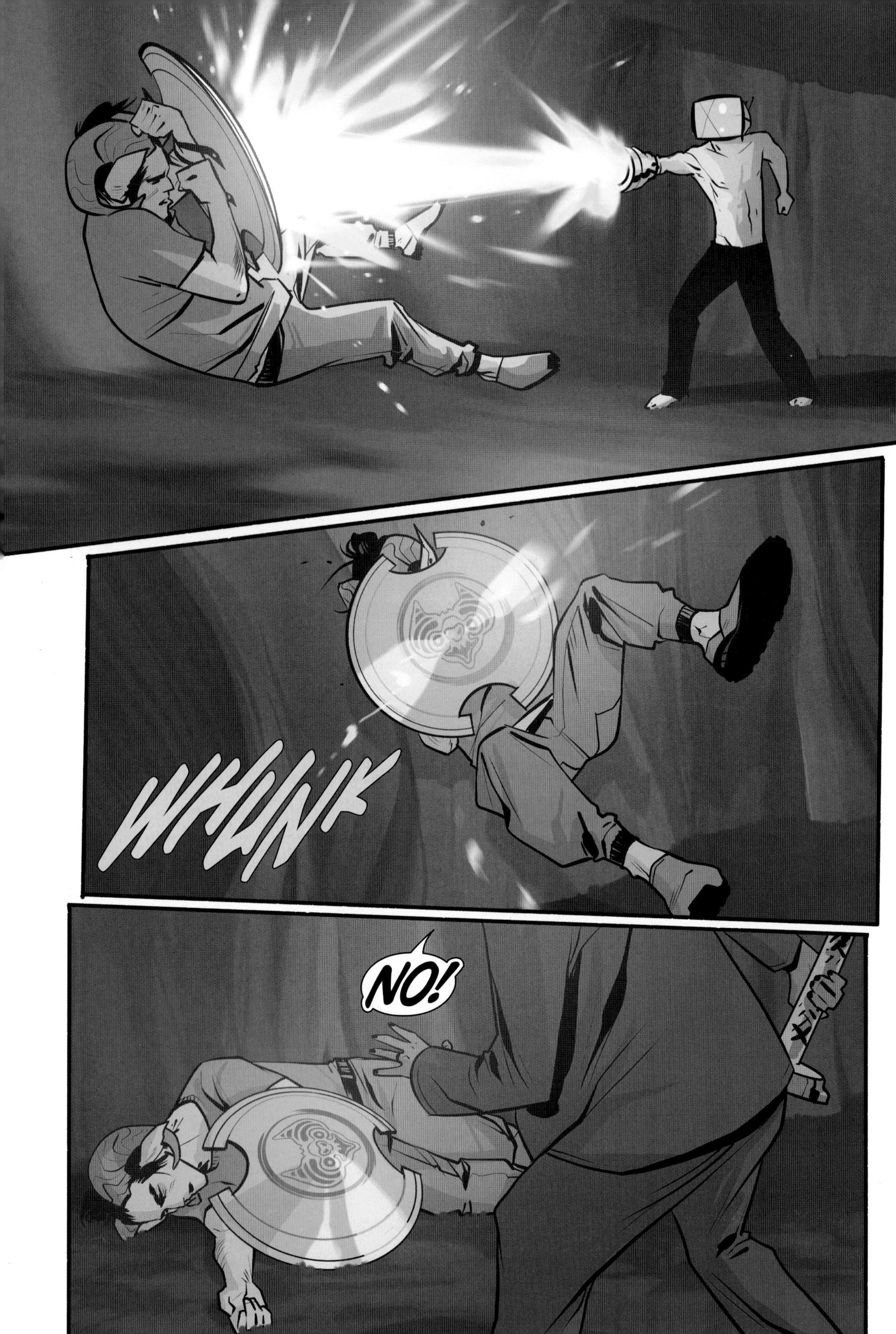
WHUNK
NO!

Oh, God.
What have I --

KALANK

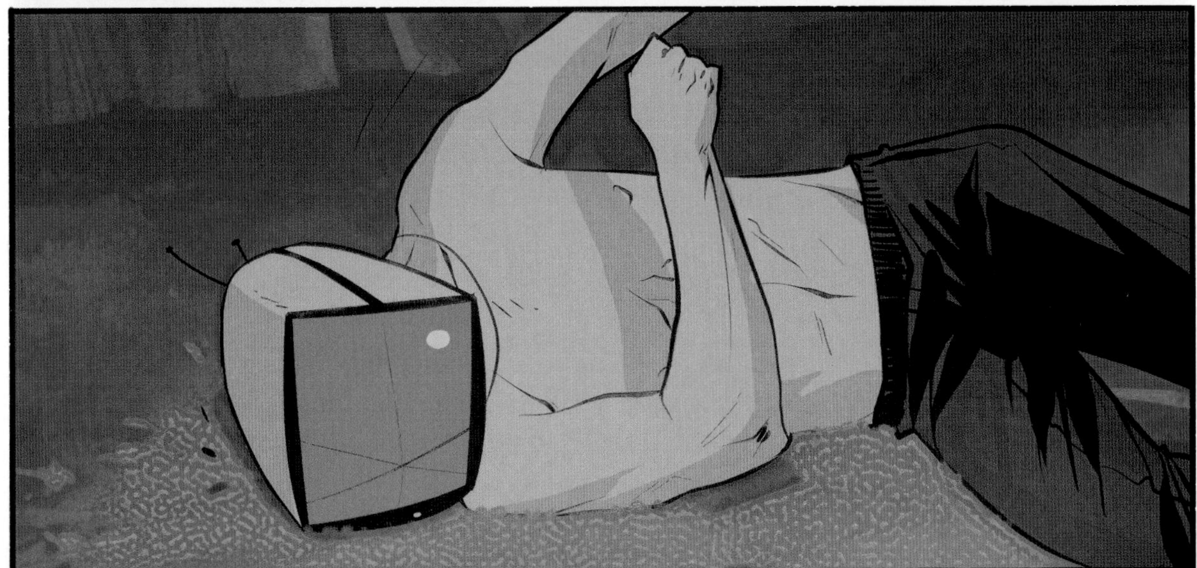

By the time they're out of preschool, most children have already seen thousands of acts of violence.

Granted, for the average kid, those acts are mostly FICTIONAL...
Thirty-eight.
Thirty-nine.
Forty.

...and unlike the real deal, fictional violence is cool as shit.
Ready or not, here I come.
And if you jump out and scare me again, I *will* punch you.

So, we playing hide-and-seek or sardines?

I always hated sardines.
I mean, why mess with a classic?

If that's how it's gonna be.

Ladies and gentlemen!

As duly licensed representatives of our clients in Wreath High Command, we kindly request an audience with **Foot Soldier Marko**!

Dammit.

God fucking dammit.

We know you and your blood are here.
Bootstraps followed the stench of your **pet ghost** straight to this dump.
HNNRK

Oh, and by the by, we already **executed** your little phantom.

And you best believe we'll do the same to this brat...

...unless you and your fam come out, come out, wherever you are!
The sight of actual violence sucks, but it's the SOUND that always bothered me most.

To this day, I still prefer the silence of space to the rhythmic din of worlds like my mom's and dad's.

Peace always sounded nice... but peace and quiet is the dream.
So now we're *collaborating* with Landfall?
No, for the good of Wreath, we're strategically coordinating with associates of opposition forces on actions involving a third-party world.
MRRN

Yeah, sounds like a fancy way of saying we're helping the enemy.
Be that as it may, talk like that will get us both thrown in a labor camp at *best*, so keep your mouth --
Sophie.

You're all grown up.

The Will?
Is that really you?
You look... unwell.

Don't be cruel now.
Just goin' through a rebuilding phase is all.
What the hell are you doing here?

Haven't been the same since me and my old **partner** went our ways.
Was hoping to make things right with her again.

Will, you can't do that to Sophie.
It's been ***years***. She and Lying Cat have ***bonded***.
Which is why I thought the girl could also come along, learn to be a proper Freelancer like me.

LYING?

Well, technically I ain't fully licensed at the moment.
But I could start fresh with Soph, show her the ropes as I set things right with my union.
You make it sound like she'd be a fucking plumbing apprentice.
I'm not letting you turn this child into a --
The Will's right, Gwendolyn.
I'm grown now.
Old enough to make my own decisions, at least.
Sophie...
I will always be in your debt for rescuing me from the nightmare I was trapped in, The Will.
But working with Gwendolyn has shown me there are ways to change the lives of millions, not just the individuals men like you are paid to hurt.
My place is here on Wreath... but if L.C. wants to go with you, I won't stand in her way.

Well?
What do you say, Cat?

Fair enough.
Wait!
You can't just show up out of the blue and then *disappear*, Will!

That ain't my handle anymore.
Good luck with your politicking, ladies.
ARF

Last warning, creep!
Get out here with the rest of your freakshow before we slice this mammal open!

What am I gonna do? What am I gonna --

--mmf.

Let him go, Freelancer!

Hurt the boy, and I **separate** you two.
Painfully.

You must be Marko's twisted **fuck buddy**.
And hey, it looks like she let him knock her up **again**.
Whoever is paying you people, I can get you **double** to leave us alone.

Then you clearly have no idea how much the moonies are willing to spend to have you and Marko **eliminated**.
Still, you're lucky we found you before someone working for **your** side did.
Unlike the wings, the horns actually want your filthy half-breed kid **alive**.

That dickbag Marko took off with our girl **weeks** ago.
But if you promise to let the rest of us live...

...maybe we can cut a deal for the other *"half-breed"* he left me with.
Huh, that's actually a pretty fair proposal.

But we'll pass, thanks.

NNH
Our intel says we're on a bit of a **ticking clock** here, so why don't you cut the bullshit and tell us where your firstborn is stashed?

Blast radius is too tight.
Can't squeeze off a shot without killing the boy, too.
Creator, I beseech you, help us in our hour of --

AHHH!

EKSPLODIS!

Fuck!

Run, Kurti!

Cute prank, shorty.
Now get your narrow butt down here and kiss your mama...

...goodbye?

...brother...

The late D. Oswald Heist once said that the opposite of war is FUCKING, but I'm not so sure...

...especially because violence seems to have so much in common with an untreatable VENEREAL DISEASE.

It burrows deep inside of everyone it touches, flaring up again and again to hurt others...

...until the day it finally consumes its host.

end chapter forty-one

CHAPTER

FORTY-TWO

24 HOURS
What do you think hell will be like?

We aren't *damned*, Sophie.
Not unless one of the countless lives we just saved on Phang turns out to be a *mass murderer* or something.
But, that jerk with the wings said they might not be able to get all the civilians off my old comet before... you know.

True, but like your own family, how much longer would those poor souls have lasted?
Trapped in the endless crossfire of some asshole despot and whatever underfunded resistance he's up against this month?

I recognize that a war can't be won without casualties, Gwendolyn.
It's just, how do you know how many are *too* many?
It varies by battlefield, obviously. I can't give you an exact number.

But there are some things you do know for sure?
Like, there really being a *hell*...?

Of course hell is real.

But it's reserved for the bastards who **started** this.
Mielo, mi estas hejme!

Not a word of this in front of Velour.
Yes, ma'am.
I wouldn't have even mentioned it, but I've been having these bad dreams, and I --

Kaj mi alportis deserto!

Cupcakes.
I've always had a difficult time with the concept of "evil."

That's how everyone used to describe my own family, so the word kind of lost its power over the years.

Oh.
Oh, no.
Alana...
her baby...?
Alive,
no thanks to
you. You nearly
killed me, Robot.
You nearly got
us *all* killed.

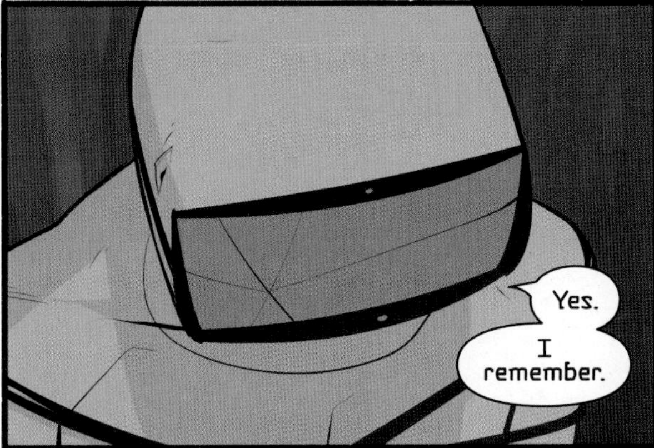
Yes.
I
remember.

So why the
bloody fuck
haven't you cut
off my head
yet?

Good
question.

Marko,
wait!

He'll be cleaner to execute once we're out in a vacuum.

You found fuel?!
Thanks to your late baby-sitter.
If she hadn't encountered those Freelancer dicks, I might never have found their *vehicle* outside our camp.

Petrichor, you just saved our --
Hold your congratulations for if and when we've escaped that *Timesuck*.
Wait, we're headed *towards* one of those monstrosities?

Why in the name of all that's sane haven't we fled yet?!
Because Marko's wife and child are waiting for the pack of locals they foolishly offered a *ride*.

As if this overcrowded treehouse couldn't smell any worse.

What are you working on, sweetheart?
A thank-you card. For Daddy.
For shooting up the bad guys who killed Izabel.

That's... that's so nice, Hazel, but I'm not sure your father will want to --
You're still here!

Praise be. I feared I wouldn't get a chance to return Marko's blade.
Miss Jabarah?
Where's Kurti? Where's *everyone*?

I'm afraid we won't be coming with you, love.

What?!
We appreciate the invitation, but my family has no intention of ever leaving Phang.

Phang is fucked!
I'm sorry, but open your eyes! This world is about to *end!*

Our home has been spared annihilation before, and I have faith we will again escape the worst.
Jabarah, even if you do somehow survive this, there's nothing here for you.
Your grandchildren deserve more than... than *ruins*.

I'll miss your family, but don't fret for mine. The creator will provide, just as he did when he sent us *you*.
We don't have time for this.
Call your people back here.

Now.

Farewell, Alana.
I pray your second child will be as perfectly joyous as your first.
Jabarah, don't do this!

If you're still looking for a name, might I suggest *Kurti*?

In our tongue, it means *"sunshine!"*
Mommy?
Where... where is she going?

I didn't even say goodbye to my friend!
JABARAH!

I didn't get to say goodbye!
The more you care about someone, the more likely it is that your eventual parting of ways will be as sudden as it is baffling.

And you can forget about "closure."

Trying to figure out how and why a loved one exited your life only ever leaves you with more questions.
You know how to get them back, don't you?
Lying Cat? Your whole little harem?
Shut up and let me finish.

You come when I *say* you come.
And if you want your old Sidekick, you need Sophie on your side, and to get her, you have to win over Gwendolyn... and we both know what that means.

I'm done chasing after her sicko ex, Stalk.
All that chick cares about is moving up some bureaucratic ladder, which you can help Gwen do by *expunging* the blackest mark on her permanent record.
Ain't in the expungin' business anymore either.

Maybe not, but if anything will get you back in the union's good graces, it's bagging a big score like that race-traitor Marko.
Honestly, Billy. There has *got* to be a more efficient way to masturbate than gnawing on tainted meat and fantasizing about old --
Quiet, all of you.

There's someone here.
Someone *real*.
RRRRRR

BRAM

Sweet Boy.

Hi there.
We don't know each other, but you murdered someone I love...

BRAM
Hng!

...so this is gonna be kind of a *process*.
The only action that has vaster repercussions for the universe than making a life is TAKING one...

...which is why I'll never understand why most people put so little foresight into doing either.

A close shave, but she'll pass right through the Timesuck's rings unscathed.
Told you the Landfallians were foolish to abandon ship.
Phang Central, this is *HMS Observer Royal*, confirming that you are on course to safely traverse the length of the...

Ma'am, incoming vessel!
Looks like ancient Coalition hardware, probably stolen.
The Last Revolution? What are those terrorist arseholes doing this far from --

We... we just executed a ***friendly***.
We executed ***orders***, Gibson.
And you know they probably had to run this ***false-flag*** shit all the way up to the commander in chief.

So what? I didn't vote for that fucktard.
It's not about him, dude.
We're releasing this payload for Aftel and Chordo and McDirk. For motherfucking Hippo Company!

This is for all the guys Phang took from us.

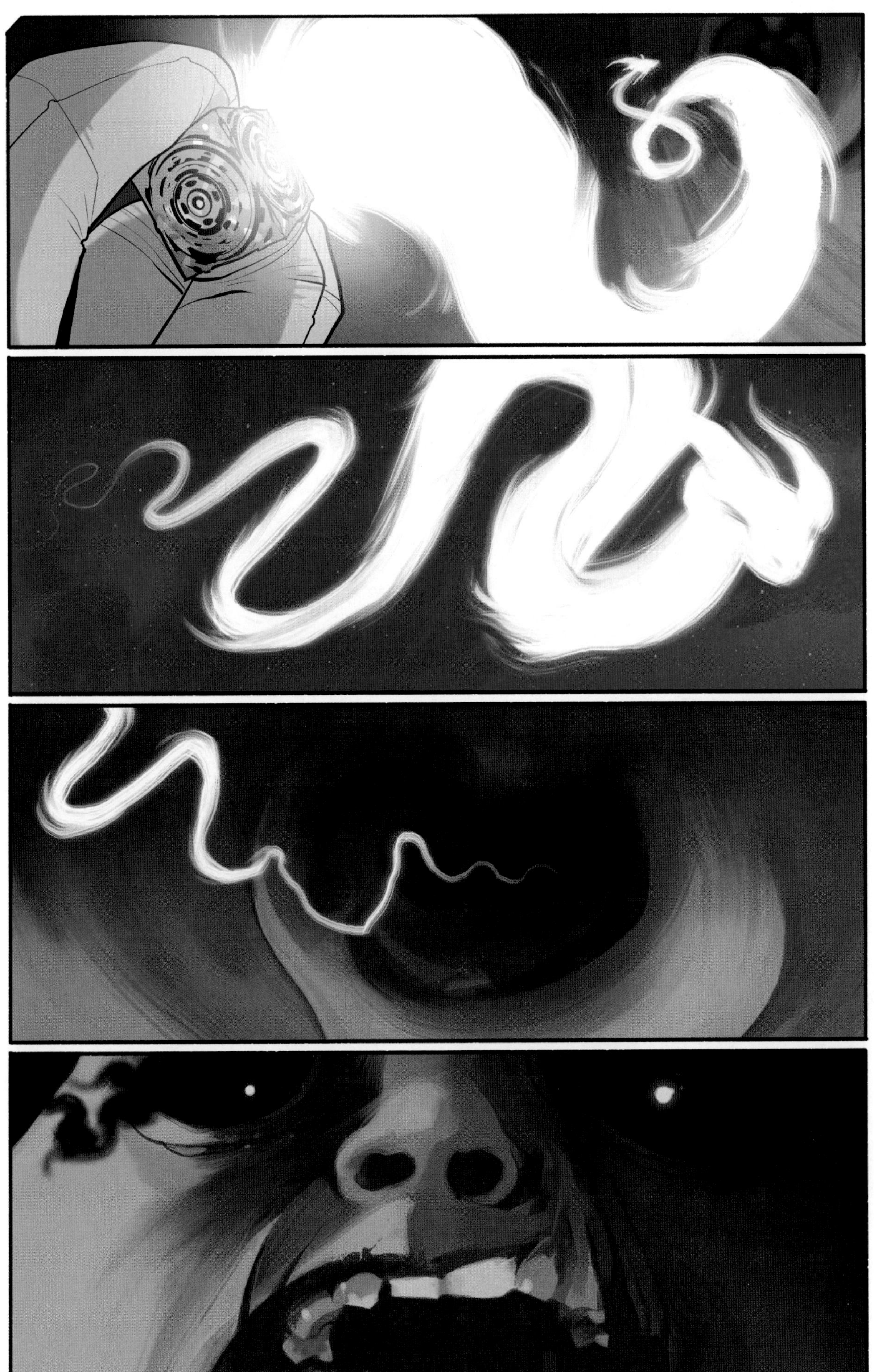

Trust in the lord!
He will never forsake your homeland!

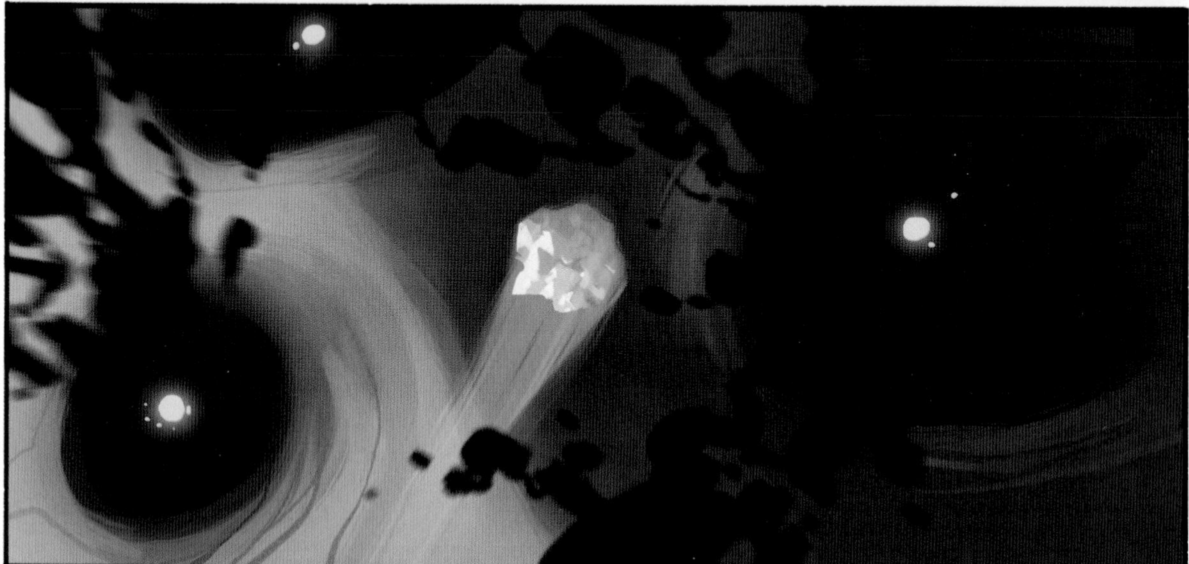

Holy...
PETRI, GO FOR LAUNCH!

Fucking finally.

We can't just leave Kurti!
I'm so sorry, Hazel.
Mommy doesn't know what else to --
UHNN!
Alana!

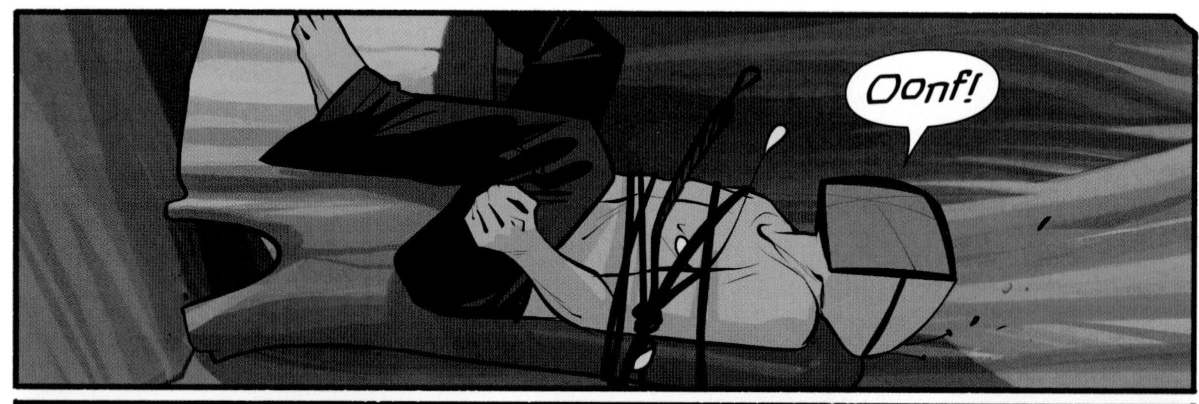
Oonf!

The fuel!
Careful, woman!
That cube is hotter than a --

NRAHHH!
tssssss

Blast off, goddammit!

hnn

Don't try to move, love.

Are you hurt?

I... I don't think so.

But our boy.

I can't feel him kicking.

But, you can still hear him.
You can still hear his ***heartbeat***.

Right?

Marko?

Marko?

If that's true, what is it when you lose something that never even had a chance to be born?

I guess I'm just haunted by all that potential energy.

One moment, the universe presents you with this amazing opportunity for new possibilities...

... and then...

end chapter forty-two

CHAPTER

FORTY-THREE

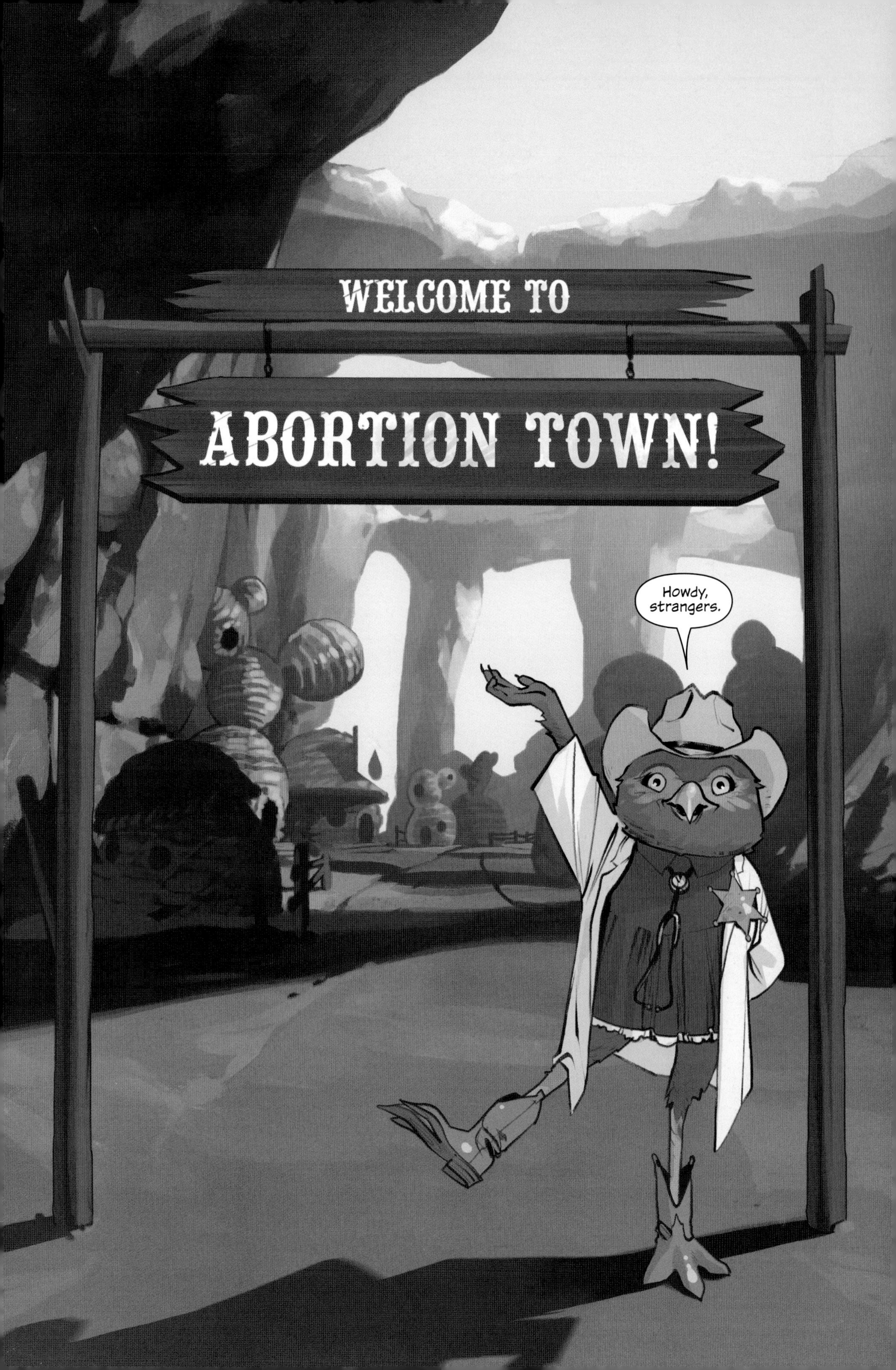

WELCOME TO
ABORTION TOWN!
Howdy, strangers.

A very pleasant morning to you, Doctor Sheriff.
My name is Earl Robot LI, and I was hoping you good people would be able to assist one of my young soldiers with her... situation.

But... I didn't think his kind and... and wings could... you know...

We were under the same belief, but let me assure you that procreation between our races is unquestionably possible.
Still, our unplanned offspring will likely suffer horrific mutations, so for the good of both our worlds, we need the fetus terminated and its remains ***discreetly*** disposed of.

Huh.
How far along are you, darling?
Um, about eight months.

Your third trimester?
I'm powerful sorry... but there ain't a thing we can do for you.

I beg your fucking pardon.

Simmer down, Earl.
Wish it weren't the case, but we're under Landfall jurisdiction.
You don't like their rules for a woman's body, you can take it up with the wings' elected officials... most of whom ain't women, mind you.

This isn't about your utterly banal political sentiments, this is about our lives.
Please, we came as soon as we could, but we were very far away from the only planet that offers this... procedure.
Isn't there anything you can do?

On the other side of this rock, there's a place called the Badlands.
Hell of a dangerous trip, but the "doctors" out that way are willing to do just about anything, no questions asked.

But y'all didn't hear that from me.

Never fear, Alana.
No matter how long it takes, we will journey to these Badlands and finish what --

We aren't doing shit, Sir Robot.
The only reason I let you tag along is so we could try this stupid ruse of yours... and now that it's predictably gone tits up, you and I are ***finished***.

But... where am I supposed to go?
I don't give a good goddamn.
All I know is I never want to see your face again.

My name's Hazel, and this is my mother.
But that's not me in there, and this is definitely not my father.

It's kind of a long story, but I can get you up to speed.

In the beginning, there was Landfall and there was Wreath.

Landfall, the planet where Mom was born, is a restless sci-fi wonderland, always bulldozing over its past to put up something shinier.
FLAT BLACK 2.1
in store today

Wreath, Dad's home moon, is a magical fantasy realm rooted in ancient tradition, pretty much the OPPOSITE of the world it orbits.

Despite what you may have heard, opposites NEVER attract.

In time, this endless war spread far beyond where it began, forcing everyone in the universe to choose between the wings and the horns.

Somehow, these two oddballs never got the memo.

In the years since they both went AWOL from their respective militaries, my parents had plenty of adventures...

... including making ME.
Why are you crying?
Is my little brother okay?

But there are few things more challenging than a sequel.
No, my heart.
Mommy got hurt and we... I'm afraid we *lost* him.
Is everyone all right?

I was just about to kick this worthless drone out the front hatch.
Still, if there's one thing I learned from the unlikely allies we made over the years, it's that family is about much more than blood.

Petrichor, what... what happened to your hands?

She sacrificed her own flesh to launch us to safety.
You owe this woman an extraordinary debt of --
Shut your filthy screen, you manipulative little...

Snf
Snf

Sankta vazo.

I am blessed to be in your presence, Most Holy Mother.

What the hell is this?
Petri, he's *gone*. My baby is --
Some faiths on Wreath *revere* women who have suffered... what *we* just have.

Your wife is no longer a mere "*woman*," Marko.
Anyone carrying the remains of an unborn Wreath child is a *sacred vessel*.
Bullshit.

I'm a fucking coffin.

But, the little boy in Mommy's tummy...
...will not exit on its own, and must be *removed* before it threatens Alana's health.
We'll have to visit a High Cleric for the dilation and curettage ceremony.
Are you out of your mind?
Those sorcerers are all on Wreath, and they'd sooner take their own lives than help a woman with *wings*.

So what, I go to one of *my* people's OB-GYNs?
As soon as they see that the child I'm carrying has... *had* horns...
Indeed.

First of all, I am dreadfully sorry for your loss.
And I am well aware that my recent actions have been inexcusable, and yet...

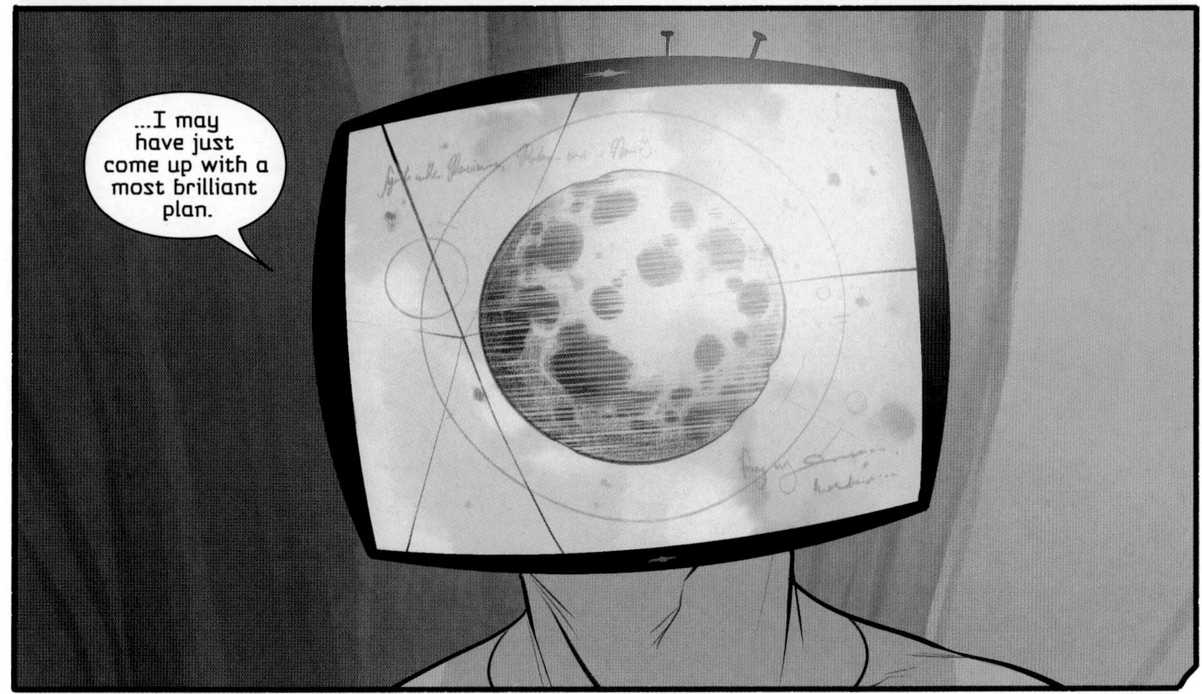
...I may have just come up with a most brilliant plan.

But some folks bounce back faster than others.

Ow!

Oops, sorry, Petrichor.
You're doing fine, little one.
Just tie my dressings as tight as you can.

You sure you don't want my dad to do this?
Marko is busy making a new septic line to remove the waste from your rocketship.
Waste? Like, pee and poop? I thought we just flush that stuff out when we're in space.

As did I.
Then, why has he been digging like that all week?
You're asking the wrong person. I'll *never* understand why men do the things they do.

That reminds me.
Can I ask about your penis?

You most certainly may not.
Because what you learned when we were imprisoned together is *private*.
Oh. But, how come?

More importantly, I refuse to be defined by my genitalia.
When you question the biology of some-one who happens to be transgender, you don't just objectify us, you make us feel illegitimate and...

What in the world is the matter?
I didn't mean to hurt your feelings, Petrichor.
I'm just... super, super scared.

Of what?
I, I, I have wings like Mommy, but also horns like Daddy.
But, but, but I have girl parts in my swimsuit places, and I don't know if maybe I'll grow boy parts next. What if everything in my body goes wrong and I *die*?

Ah.

I just wish... I just wish I was normal.
Little one, you are unlike anyone who has ever existed, and that makes you ***exactly*** like everyone who has ever existed.
I don't know what the future holds for you or your body...

...but I promise that you will never be alone.

Also, can I ask you a question about nipples?
Er...

Hey, look!
Mommy's back!
Oh, thank God.

Whoa.
Easy now, Button.
Alana!

How did it go, my love?
It didn't.
I was too far along for the powers that be, but at least they pointed me in the direction of this planet's creepy back-alley option.

Wherever it is, I'm coming with you.
Not with those horns, you're not. This is still Landfall territory. You need to stay with Hazel here on the outskirts.
But there are ways for us to travel inconspicuously and --
I appreciate the offer, handsome, but this is something I need to finish on my own.
I can't let you do that, Alana.
Not when this is all my fault.

Hey, it took **both** of us to make this happen.
And there's nobody to blame for our pregnancy ending but a shitty universe that's cruel and random.
Violence always has a cost, and we lost this child because of the life *I* took.

What, that mercenary douche you killed on Phang?
Marko, we'd ***all*** be dead if you hadn't done what you did.

...maybe.
I'll just never understand why war is easy, and peace is so god-damn hard.
Mommy!

Are you all better now?
Where's Sir Robot?
Oh, he... he needed to keep moving, honey. His ***son*** is still out there, so he decided to --

Behind you!

OH, FUCKING!

Hazel, that's not a nice word, remember?
And you're still using it wrong.
What *are* those things?!

Dung People.
Some kinda microbes in the soil that animate *feces*, turn it into a gross approximation of whoever shat it out.

I accidentally made one the first time I got stuck digging trenches for my platoon to crap in.
You used to get latrine duty, too?
That's how my first commander would punish me for --

SQUACK

Marko!
VNNAX
Your planet's garbage weapons are useless against these monsters!
We need proper **spellcasting** to --
gwuhl
Mommy!
They're gonna make us all dead!
Like hell, baby.
Here's the thing about miscarriages.

They are painful, they are horrific, and they are very, very common.

...it's actually just the beginning of a new one.
Wait, what?

end chapter forty-three

CHAPTER

FORTY-FOUR

"I'm allergic to condoms," he says.
"I promise I'll pull out," he says.
Fucking let it go, will you?
Yeah, look where that got us.
You think this is fun for me?
I used up every last day of leave I had left to tag along to this suck-ass planet.
Partner, there's a **tax** on bad-mouthin' my home.

And I intend to collect.

What the hell are you?!
The handsome devil who's relieving y'all of your valuables.
And soldier boy, you so much as *finger* that heater, you're a goner.

Try me, you sick --

KRA-BLAM!

ROBIN!
Mighty sorry you had to see that, ma'am.
I really did try to --

RAHHH!

KABRAM

Bad form, Kidd.
Sexist to presume the girl didn't have a piece, too.

Dammit, Maw.
That lady was ***with child***.
Not for long. Wicked creature was about to have that poor baby ripped right out of her womb.

Just like them evil doctors told me I should do to ***you***.
Enough jawin'.

Either of you notice these *tracks*?

Probably just other bandits, Paw.
Nah, these belong to a well-heeled gentleman.
And him and his boots were headed **west**.

Nothing out there but the valley.
Why would outsiders risk comin' all the way to Pervious... only to move **away** from those Abortion Town butchers?
Decent question, son.

What say we go find the answer?
Every culture in the universe has a very different opinion about exactly when life begins.

No, it's ***impossible***. Spells can only be cast by those with Wreath blood.

Obviously, when the child you two conceived... passed, it must have transferred its capabilities to Alana.

So can Mommy make bad guys' heads explode?!

Hazel, we've talked about this.
No matter what mistakes you've seen your daddy make, violence -- magical or otherwise -- is never acceptable.

Nonsense, Marko.
Violence is often ***essential***: in self-defense, the arts, foreplay...
I want to four-play!

I feel stronger... but also weaker.
God, it's like being pregnant all over ag--

GHWARR

That settles it.
We have to get that fetus out before it kills you.

I told you, ***I'll*** take care of it. This world isn't safe for your kind, Marko.
It's not safe for either of us ***anywhere*** in this universe, love.
But we've always been better off together.

What about me?!
Please, wherever you guys are going, I have to come with you!

She's right. This isn't the time to be splitting your nuclear family.
Besides, I already whipped up attire that should help conceal Hazel and Marko's modest horns.
"Modest?"

No offense, Petrichor, but why should I believe you won't just blast off with our rocket the second we leave you alone?
Because I'd like my ***sewing hands*** back before I take leave of you people.
If I hold down your fort, perhaps you'll inquire about a ***healing elixir*** for me from whatever quacks you find to perform your operation.

In that case, I'll leave you with ***this***.

You're giving her your ***wedding band***?
Is this some kind of kinky thrupple thing?
Because I'm not necessarily opposed.

I'm lending Petri one of our ***translation rings.***
If she runs into trouble with any of the locals, it'll at least give her a chance to talk her way out of it.

"Talk."
Hilarious.

I agree, everything about this is ***ridiculous.***
We're all just gonna put on matching cowboy hats and ***hope*** that'll be enough to let us prance across the Badlands unscathed?

Who said anything about prancing?

That's an old Coalition model.

I spotted it while you and Sir Robot were in town.

Guards?

Only on the return route. It must pick them up with whatever laser-powder your people have them hauling out.

One.
Two.
Girls, *wait!*

WHEEEEEEEEEE!

Forgive me, Dad.

I had no idea how hard your job was.

Uhn!
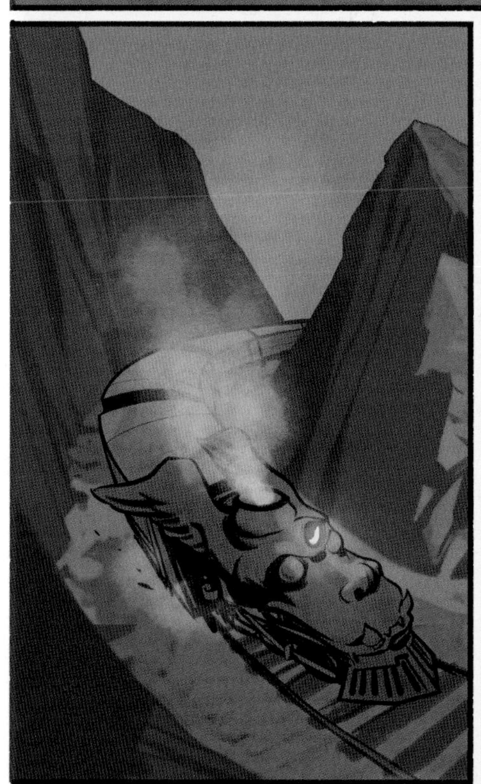

MARKO!

Fadenoj!

What she said!

hnnf

Mommy?
Yeah, sweetheart?
After they take out the dead baby, will Daddy put a new one in your tummy?

I... I don't know, Hazel.
We'll see, okay?
Every kid who's ever had a parent knows exactly what "we'll see" means.

Play your cards right,
and it's a sixty percent
chance of YES.

I've held you in my heart since the day you left me.

But you're too heavy to carry another step.

And I need to keep moving.

Saints above, I beseech you.

In all my years, I've asked for nothing.
But if you feel I've lived a decent life, hear this, my one and only prayer.

Please.
Send me someone to fuck.

Petri, you are a pathetic old hag, and you deserve to die alone.

It's a Wreather, all right.

A real one?
You're sure, Paw?
The hell is one of them doing in wing country?

Dunno.
But looks like she can spell something fierce.
Okay then.

Best do her before she can do us.

Whether we like it or not, most of our deepest-held beliefs come straight from the people who made us.

Even when we turn against them, our parents still help define exactly what kind of "rebels" we'll be.

Don't stop, I'm so close.
Yeah, suck my clit hard...

Hey, Alana.
You ever think about having *kids*?

What the fuck, Heath?
We've only been dating for, like, three weeks!
I don't mean having them with me! I mean, not necessarily. Just, you know, in general?

Dude, can you *picture* me with a baby?
Even my best friends say I'm a selfish bitch.

Actually, I think you'd be a great mother.
Also, the fact that you're a *junky*.
Well, my empty bank account and the last three houseplants I killed tell a different story.

What did you say?
You still dream about getting high on Fadeaway every single night, don't you?
I... I've never even tried that shit.

But you will.

No.
That's probably why you *miscarried*, right?
Because of all that ***poison*** you put into your body when Hazel was little.

You're a goddamn drug addict, and you ***killed*** your baby boy.

No.
It was an ***accident***. It was just a...

...mn?

Oh.

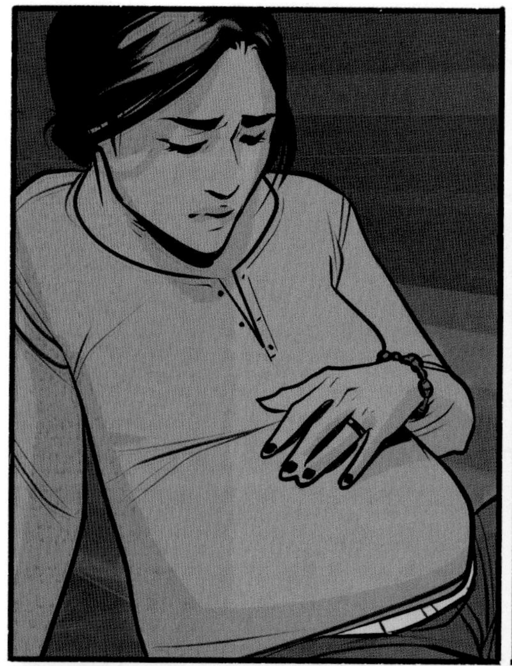

I don't deserve you.

Mom?
Sorry if I woke you, Hazel.
Mommy just had a bad dream.

"Hazel"?

I'm your son, silly.

end chapter forty-four

CHAPTER FORTY-FIVE

Bother.

This is your last warning!

Elvenu nun!

Aŭ ni bruligas vian arbon!
How in the sweaty hell does our boy suddenly speak Blue?
It's just a translation app, Paw.

Real question is, how's he getting reception out here when I can't get it in our own gee-damn dining room?

Please, take whatever you want.
Just don't hurt my home.
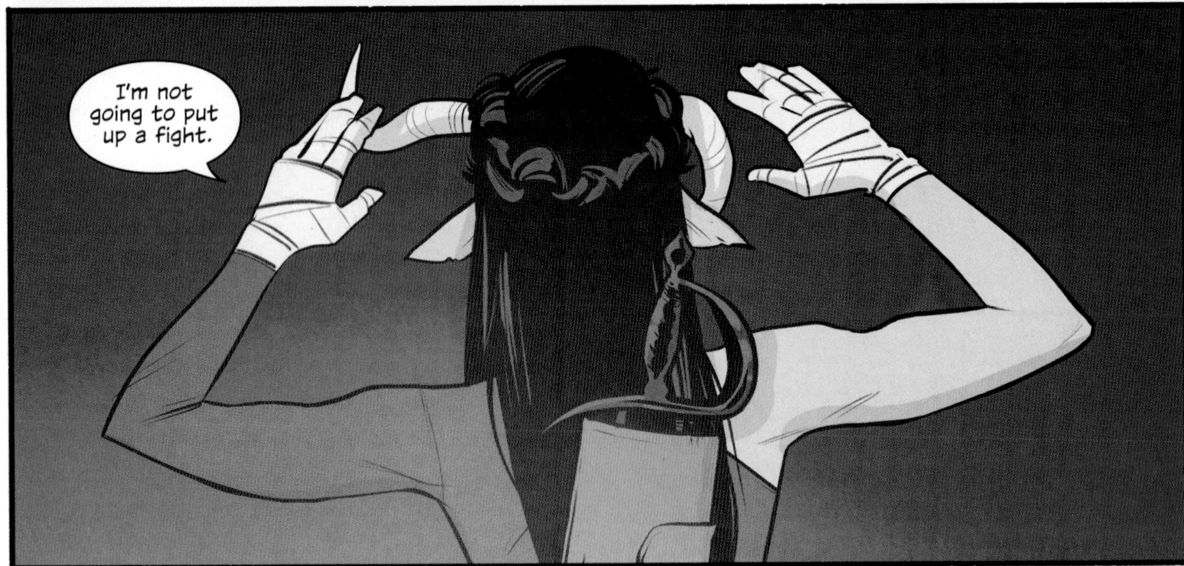
I'm not going to put up a fight.

Lord.
Never seen one of them up close before.

Enjoy.

UHN!
Kidd!

You filthy cunny!
SHOOM

Gross!

Our dear child still breathing?
Just got his bell rung.
Boy's dragon-hide coat took most of the brunt.

hngh
We know you ain't out here by your lonesome, longhorn.
Tell us who you're with and exactly what they got of worth...

...or we hang you from your own tree.
When did you first know that you'd give up your life for someone?

Okay, maybe you've never felt that way, but parents usually say that about their offspring, right?
KSSSSSSS

Personally, I think it's almost always a dumb idea to sacrifice your own existence for others.

Or worse, for some "cause."

If we were all a little more selfish with our own lives instead of being in such a hurry to defend everything to the death...
I can't fall asleep.

...the universe would be a much less scary place.
Will you sing me a song?

Marko.
Marko, am I dreaming?
Mmn?

Well, *I* was.
I have this recurring nightmare about my teeth climbing out of my head and turning into little...

...kiu?
So this ***isn't*** me having a psychotic break.

Alana, who... who is this boy?
It's me, Daddy.
It's ***Kurti***.

You know how to Forecast?!
I don't even know what that means!

It's a... a very powerful projection spell.
Our High Clerics use it to *simulate* long-term outcomes before going into battle.

That tickles!
This is your vision of the future.
A possible one, anyway.

Except it isn't.
That might be what I'd *hoped* for, but our baby is --
Holy smokes.

Is that a nice ghost?
Like Izabel?

Or a scary ghost?
Like from the creepy book cover I'm not supposed to look at before bed?

I'm not a ghost, ding dong.
I'm your favoritest brother.
Scary ghost.

He isn't dangerous, sweetheart.
He may be to you, love.
Every spell has a cost, and this one is particularly expensive. Forecasting hurts the ***heart***.

No shit.

You don't understand. The longer you keep this enchantment going, the more you risk ***cardiac arrest***.
But, I don't know how to make it stop.
And even if I did...

...how could I?

khh
No sense playin' noble.
Whoever your friends are, I guarantee they'd give *you* up before drawing their last.

...swear... I'm here... *alone*...
Bull. Your hooves are big, but not big enough to fill the fancy footwear we followed here. There's at least one man with you, a man with *money*.
Where's your whoremonger off to, harlot?

She's not going to spill, y'all.
Just snap her neck already.

...please...
...please don't hurt... my *dear child*...

Come again?
The bastard who knocked me up... demanded I get an **abortion**.
Said the doctors out in your Badlands would take care of my kind, no questions asked.

But when I got here, I... I just couldn't go through with it.

Second I told my boyfriend, he said we were finished.
Haven't seen him since... but if you find the son of a bitch, I hope you rob him blind.
Heh.

You made the right call, not going to the Badlands.
Your baby **and** you would have been slaughtered soon as you got there.
What... what do you mean?

That place is run by **monsters**.
And that ain't a figure of speech.

This looks fun!

Race you to the front door, Hazy?
Don't call me that.
And I'm real fast, so don't cry when I beat you!

I can't do this.

You're stronger than you think, love.
I think I'm plenty fucking strong, thanks.
I mean I can't do this to *Hazel*.

All she wants is for her mother to be healthy.
Maybe.
But after this... operation, I'm going to lose my awesome new superpowers, aren't I?

And that means we're going to lose *him*.
Again.

Alana, that is *not* our son.
Obviously.
He's everything I *thought* having a child would be... not the messy, beautiful reality.

But how do we explain that to *her*?

No fair!
I haven't learned to fly yet!

Can I ask you something?
What do you like best about being... you know... *alive*?

I dunno.
It's mostly boring, but then sometimes it's scary, which is way worse than the times when it's boring, so --

PBFFFFFFT

That.
Fart.
Was.
GREAT.

I know it's only temporary, but you let our girl learn who her little brother might have been.
That is a *gift*.
If introducing her to people she's just going to lose is a gift... I'm worried we're starting to *spoil* the kid.

Hazel is shockingly resilient, like all children.
The more loss she experiences now, the stronger she'll --
hngh

Alana?

Uh-oh.

Mommy...?

We don't want to hurt you *or* your unborn, miss.
Matter of fact, you tell us which way your rich ex ran off, we might be able to do you a kindness.
You're... you're going to kill him, aren't you?

Only if he puts up a fight.
But you said yourself, the man is a scoundrel.

Don't be shy.
We're doing this for the good of you *and* your bundle of --

HRAH!

NGH!

NAAAAAH!

HELL-
BITCH!

ptoo

...not afraid -hkk- to die...
...just wanted to -kkh- spite her ugly face first...
We're gonna end you **twice** for that, you vicious --

GAHH!

When it comes to life-or-death situations, I'm a big fan of the "live to fight another day" strategy.
Evening.

The first half of that plan, anyway.
Just stopped by to return a few things.
D. OSWALD HEIST
PETITE DEATHS III

But "live to sleep past another noon" doesn't sound nearly as inspiring.

What's wrong with Mommy?
Why aren't you helping her?!
I... I can't.

We need to **shock** her heart awake.
But I only know how to cast ***lightning***, and that much current would kill your mother for sure.

Which is why ***you*** have to help her.
What?!

Just... just please listen to me, Hazel. Please listen.
Someone your age will create much less current than an old man like me. All you have to do is, is spell *fulmo*.
I don't know how!

Good, that's good, because this incantation is fueled by ***doubt***.
You know what doubt is, don't you?
Kinda?

Everyone feels it, even Mommy and Daddy.
Doubt can paralyze you, can... can make you not want to do anything.

But if you learn to ***channel*** it, to turn those feelings away from yourself and out at the world...

...you can doubt what's impossible.

F... U... L... M...

O!
KRAKOOM

HWUH

Sorry, sorry, sorry!
Don't be, honey girl.
You just saved our family.

But we still have to get your mother to a *professional*...
YES YES YES, MY DARLINGS.

YOU'RE IN SUCH VERY GOOD HANDS.

end chapter forty-five

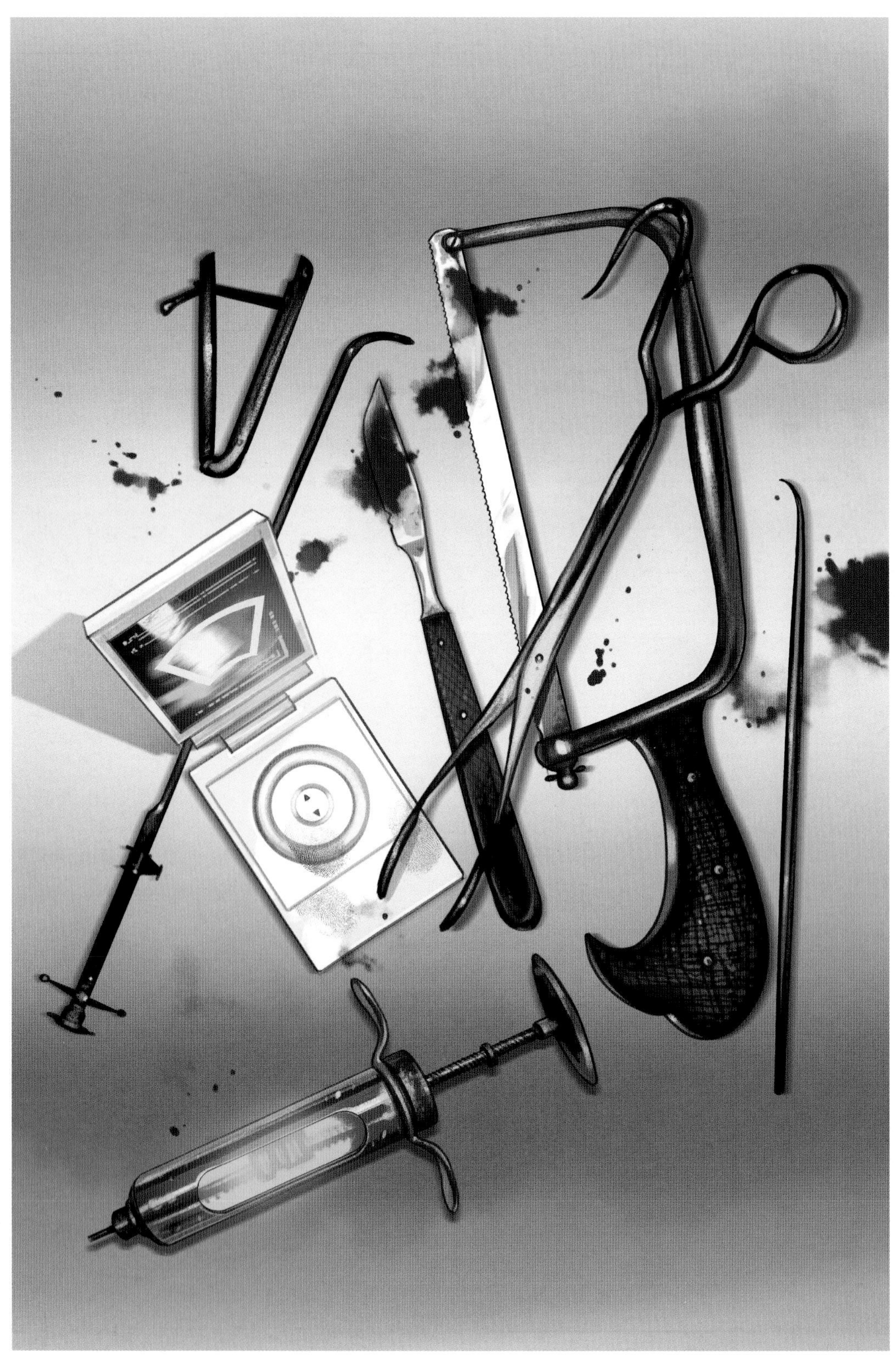

CHAPTER

FORTY-SIX

Pease!
Wee suffhurr ennuh!

We're beggin' you, sir.
Kindly show a little **mercy**.

Fuck your mercy in the face.
=koff=
=koff=
=koff=

You ignorant hayseeds thought you could *lynch* an innocent woman?
Woman? Sir, she's just a *Wreather*.
I... I was thinking her kind was your mortal enemy.

Yes.
Well.

Kill Maw and me if you have to.
S'pose we got it coming.

But won't you please spare our darling son?

Son...?

I ain't a child, Paw.
I'm as ready to meet our Maker as --
Shut your mouth when the adults are speaking, gelding.

You arseholes aren't worth the shallow graves I'd have to dig for your corpses.
Go on, get the hell out of my sight.
...what...?

But set foot around these parts again, I turn your entire family to ***glue***.

Yes, yes.
"This ain't over," etcetera.

Drone piece of ***SHIT!***

Would you care to repeat that?

Fuck your white knight act!
I didn't need you to save me!
That hemp necklace tells a different story, you ungrateful moony slag!

If it weren't for my timely intervention, you'd be a goddamn **bird feeder** right now.
No kidding, Robot.

But you just had to go and ruin a good thing.
My parents taught me never to get too attached to new people who came into my life, since attachment is the root of suffering.

Stay the hell away from my family.

AHH, YES, WHAT SIGHT I MUST BE!
APOLOGIES, HAVE NOT YET HAD CHANCE TO SCRUB OUT SINCE HELPING MY LAST PATIENT.
Are you a doctor-lady?

OF SORT.
I AM ENDWIFE, AND I AM HERE TO HELP THOSE IN NEED.

At what cost?
MY SERVICES ARE PROVIDED ON... SLIDING SCALE.
IF YOU HAVE NO MONEY, PERHAPS YOU MAY REPAY WITH FAVOR ANOTHER DAY?

BUT LET US DISCUSS SUCH MATTERS LATER, FATHER.
FOR MOMENT, MOTHER APPEARS IN DIRE WAY, SO WHAT CHOICE DO YOU HAVE BUT TO COME INTO MY HOME?

NO CHOICE AT ALL, I THINK.

PAY NO MIND TO MY PUPS. THEIR BELLIES ARE FULL SO THEY WILL SLEEP UNTIL MORNING.
YOU TWO MAY WAIT WITH THEM WHILE I ATTEND TO MOTHER.

I won't leave Alana's side, Endwife.
MRRRN.
VERY WELL, YOU MAY JOIN ME IN MY THEATER...

...BUT I DO NOT THINK YOUR TREASURED ONE WILL WANT TO SEE WHAT COMES NEXT.

Stay here, Hazel.
I promise I'll be right back and Mommy will be all better, okay?
Okay.

Big sister?
Ahh!

Are you as afraid as I am?

Uh-uh, imaginary brother.

I'm not afraid at all.

What in fuck's name does someone like you have to be **suicidal** about?
If you really wanted to top yourself, you should have done it when you were a bloody P.O.W., not as a newly free woman.
You call this free?

At least Alana hasn't **banished** you.
After she returns, I'm sure her family will take you wherever the hell you want to be.
Like Wreath? There's nothing there for me anymore.
My own family no longer speaks to me, and the man I loved left his heart on the battlefield... along with most of his other vital organs.

Ah.
I suppose my Coalition was responsible?
No, just another hapless victim of *"friendly fire."*

Yes, my dear wife was killed by one of my own.
Frankly, it was easier to lose people I cared about to ***your lot***. At least I knew where to channel some of the old bottomless rage.

Spare me your false empathy, Robot.
You have ***no clue*** what that man meant to me. Flustro was the only person who stood by my side during an unimaginably challenging... transition.
No need to be coy, Petrichor.

I am well aware of your *"secret identity."*

How? Did Hazel --
No, and I'm sure her myopic parents are still in the dark. I, however, had a sense from the moment we first met.
Between us, I have always been rather...

...fluid.

Bully for you.
But the universe isn't as easy to navigate for those of us who weren't fortunate enough to be born into ***royalty.***
If you say so.

By the by, what the hell kind of lethal potion are you concocting over there?
Viskio.
Back in prison, one of the girls taught us how to turn bug guts into ***rotgut.***

Alcohol?
Blessed, life-giving alcohol?

Not exactly top shelf, but it'll sauté your brain, which is all I'm after.

Care for a nip before you're on your way?
...twist my arm.

To old friends and new enemies.
Chin-fucking-chin.

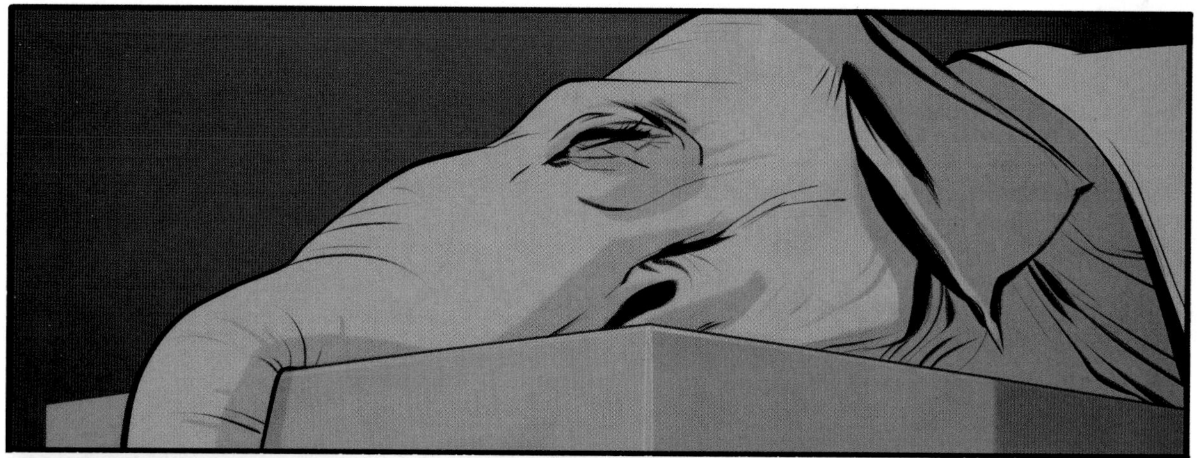

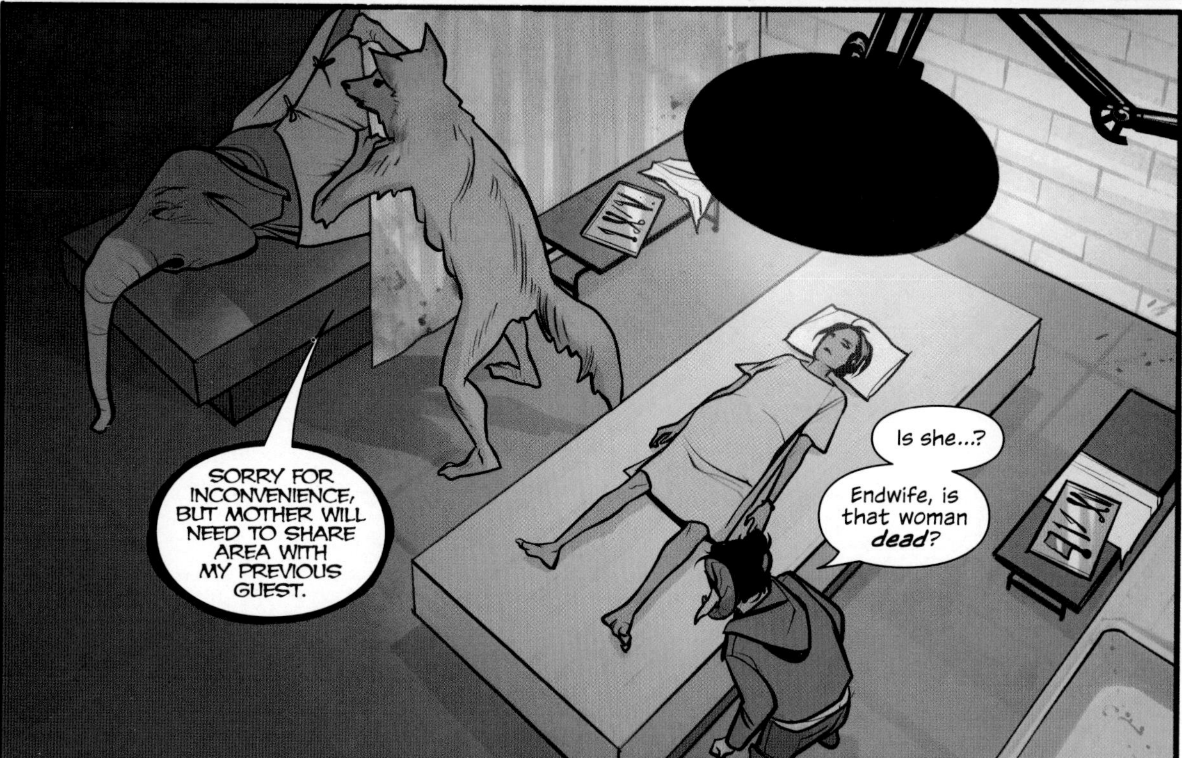
SORRY FOR INCONVENIENCE, BUT MOTHER WILL NEED TO SHARE AREA WITH MY PREVIOUS GUEST.
Is she...?
Endwife, is that woman *dead*?

FOR COUPLE WITH GREAT NEED FOR PRIVACY, YOU ARE MOST CAVALIER ABOUT PATIENT CONFIDENTIALITY.
Forgive me, I only --
AM JUST HAVING FUN WITH YOU, HORNED ONE. IS CLEAR YOU AND YOUR WINGED WIFE ARE VERY GOOD AT KEEPING SECRETS, YES?

THE WOMAN YOU SAW IS MERELY RECUPERATING.
REMOVING A VIABLE FETUS AT THIRTY WEEKS CAN BE MOST CHALLENGING OPERATION.
Thirty *weeks*?

IS THERE PROBLEM?
It's just, I remember how strong Hazel's *kicks* felt around then.
She probably could have survived out of the womb by that age...

AHH, SO YOU DISAPPROVE OF WORK I DO HERE.
I'm eternally grateful for however you can help my wife, ma'am.
But I'd be lying if I said I didn't have misgivings about this place. I mean, Alana's fetus -- our *child* -- has already passed, but other babies...

My father wasn't particularly religious, but I guess you could say he considered himself "pro-life."
And not just when it came to abortion. He raised me to be against things like capital punishment, even eating meat.

AND YET, AM I WRONG WHEN I SENSE YOU COME FROM LONG LINE OF SOLDIERS?
Dad felt that a "just war" was sometimes a necessary evil, but I'm no longer sure there *is* such a thing.
I choose to believe that the taking of any life should always be avoided.

MMN, IDEOLOGIES ARE LOVELY... BUT DOWN HERE, IS ONLY REALITY.

Whose reality?
I can't imagine every woman who comes to you only does so because her own life is in danger.
NO, LIKE MOST, MY LAST PATIENT COULD HAVE EASILY CARRIED HER CHILD TO TERM.

BUT ONLY DAYS AGO, DOCTOR WAS ABLE TO DETECT THAT HER UNBORN HAD DEVELOPED MOST TERRIBLE BRAIN DEFECT.
HER LITTLE ONE MAY HAVE SURVIVED, BUT THERE IS NO QUESTION THE CHILD'S LIFE WOULD BE SHORT AND PAINFUL.

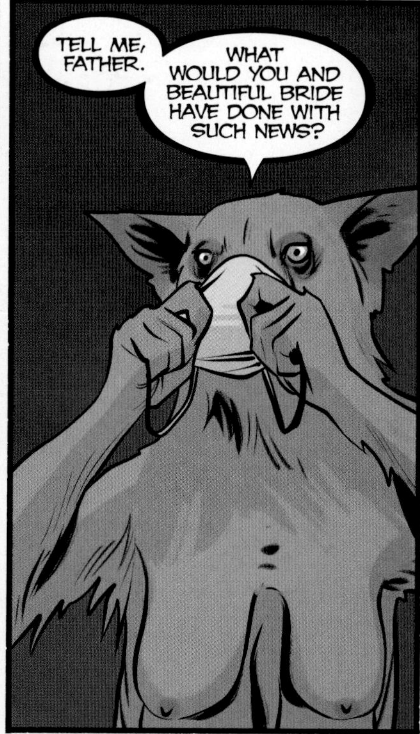
TELL ME, FATHER.
WHAT WOULD YOU AND BEAUTIFUL BRIDE HAVE DONE WITH SUCH NEWS?

MMN.
PASS FORCEPS, WILL YOU, PLEASE?

If they really fix Mama, am I gonna get deaded?

It's *die*.
And I don't know if somebody who's make-believe can even do that.
I'm not make-believe, I'm Kurti!

No, Kurti was a friend of mine who died for real.
I don't wanna hurt your feelings, but Daddy says you're more like... like an *idea*.

Can an idea get deaded?
Die.
And I don't think so, long as somebody remembers it.

Will you remember me, Hazel? Forever and ever?
Maybe... but I can't cross my heart.
I liked the other Kurti a whole lot, but I already have trouble remembering what color eyes he had and stuff.

Oh.
Then, before I go, will you at least sing me a song?

I'm... not that good a singer.
That's okay.
Do you know any lullabies?

The only ones I know were made up by my old babysitter.
Izabel.

She died, too.
Again.

I'm real sorry.
But, do you remember how any of her songs went?
...

Good night, chubby baby
I can't rock you no more

I'm sorry, chubby baby
But my arms are getting sore

Sleep tight, chubby baby
And please don't get me wrong

You're a perfect sized baby
So never accept fakey beauty standards or develop unhealthy body issues...

...from this dumb song
Heh.
"Dumb."

Goodbye, baby brother.

It's funny which random moments from the past our minds choose to cling to, isn't it?

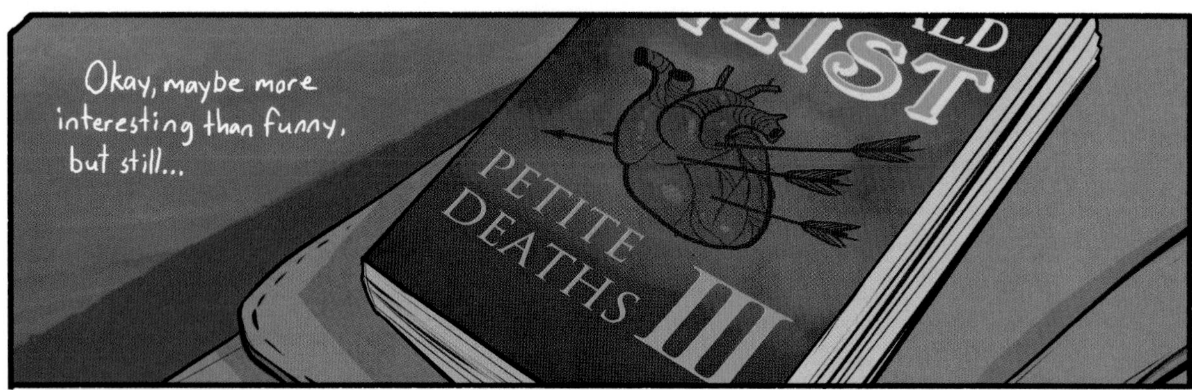
Okay, maybe more interesting than funny, but still...
HEIST
PETITE DEATHS III

You've been hacking your way through these trashy romance novels, too?
Only for lack of less boring options.
I gather the lovebirds grabbed every D. Oswald Heist book they could find before fleeing the author's home.

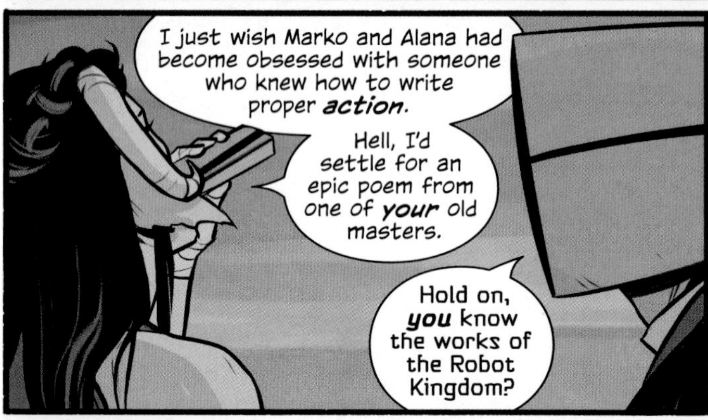
I just wish Marko and Alana had become obsessed with someone who knew how to write proper **action**.
Hell, I'd settle for an epic poem from one of **your** old masters.
Hold on, **you** know the works of the Robot Kingdom?

When I was a student, I read some of your ancient war stories... from back when your fickle world was still an **ally** of our moon.
Before you bastards **betrayed** us and sided with the wings.

Oh, please.
You're the ones who backstabbed my people centuries ago.
If you say so.

I *do* say so, you mouthy trollop.
I knew it was a bad idea to share a drink with your kind.
There's too much history between us.

History?
I barely even know you!
Clearly, you conceited fop.

Are you looking to start something, Petrichor?
Make a move and find out, Robot.

I promise you will come to regret those words.

One way to find out, bitch.

end chapter forty-six

CHAPTER FORTY-SEVEN

BILLY!

Sophie?
Help!

He's gonna kill me!
You'll wish I did.
Now fetch me a **proper** switch to use on your deceitful ass.

Dad.
St... st... **stop it**.

Fuh... fuh... **fuck off**, Bill.
Your sister's a willful brat who needs to learn some --

thwap

That's enough of that.

Good to see you, pal.

But if you please, while I'm on the clock, I go by ***The Letter***.

Uncle Steve.

The hell is this, *Steve*?
Your worthless drunk sister hire you to shake me down for alimony?
Angie's a year sober. Got her old job back and everything.

All she wants is to be a mother again.
So I'm here to take the children home.

Home? Some leaky-ass *fishing boat*?
If you think I'm letting my flesh and blood go *anywhere*, you're out of your --
Sophie sent us a letter.

About what you get up to in that cabin of yours.

Sorry.

You oughtn't have done that.

Don't, Steve!
Don't you even --

THOK

Damn, look how crisp that blood looks on your adorable psycho cheeks!

This magic VCR cost more than my first apartment, but it was **so** worth it.

Sweet Boy...?

Oh, yeah, after I shot you, I had your dog turned into a *rug!*

How's that for some super-villain shit?

...why...?

Because you murdered the man I was going to *marry*, you fat fuck.

My name's ***Ianthe***, and while I look forward to eventually decapitating you, I thought it might be more fun to make you watch me kill all your loved ones first.

But it looks like you've already managed to lose most of your *family*, so we'll have to fast-forward through some more shitty memories to find other contenders.
FREELANCER KILLED WHILE VISITING DEMIMONDE
-koff- listen to me -koff-
I did something to your kin back when I was *The Will*, you got every right to end me... but you start offing civilians, the Constables are gonna give you the *chair*.
Except they won't, you complete asshole.
I could burn down a nursing home and never even spend a night in lockup.
...you some kinda made woman?
Better.
I'm a *diplomat*.
That's just another word for gangster.
No, it's another word for gangster with *immunity*.
Long as I give my home world the occasional intel about which side of the war they should help fund this month, I can do pretty much whatever the fuck I want.
And my newest hobby is binge-watching this misery.
HNNNGH!

Ugh, so predictable.

That's what ***every*** Freelancer going through a midlife crisis does.

I ain't middle-aged.

Whatever, Stalk.
Unlike you, I could *use* an extra pair of eyes.
Just don't get something that sheds.

Why do you even care?
We almost never work the same jobs these days.
Yeah, but if I ever spend the night at your place, I don't want disgusting *hair* getting all over my nice clothes.

You own clothes?
Plural?

Har har.
I love that you ding that but don't even **react** to the suggestion of me spending the night.
Who gives a shit if you need to crash with me sometime?
Because I'm not talking about a grade-school sleepover, dummy.
I'm talking about **sexytimes**.
Call it that again, and we're never sleeping in the same **orbit**, much less --
I GIVE UP!

The hostage! The hostage you're looking for, she's down on P3!
She's alive. She's alive, I swear. And I surrender. I surrender unconditionally.

I'm begging you, I only took this job to take care of my mom.
I did it for the money, and the money *blows*.

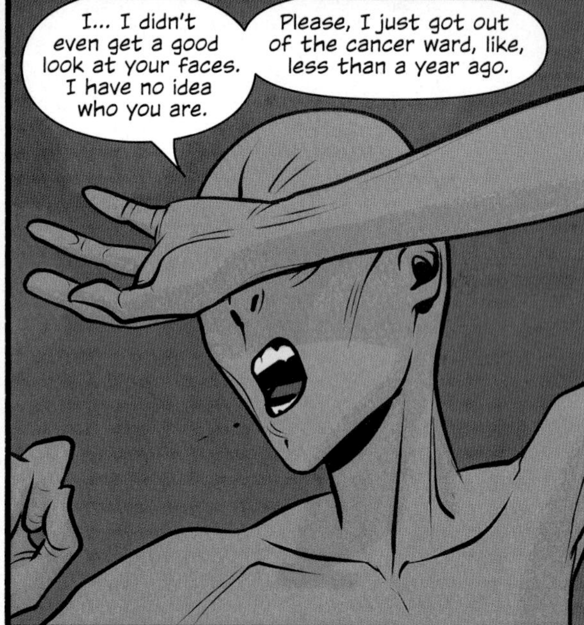
I... I didn't even get a good look at your faces. I have no idea who you are.
Please, I just got out of the cancer ward, like, less than a year ago.

Plus, I finally met someone.
I met someone and I think she might actually --

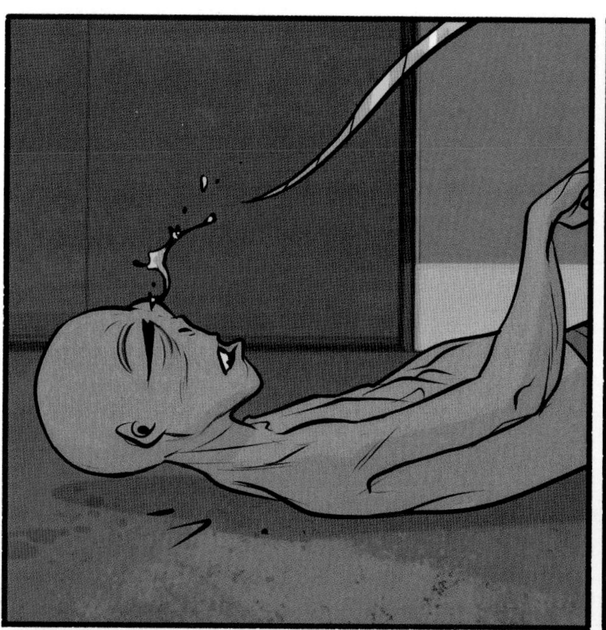

Who knows if he was even telling the truth?

And I'm not doing much later.
If you want to come over, I mean.

Okay.

Boo!
Fucking filler!

You're telling me this chick gets killed in action, too?
Does **everyone** you meet end up dead?

You'll see.

Ooh, sick threat.
Say, how about we rewatch the time you literally shit your pants in front of the entire third grade?
That Gray Gang flunky I lanced... was **he** the guy you were hitched to?

Well now.
I was going to save this dramatic reveal until we caught up to the actual moment of his death, but all right, what the hell?

Years ago, I was engaged to a young man named **Hektor**. One fine day he visited the planet Indica for work...
...and you cut his face in half.

But it used to be pretty as mine.

Sorry.
Not ringing any bells.

Are... are you fucking kidding me?
He was a private security consultant, helping his brothers on some case for Sextillion. You **butchered** all three of them.
Oh. Yeah. Mama Sun's goons, right?

Lady, your boyfriend was working for a bunch of kid rapists.
Wish I could kill him again.

You're a goddamn *liar*. Hektor was no angel, but he'd never have any part of... of hurting a child.
Keep watching.
Enjoy the show.

Fuck your moralizing. Do you have any idea how many young people I've watched you *execute*?
Whatever kind of bastards happened to be cutting a check to my fiancé, he didn't deserve what you did to him.

Maybe he was just another random hash mark to you, but Hektor was the only man in my fucked-up life who made me *laugh*.
I don't know if a woman has ever done that for you, but if so, we're going to find her.

And I'm going to feed you her severed cunt.

Excuse me.

Shit!
Sorry, Gwendolyn.
Relax, my people aren't as hung up as you prudes about nipples.

All the same, I didn't even see nothing.
LYING

Do me a favor and scram, will you?

May I ask something?
Where in the fuck did you even find such a creature?

Lying Cat?
Bought her at a pet store in some ratty old mall.
Bullshit.

Everyone told me to go to one of those *"rescue"* shelters, but most of those animals are straight psycho.
...
I can't tell whether or not you're messing with me, Will.

Anyway, just a heads-up that the repair guys are finally here.
Should be able to get my ship patched in a few hours.
Tell them we'll pay double for a ***rush job***.

Now ***you*** relax.
Settling the score with your pervert ex is gonna take as long as it takes.
I know you don't believe me, but this is about much more than Marko.

His mongrel child is nothing less than a time bomb.
If the general population ever learns that a Wreath Foot Soldier willingly ***procreated*** with an enlisted Landfallian woman --
Uhhhm, bitch, ***rewind.***

Ianthe, please.

Please don't hurt her.
Her?
Billy Boy, if what tits here says is true, I'll be rich enough to hunt down and torture everyone you've ever even *met*.

Huh?
All this time, you've known about a half-moony, half-wingnut *child*? Like a living, breathing entity? With gross little horns *and* feathers or whatever?
People in my line of work wait their whole careers to find dirt as valuable as what your portly ass has been sitting on.
Trust me, it ain't worth the cost.
Because you only know how to monetize punching.
Real power comes from *secrets*.

Think about it: every two-bit conspiracy theorist out there believes both sides of this war have long been *colluding* behind the scenes.
But if your bloated head contains proof that a couple of their soldiers are *literally* in bed together...

...I can crack the fucking universe in half.

But we have to haul ass.
What's this "*we*" crap?
Best finish your revenging now, 'cause I'm not going ***anywhere*** with you.

Oh, Bill.
You profoundly stupid person.

We're already on our way.
NAHHH!!

You know, I'm almost grateful Hektor brought you into my life.
AHHHHH!!

We're going to do something right with everything you've done wrong.

Now shut up and let me finish my show.

end chapter forty-seven

CHAPTER

FORTY-EIGHT

I'm sorry you had to see this.

Don't you dare, Mister Upsher.
Don't you dare hurt one hair on that girl's head.

It's not a girl, it's an animal!
And I'll be goddamned if we let *actual people* starve to death while what's left of this blubber rots!
I'm hungry as you are, but Ghüs knows we just gotta hold out hope that Marko and Alana and their rocketful of food will be back real soon.

You've been saying that for *months!*
I'm sorry, but much as I'd kill to interview your freaky friends, you have to accept that they're *never* coming back to this blighted shitstain.

Face it, those fugitive lovebirds are *dead*... like my boyfriend's going to be if we don't get him something more to eat than wilted fucking crops.
...too much smoke... in the darkroom...

What if we slayed a Dread Naught?

The hell is that?
A wild thing, big game with plenty of meat on its bones.
Heard one howling a few weeks back.

Then why in god's name haven't you hunted it down yet?!
'Cause the tricky beast is *invisible*, least until the day it dies.

Not to my kind.
We can see their ***insides***.
Now how do you know that, Squire?

Because I saw one last night.
In the Barrens.

Gosh darn it!
How many times has Ghüs told you ***never*** to go in those woods?
You actually believe ***anything*** this little sneak says?

Yesterday, I caught him stealing from Doff's share of the rations.
On my oath, he... he ***gave*** me those berries!
Enough.

Gimme one night to see if I can make a meal out of Squire's monster.

If I don't catch nothing... then I'll carve up sweet Friendo myself.
RRRMMM

Of course, I shall be joining you.
Don't want to hear it, son.
Swore to Sir Robot I'd keep you safe until he got back, and the thing we're after is a ***killer***.

I've spotted the Dread Naught once, and I can spot it again.
Besides, I'm safer with you than I am with the newspaperman and his picture-maker.

He's not wrong.
If the fat-ass Freelancer who stranded us here ever comes back, it'll be to finish making that kid pay for his father's sins.
...don't have... The Will...

Hmf.
You gotta promise to do ***whatever*** Ghüs tells you.
I vow on the soul of my late mother.

Then fetch your weapon already.
One day, a boy decided to break the rules.

Like in most children's stories, he then had an adventure.

This experience taught the boy that those aforementioned rules were there for a reason.

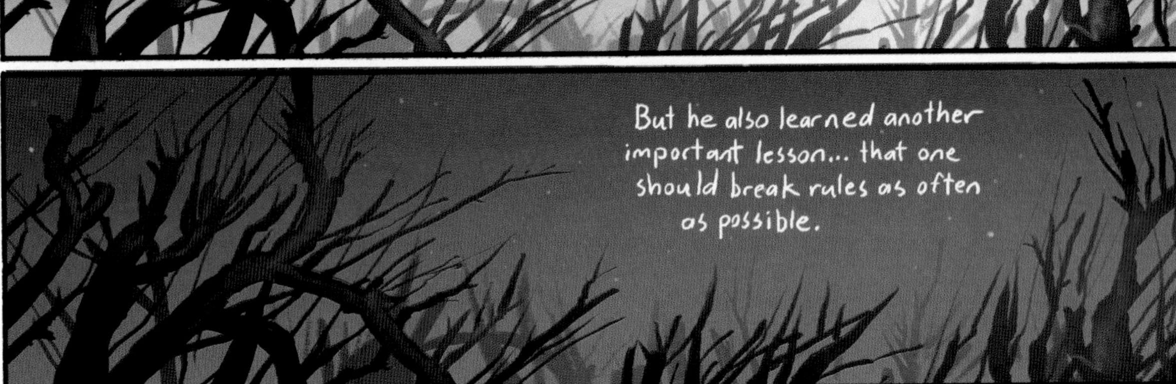

Say what now?
And I'm not speaking of the last of the *birds* we slayed.
Have you ever killed a walking, talking someone like us?

Don't have to chitchat to hunt, you know.
Silence is plenty good, too.

It's just, the bounty hunter who came here, he said that my father has killed *women*.
You don't think that's true, do you?

Ghüs can't speak to any of that.
But best not dig too deep into your old man's past. Sir Robot was born into an awful bloody war.

Who wasn't?

I suppose.
Either way, bad things need doing when folks are at war.
Don't matter if you're a he or a she or what have you.
ow
Sometimes, killing is the only thing to be done.

Did you see that?
A shooting star!
No such thing.

But, I saw it with my own eyes!
Maybe, but it ain't a star.
Just a clump of space dirt catching fire.

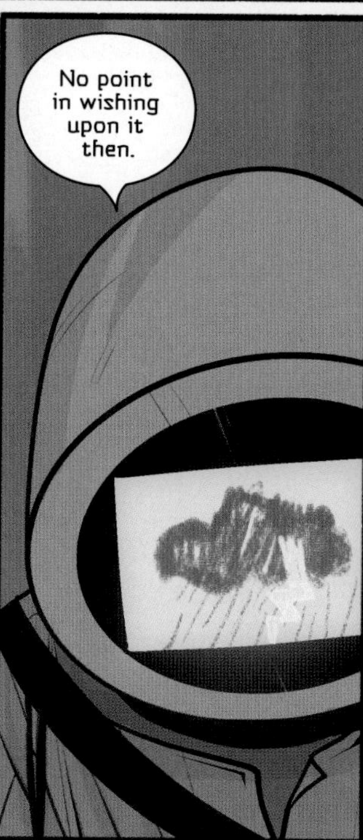

No point in wishing upon it then.

Aw, don't listen to Ghüs, little fella. I'm just tired and hungry.
No, you're quite right.
I'm all alone in this universe, and nothing in the heavens will change that.

Don't you talk like that.
No matter what, Ghüs will always be there for you.
But I'll never marry a beautiful princess like my father did.

Father says a true knight's most important duty is to his romantic partner.
But so long as we're unwelcome in the Robot Kingdom, I can't even visit the one world where my courtly love might be.
Aren't you a little young to be worrying about that kinda stuff?

Well, for what it's worth, I don't think folks gotta get ***hitched*** to be happy.
Ol' Ghüs has always kept his own company just fine.

Then why go to all this trouble just to spare your ***pet?***
Friendo is a lot more than that to me.

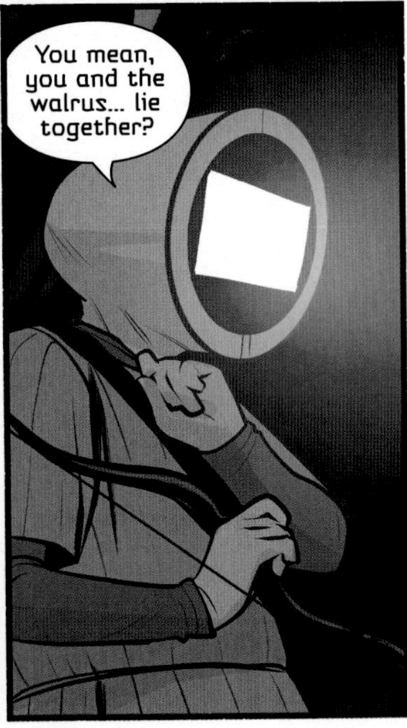
You mean, you and the walrus... lie together?

Huh?!
No, geez, nothing like that!

I mean, my people, we got a strong bond with all our livestock, but there was always something special about Friendo.
Ah.
Got her from my **sister**, after she passed from the lung disease.

Wasn't a very good brother to her, never called enough or nothing.
But when I look into her animal's eyes, it's almost like...

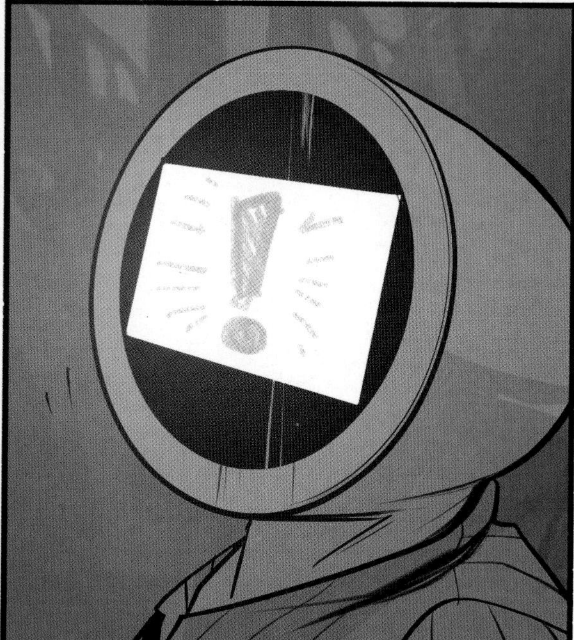
!

Squire?

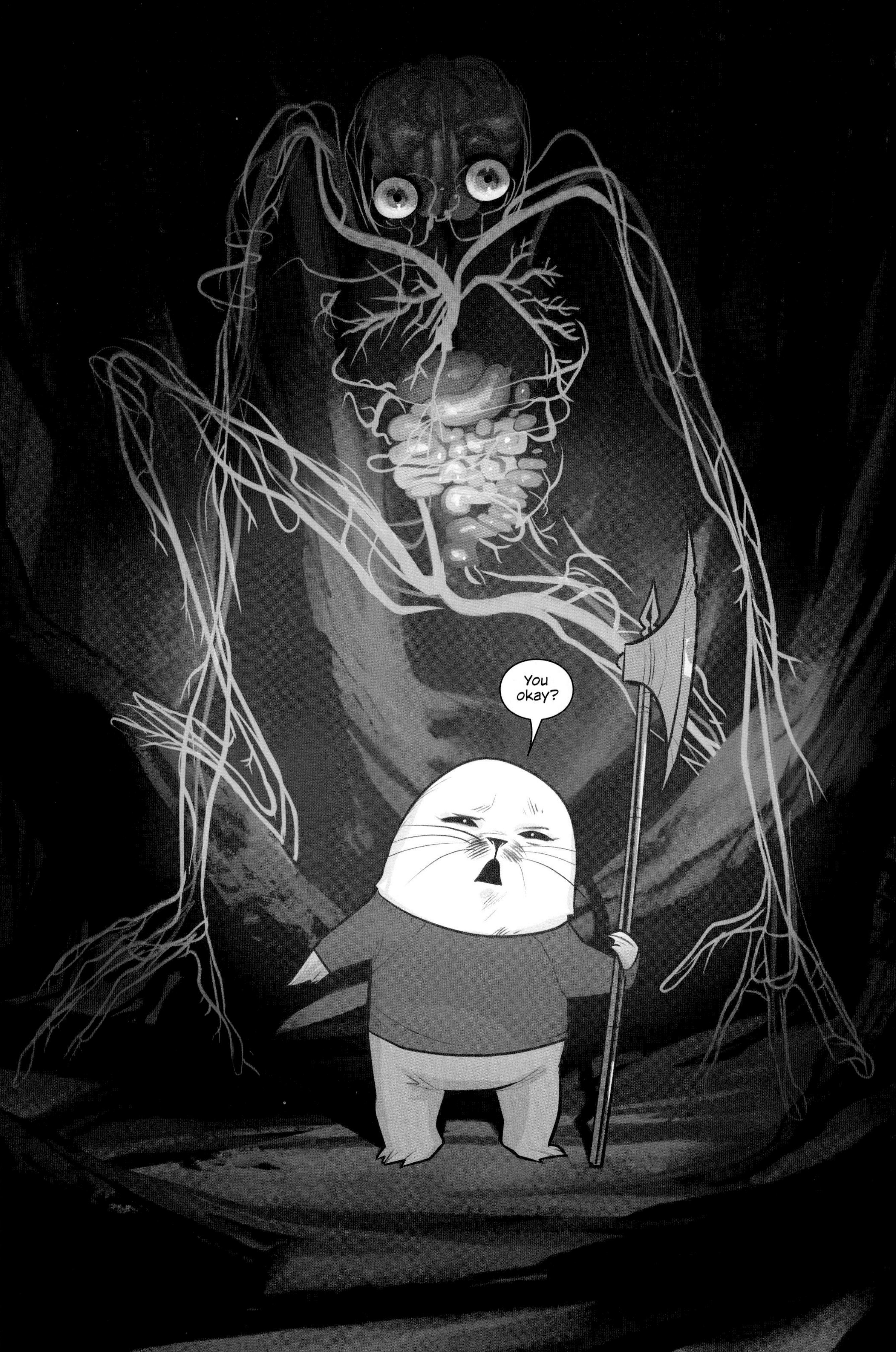
You okay?

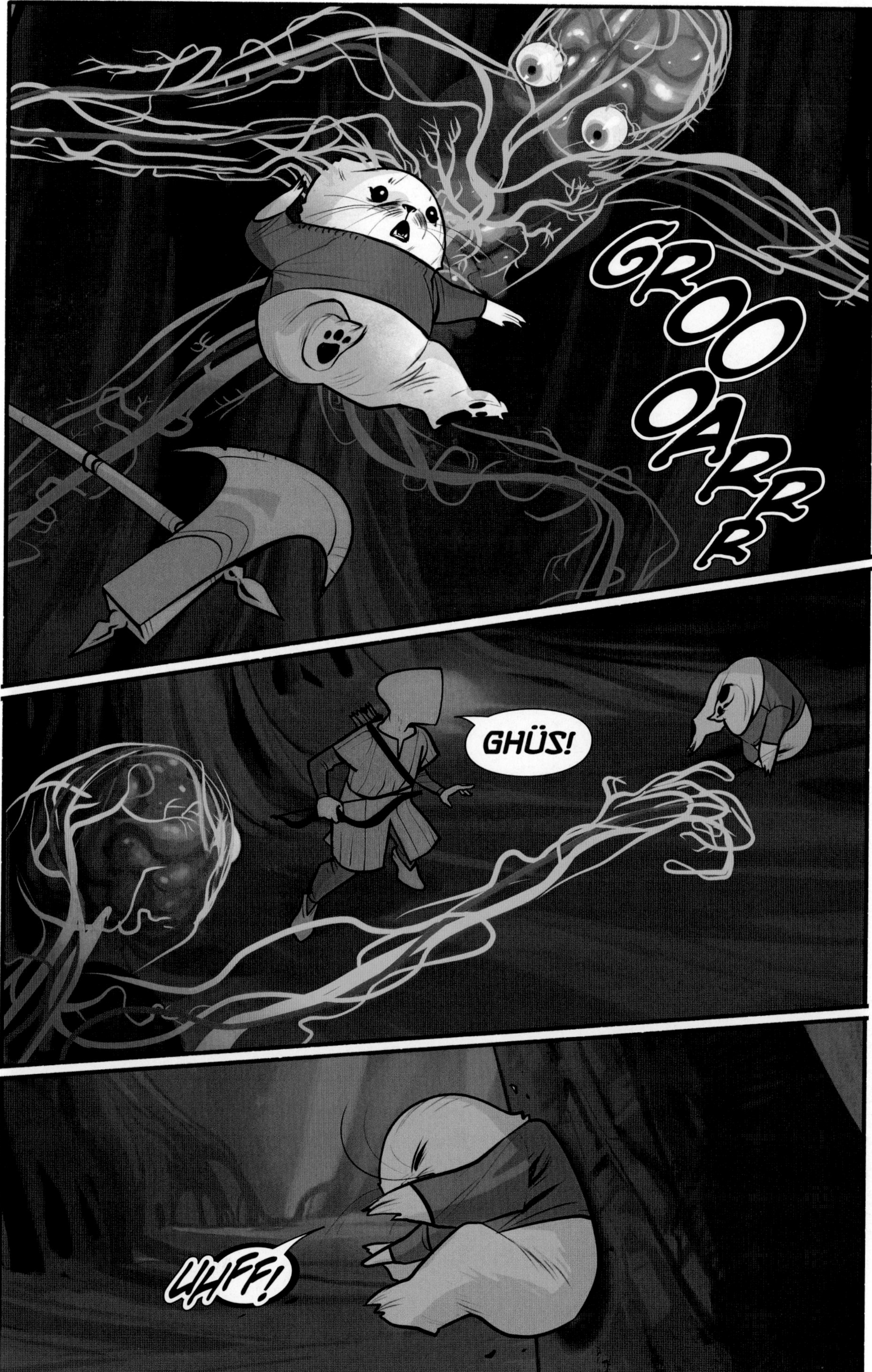
GROOOARRR
GHÜS!
UHFF!

Are you...?
Nnh.
Keep your eyes on it, dammit!

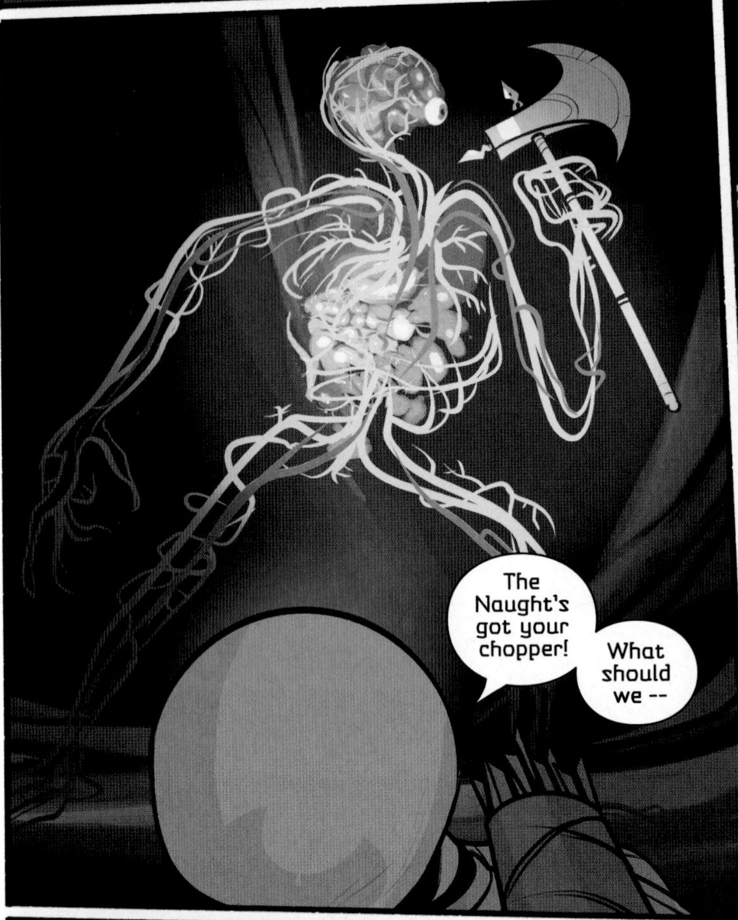
The Naught's got your chopper!
What should we --

KERRACK

Listen good, boy.
It's up to you now, understand?

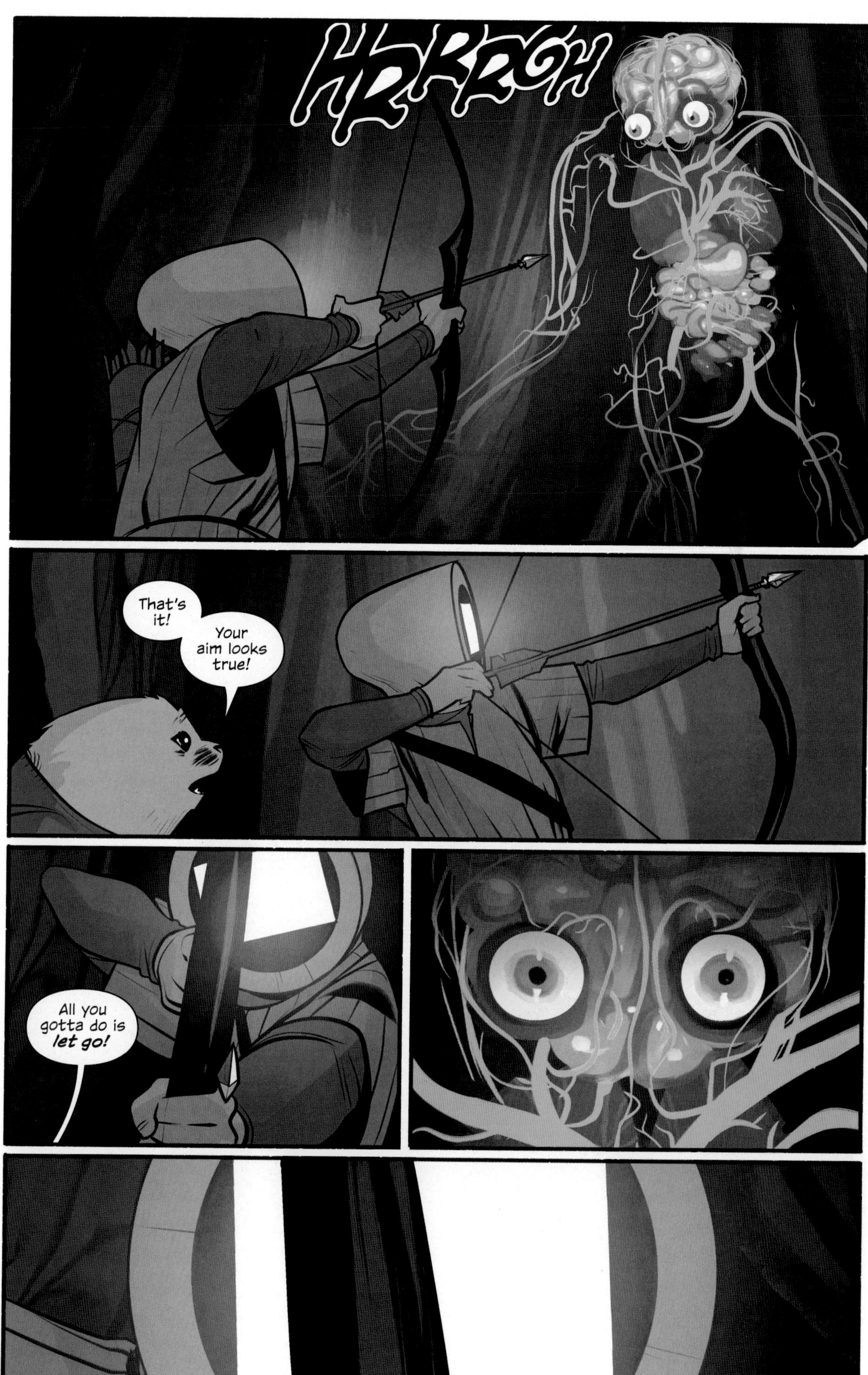
HRRRGH
That's it!
Your aim looks true!
All you gotta do is *let go!*

I cannot.

What are you doing?!
Don't look away! You'll let it...

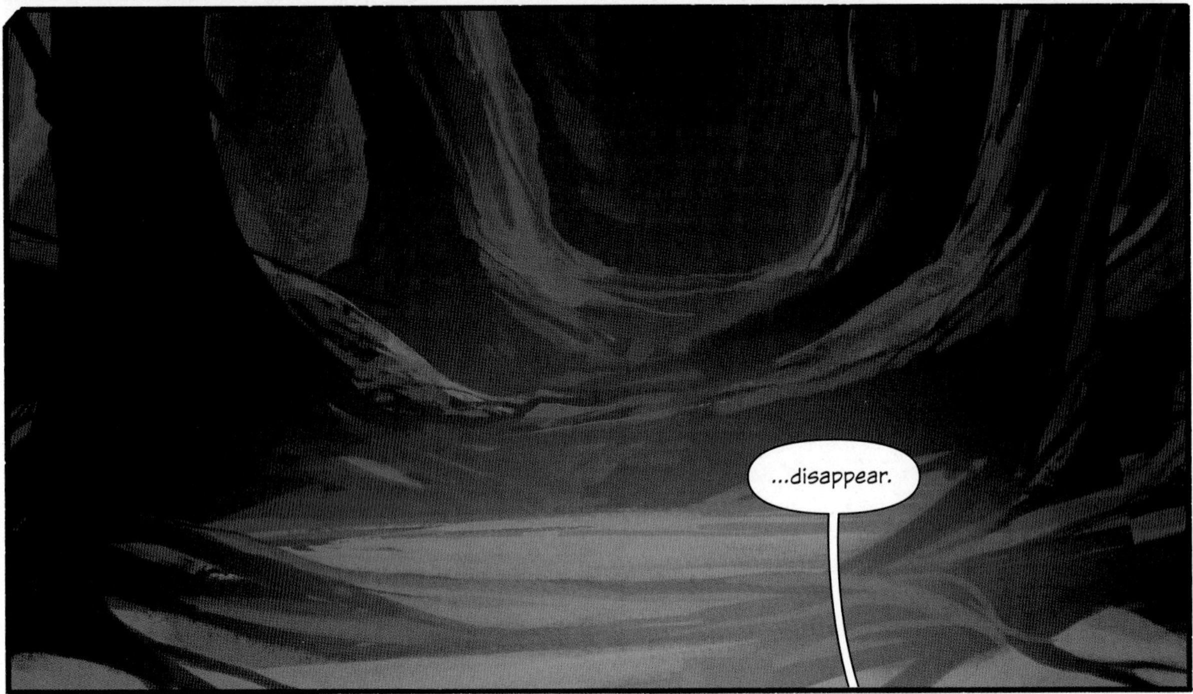
...disappear.

Forgive me.
I... I thought I could slay it, but --
You did your best, Squire.

And that'll have to do.

Ghüs...
I told you, I'm not cross.
Just sad about what's gotta happen next.

Is that **smoke** coming from our grounds?
No, look.
I'll be darned.

You don't think they cooked Friendo already, do you?
What we saw in the sky last night.
That weren't a shooting star **or** space dirt.

It was them.

Squire?

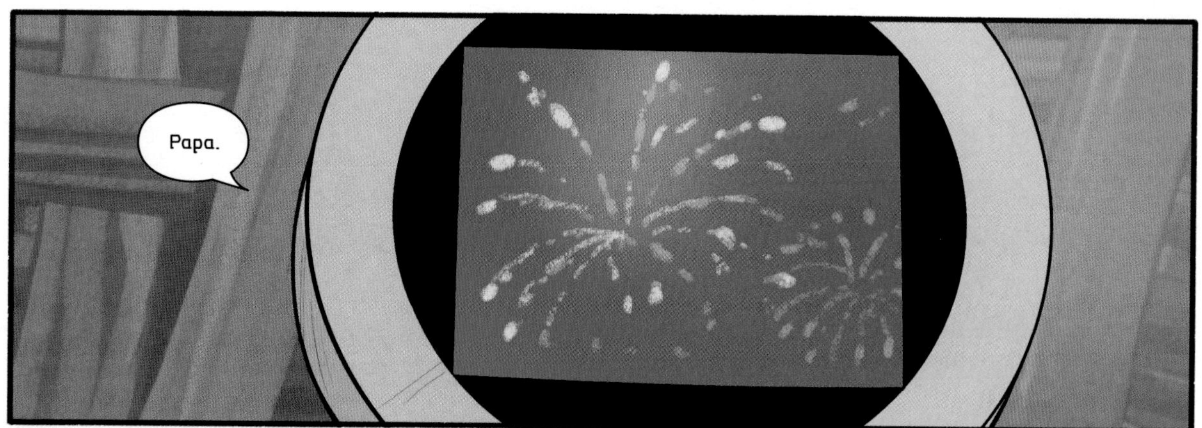
Papa.

Welcome back from your quest, Sir Robot.
On your bloody feet, young man.
Let's see how much you've grown.

My word.

It is... it is ***very good*** to see you again, lad.
Yes.
It is very good to see you, as well.

I only wish I could have returned sooner.
Our journey was a complicated one, but I owe a tremendous debt to my new friend Petrichor for persuading --
Why aren't you ***hugging*** him?

Boys are weird.
Be nice, dear.
Though you're not wrong.

Squire, it is my great honor to introduce you to Marko and Alana's daughter ***Hazel***.
That's her?
The fair maiden?

You don't ***look*** like a fair maiden.
So what?
Do you even know what a fidget spinner is?

Of course I do.
Then what does one look like?

I have no idea what a fidget spinner is.

Come on, squirt.
I'll show you.
One day, a boy decided to break the rules.

And that boy would
become my brother.

end chapter forty-eight

CHAPTER

FORTY-NINE

Hurry up, Slave Boy.

I can fucking *taste* how close we are.
Wasting your time, Ianthe.
Marko and his gang ain't here.

Maybe not, Little Willie, but the two *tabloid hacks* you abandoned were.
And they seemed much closer to finding this mixed-species cult than your stoned ass ever was.

You're a dead woman.
And the longer you keep me alive, the worse it's gonna --
Ugh, mute this boilerplate tough-guy shit.

HNNNGH

Now drop and give me another thousand.
And while you're down there, keep an eye out for, I don't know, clues? Maybe one of your newsboy pals left behind a scrap of...
gnh

Fuck me crooked.

Our race-traitors and their kid.
You said they boosted a ride from the Rocketship Forest, yeah?
...so...?

These scorch marks are dusted with ***pollen***.
Marko and his bitches ***were*** here... and we just fucking missed them.

On your feet, Bill.
I bet we can still pick up their trail.
Don't need *me* for that. -Nnn- Just slit my damn throat already.

Oh, my dear, handsome-ish manservant.
I'm not just using you to help me find some career-making diplomatic intel!

Every minute I get to *torture* you is one I don't have to think about what you did to the love of my life.
You still holding out for an apology?
No, I realize Hektor was just another rando bit player in whatever bullshit *"hero's journey"* you think you've been on.

But when this is over, you'll finally realize that you're not even the star of your own story.
You're a goddamn *black hole.*

And you're going to help me pull every last world off its axis.
The forces that wanted to destroy my parents and me were closer to their goal than they had ever been...

Because while our enemies were close, we were closer...

...closer as a family, and closer to the new companions we'd gathered along the way.

Yeah, you like that, don't you?
Uhn!
Yes, mistress!

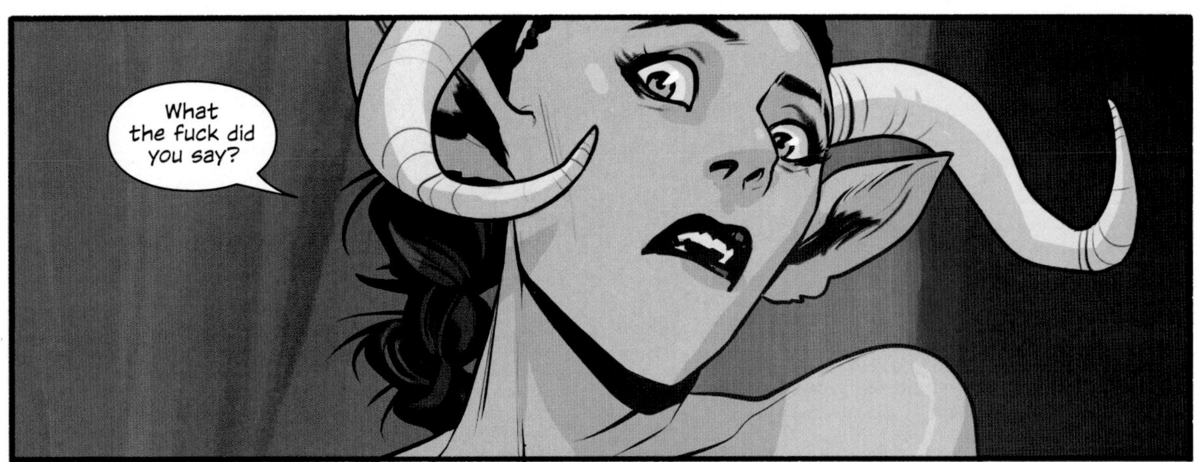
What the fuck did you say?

Forgive me, Petrichor.
Did... did you want me to delay orgasm?
Your face. Your dumb face just told me you *loved* me.

Ah.
Yes, well, kindly **ignore** that gibberish. In moments of passion, my people's physiology can sometimes display signs that might be misinterpreted as...

You know what? Fuck it.
Petri, over the past several months, I must admit that I have developed certain **feelings** for you.
...

Have you not for me?

What would it matter, Robot?

I've had a lovely trip with you so far, but it's just a *trip*.
When it inevitably ends, so will... whatever this is.
But why?

Because I'm from Wreath and you're a motherfucking drone!
I could never even be *seen* in public with you... with your *son!*
Squire adores you!

Silly Robot.
Though it pains me to say so about one of your kind, you're a good guy. But you must know that the two of us have no future.

So we may as well enjoy the present.

They'll never go for it.
We can't know unless we ask, Doff.
So ask.
I would, but he scares the salty piss out of me.
Uh-oh.

Never good when you two are scheming.
Oh, good morning, Alana.
Wait, is it morning? We've been out here so long, I've lost all sense of --

Upsher wants to know if you'll let us tell your family's story.

What?!
The only reason we agreed to let you two come with us is because you swore to keep whatever Marko and I told you ***off the fucking record.***

And we fully intend to honor that agreement... unless you change your mind.
My wife and I are the two most wanted people alive.
Why would we help your scandal rag ***expose*** us?

Because we could offer you and your daughter a chance to finally stop running.
Guaranteed safety and security for the rest of your lives.

Go on...
The Hebdomadal has something called the ***Source Protection Program.***
In exchange for coming to Jetsam and granting us an exclusive interview, our paper would secure you with new identities.

And we're not talking about fake IDs and bargain-basement disguises.
Through an ancient enchanted process, you'd each be given a completely ***new body.***

Bullshit.
No kind of magic can do what you're describing.
It can and it has.
The spell's called Transubstantiation, and it's expensive as fuck.
But over the years, our publisher's offered it to a handful of high-value sources from both Wreath *and* Landfall, and those folks have all blended in seamlessly with our general population.
You're saying we could live happily ever after... as fish people?
Trust us, it's the best of both worlds.
The best of *a* world, anyway.
We prefer *amphibians*, but yeah.
Think what it could mean for your daughter.
She could go to school, have friends, lead an ordinary life.

No.
Our daughter's biology isn't a liability.
It's a *gift*.

I understand... but consider what effect billions of our readers learning the truth about your family could have on the *war*.
When people find out that you're all living together in harmony, maybe they'll realize that... that *peace* is possible.
Except it isn't.

As D. Oswald Heist said, "War can't be ended any more than the rain.
"All we can do is help each other stay dry."
Heist was a man of *privilege* --
What my partner means to say is, we appreciate you hearing us out.
And if you're really still willing to take us all the way home...

...we'll still take your story to the grave.

You are so dead!

Oww, you bit me!
You're ***biting*** me!

Guhme ahh muhayay!
WHAT?!

GIVE ME BACK MY BABY!

What, your stupid dolly?
Ponk Konk isn't a doll!
She's my friend!

You're mental, Hazel!
I haven't even seen that thing!
I **know** you took her, you big... fat...

...LIAR!

MURRN

I am **not** fat.
HEY!

The heck is going on down here?

She started this row, Ghüs!
That don't matter!
You **never** fight a girl, Squire!

Why not?
Petrichor says that kinda talk is **sexes**.

Look, if you two got problems, work it out like grownups.
Use your dang **words**.

These days, I guess a lot of kids interact with each other over screens.
Fine.
Hazel, you look **dumb** without that front tooth.

But I'm grateful that all of my early interactions were in person.
Yeah, well... you look dumb without a ***mom***.

It's a real gift for young people to be able to see the face of someone they've just hurt.

In that moment, you learn whether or not you have what it takes to be a killer.
I.
I was just kidding?

You told us to use words.
Not like that, darlin'.

You're a terrible baby-sitter.

Ghüs cannot argue.

Knock, knock.

Not a good time, Robot.
Behold the crest-fallen muckrakers, forced to sit on the biggest scoop of their lives.
But what if I told you that I possessed a bombshell of similar magnitude?

We graduated from the royal beat a long time ago.
WHOREHOUSE
I'm a *former* royal, properly disgraced, thank you ever so much.
And my information comes from a house of ill repute I visited shortly after Alana and I parted ways back on *Pervious*.

I'm not ashamed to admit that I've visited my fair share of sex workers over the years, but this was the first time I'd encountered one from my own kingdom.
A commoner, but still. I was mildly annoyed she didn't recognize me.

I think she may have been high on something...

So you're like a real earl?
I... I suppose I am, yes.

And you fought for His Majesty's Army and every-thing?
Indeed, though I would prefer not to discuss such matters during our hour together.

Aww, you're not gonna break down on me, are you?
Last soldier boy I had in here cried like a baby.

Well, I should hope for a great deal more discretion following ***our*** time together this --
He said he killed millions of people.

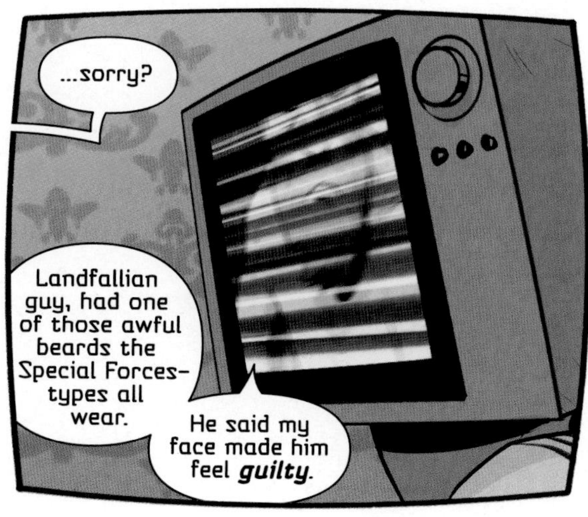
...sorry?
Landfallian guy, had one of those awful beards the Special Forces-types all wear.
He said my face made him feel ***guilty***.

I think he may have been high on something...

When I look at you, it reminds me, like... you people have souls, too.

That's mighty sweet of you, honey.
I mean, I don't care about whatever filthy animals we helped exterminate, but I'm sorry some of *your* folks had to get caught in the crossfire.

Say again?
You've heard of *Phang*, right?

The comet?
It wasn't some natural disaster that ended those poor fucks.
It was *us*.

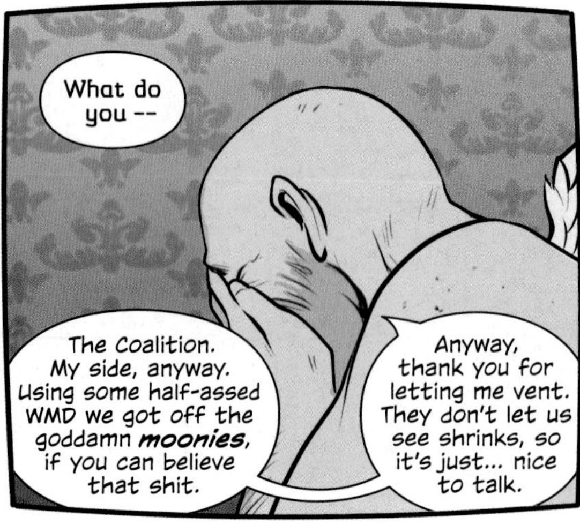
What do you --
The Coalition. My side, anyway. Using some half-assed WMD we got off the goddamn *moonies*, if you can believe that shit.
Anyway, thank you for letting me vent. They don't let us see shrinks, so it's just... nice to talk.

How much extra if I don't want to use a rubber?

There's more where that came from.
If you feel it's newsworthy, of course.

Why the hell haven't you told anyone about this before?!

I had nothing to gain by volunteering dirt about a war I no longer have anything to do with.
Still, if you would be willing to extend the offer you made to Marko, Alana and Hazel to ***Petrichor, Squire and myself***... I might be open to cooperating.
Do you even know if that's something those two want?

I'm confident Petri will be persuaded.
And my son... my son will do as he's told.
Anyone can kill you, but it takes someone you know to really HURT you.

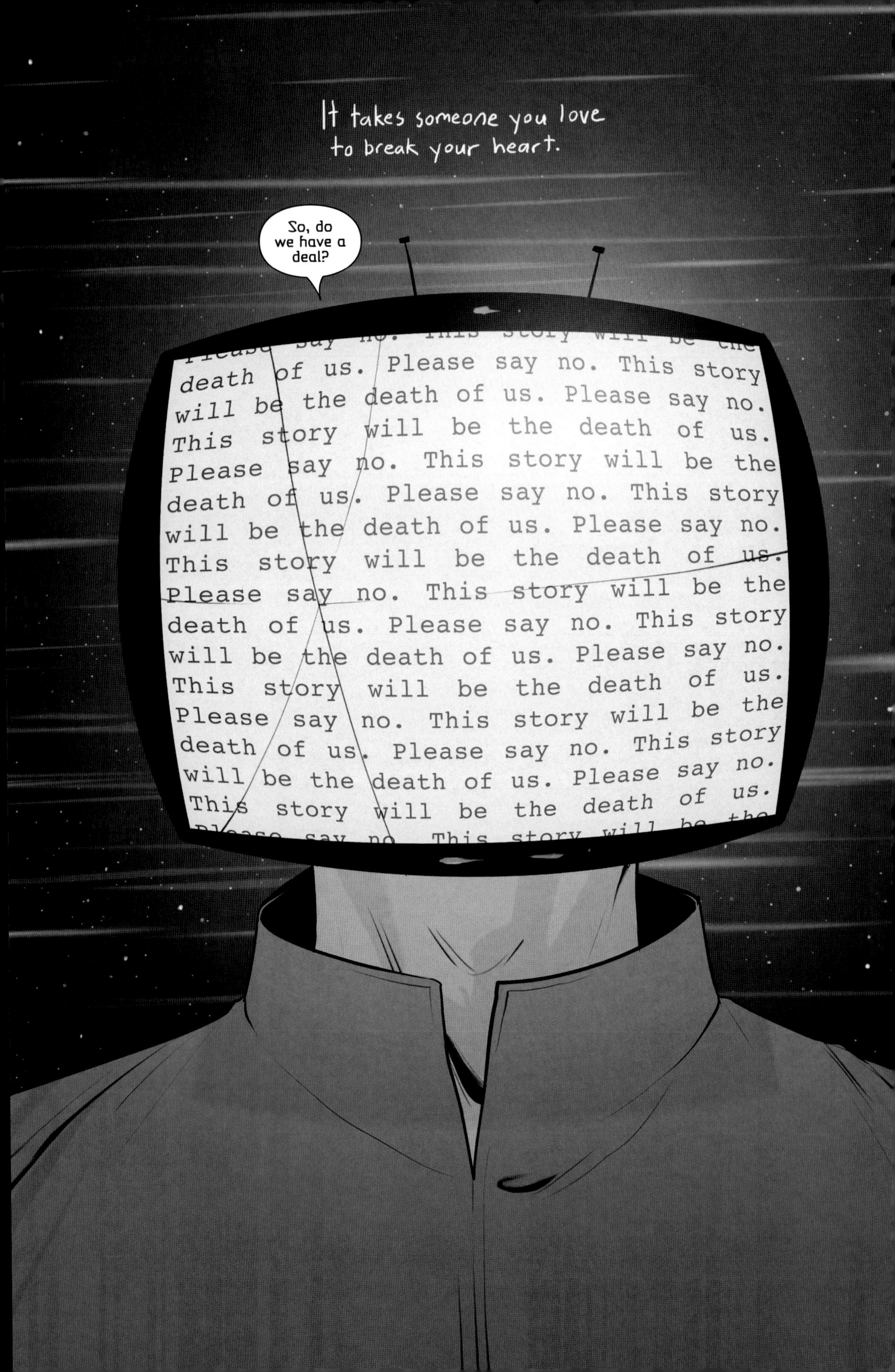

It takes someone you love
to break your heart.

So, do we have a deal?

death of us. Please say no. This story
will be the death of us. Please say no.
This story will be the death of us.
Please say no. This story will be the
death of us. Please say no. This story
will be the death of us. Please say no.
This story will be the death of us.
Please say no. This story will be the
death of us. Please say no. This story
will be the death of us. Please say no.
This story will be the death of us.
Please say no. This story will be the
death of us. Please say no. This story
will be the death of us. Please say no.
This story will be the death of us.

end chapter forty-nine

CHAPTER

FIFTY

Yes.

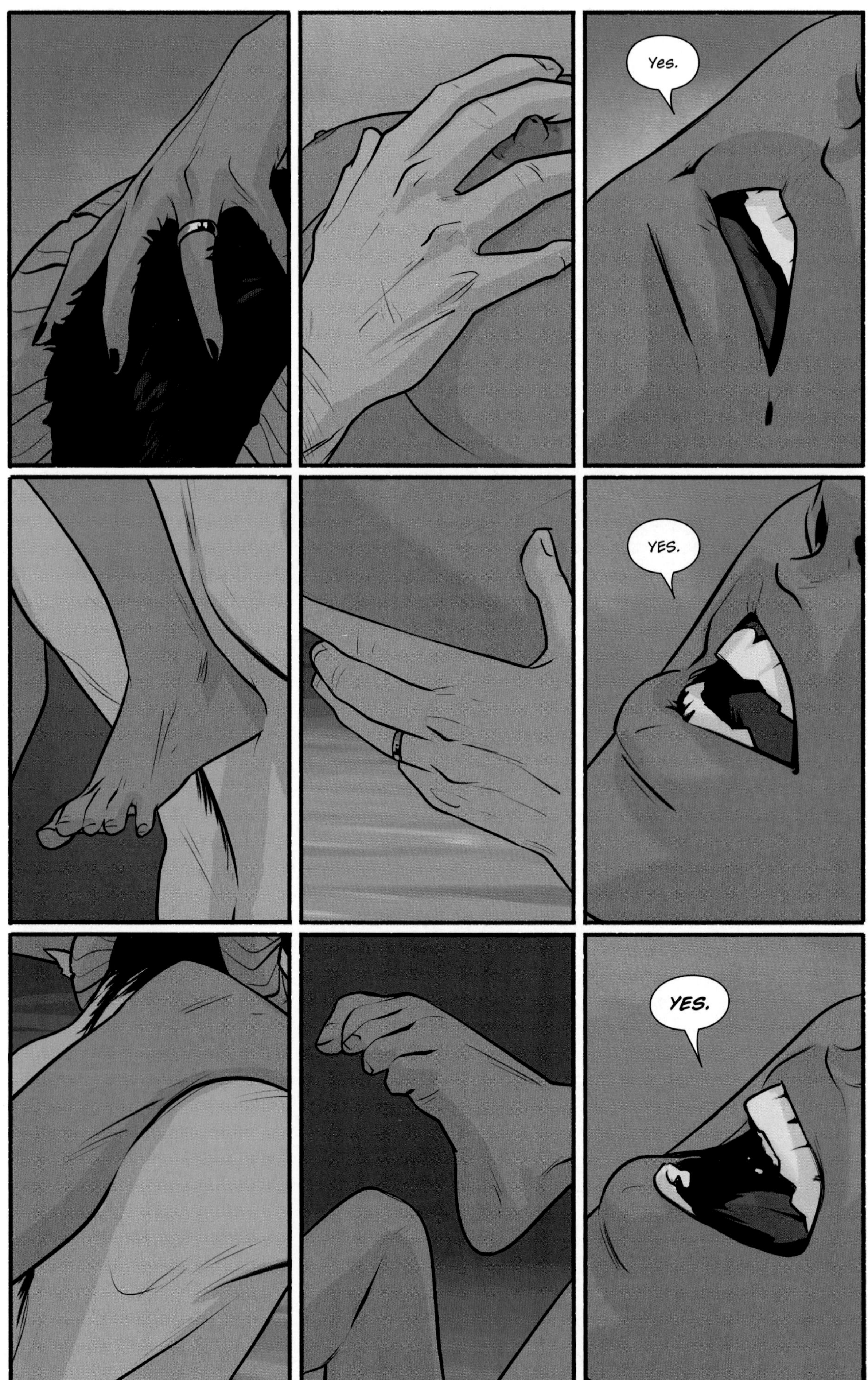
Yes.
YES.
YES.

SPLOSSH

Sorry!
I promise that wasn't pee!
I'm pretty sure that wasn't pee.
mmf

You have nothing to be sorry about, love.
I know all about female ejaculate.

Then please find a sexier word for it.
Also, where did you learn that wizardry, and why haven't you used it on me before?
I would never perform a spell without your consent.

So that was all you?
It was *us*, Alana.
I just tried to listen to your body.

God, are we making a horrible mistake?

Sorry?
Not *moving* here, I mean.
It's not too late for us to take the newsies up on their offer.

I've loved our stop on Jetsam as much as you, but once we finish refueling, I still think we need to keep moving.
Upsher and Doff can give all the assurances they want, but we both know they could never *guarantee* our safety here.

Besides, Hazel would get bored having to spend the rest of her life on one planet.
And so would her mother.
I haven't gotten tired of you and your weirdly hairy ass yet, and we're not exactly newlyweds.

Believe it or not, it's been almost *seven years* since I proposed.
Get the fuck out.
Feels like just yesterday you knelt down behind that flaming garbage pile and shoved this on my finger.

To be fair, we were on the run.
My parents were never big on anniversaries.
And here's hoping we always will be, my sweet Ejaculate Face...

AIRLAND
Any day they both managed to stay alive was already more than enough cause for celebration.

This is why no one gives a toss about newspapers anymore.

Shootem
Real journalism takes time, Robot.
This isn't journalism, it's low-grade torture.
I was promised a new life in exchange for my story, and instead, I've been sequestered in this nigh-haunted dump, forced to rehash every salacious detail.

Trust us, it's the salacious details that are gonna convince our bosses to *give* you that new life.

I have irrefutable proof of military collusion between the most formidable superpowers in the universe.
Who the hell cares that I happened to acquire this information from some prostitute?
Um, every reader ever?

Marko and Alana having a forbidden love child would have been a slam-dunk Page One, but the kind of insider politics *you're* peddling needs to be a little... sexed up.
Yes, well, I'm sure Phang's countless dead are grateful you've found a way to make their extermination palatable to the supermarket checkout crowd.

Look, as soon as editorial decrypts everything we're about to wire 'em, I'm sure they'll want to publish within the week.
And before they do, they'll send us everything you'll need to complete your... makeover.
I'm sacrificing my entire body, not getting a bloody nip and tuck.

If you're having second thoughts about the transformation spell...
Please, I'm done with this battered husk.
But before this story explodes in print, my hopefully chiseled new face and I will have the luxury of ***disappearing***.

What happens to you lads?

Me and Upsher win a couple of meaningless awards?
If we're lucky, management might not cut our salaries next year.

Mm, very whimsical.
But you do realize your report is going to lethally piss off every powerful cunt on Landfall ***and*** Wreath... to say nothing of my own former Kingdom.

You don't think they're gonna like seeing you in your old duds again?
While it may lend a whiff of credibility to your boyfriend's writing, seeing me gussied up like this is only going to make my estranged father more ***cross***.
And when King Robot is cross, mother-fuckers get ***headless***.

We're not afraid of some backwater monarchy.
Then you should try cracking open a history book.
I'm being quite serious when I say the words you just typed may very well be your last.

Robot, since Doff and I started covering this war, we've been threatened, kidnapped, poisoned, shot at and/or ***actually*** shot.
No offense, but we were ready to die on the job long before we ever met ***you***.

Why, for the love of fuck?
Ehn, who knows?

Guess I just got sick of all the bullshit.

Don't listen to this old byline whore.
Upsher's been chasing an obituary ever since he realized it means he'll finally get his name in an actual headline.

As long as they don't use that sucky photo of me you took at the goddamn roller rink.
You looked adorable with that haircut, stupid.

Brilliant.
I've once again entrusted my future to a pair of lovesick imbeciles.

TUNNEL OF LOVE
Hurry!

It's getting closer!

Take its head off!
I can't kick that high, *majstro*!
Not with that whiny attitude, you can't!

KAPOW!

I did it.
Yes, very nice.
But let's keep working on not saying "kapow" with every strike.

You know how I pulled it off?
I tried to imagine that dummy was **Sir Robot**.
I realize he and your parents have had their differences, but what the hell has that man ever done to *you*?

He's forcing Squire to ***move.***
I finally have somebody my own age to play with, and he gets taken away by his evil dad.

Robot is a lot of things, but he's not evil.
Besides, you'll still have Ghüs and Friendo.
And my *memdefendo* coach.

Yes.
About that.

Hazel, I've decided that I'll be ***joining*** Sir Robot and his son.
Ha ha, Petrichor.
I'm not kidding, kid.

But... but you told me to always be proud of ***my*** body.
So why are ***you*** leaving to... to get yourself a new one?

No, *uh-uh*, eff this.
I am not going to be manipulated into another wildly inappropriate adult conversation with you.
I just --

You're an adorably precocious child, but you're still a child.
I'm staying here on Jetsam because... because the universe is ***complicated***, and I don't owe you any explanation more than that. Do you understand?

Jes, majstro.

Then let's finish this lesson strong, before your parents get back from their *"date."*
I want you to focus all of your negative emotions on this next dummy and --

VAPORO!

KOFF

You're a dangerous little girl, Hazel.
I'm going to miss you.

The most important moments in our life rarely take place on some numerically significant date.

Most of the time, we don't even realize we've lived through something worth commemorating until long after it's already ended.

You still awake in there?

Oh, good evening, Ghüs.
Yes, just taking stock. Mister Upsher told me I won't be able to bring anything from the *past* after I'm enchanted with my new identity.
Big changes afoot. Ghüs just wanted to see how his little buddy was feeling about 'em.

That doesn't really matter, does it?
A child's duty is to obey his parent.

Son, if this is something you don't wanna do...
I *want* to honor my father's wishes.
I'll be all right, Ghus.

But I was wondering if you might be able to look after this for me?

Aw geez, Squire.
Ghüs is mighty grateful and all... but Ghüs isn't exactly built to use one of these.
Nor am I, it turns out.

Anyway, let's have a proper farewell when the time comes?
Oh, *uh*, sure.
Thanks for the swell bow and all.

Sweet dreams.
We'll see.

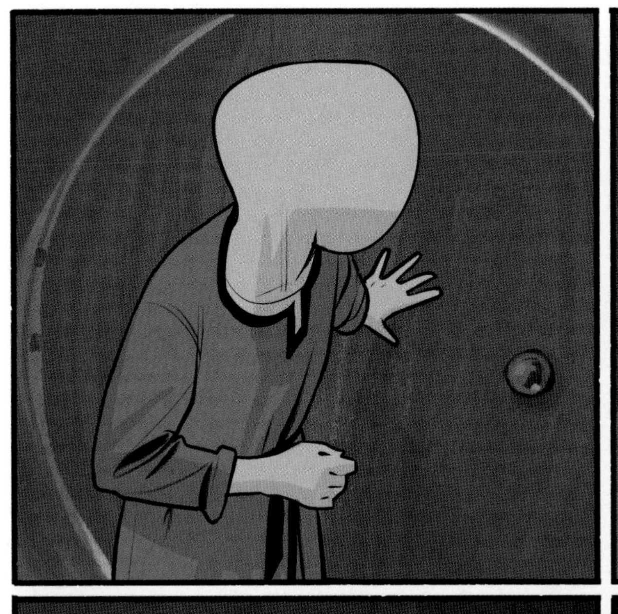

Why did you lie to that man, Squire?

I didn't have a choice, Ponk Konk.
If I told him my real plan, Ghüs would have warned Papa.

And what ***is*** your plan?

We're going to do what the grownups do when ***they*** get into trouble.
We're going to run away.

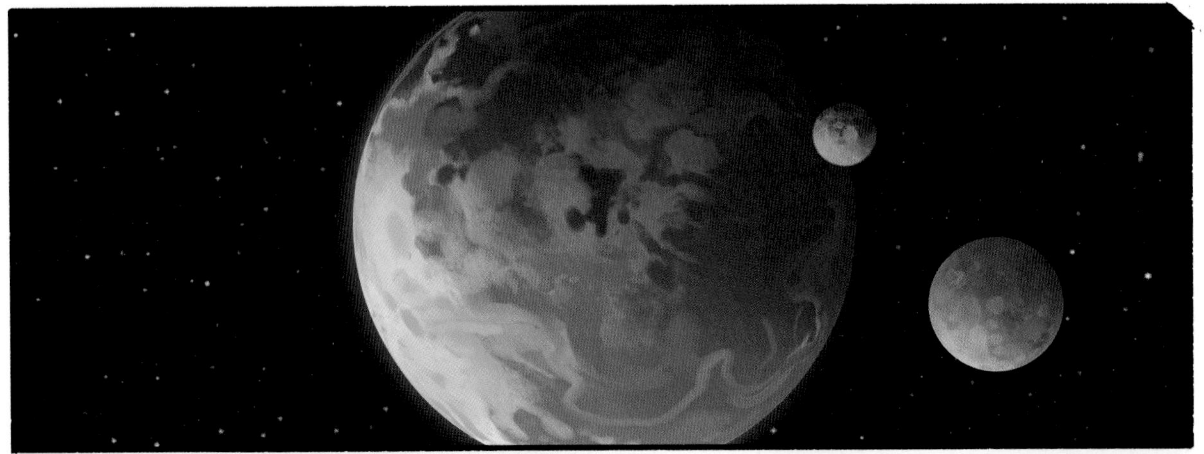

That's so hot, dude.
Mmm, spit on his hairy asshole...
Excuse me, Mister Zlote.

Is now an okay time to talk?

Gah!
The fuck are you?!
Make a move, and I shoot your tiny cock off before you can.

There's a hundred grand and two kilos of Brainpower in the vault behind that masterpiece.
Take it all.

Thanks, but I'm not some two-bit stickup bitch.
The name is *Ianthe*, and I'm visiting Jetsam on a diplomatic mission.

Diplo...?
And my very reliable spook intelligence says that you were once a colleague of a *Hebdomadal* photographer by the name of **Doff**, isn't that right?
Oh, fuck.
You're a fucking *spook*.

I quit that rag ages ago.
Yeah, I'm aware of your new line of work.
But you must be familiar with your former employer's *tradecraft*.

See, I have reason to believe that your pal Doff and his buddy Upsher may have stumbled across an extremely valuable story.
So tell me, is there some kind of, I don't know... *safehouse* where you people might stash a couple of VIP sources?

QUEENIE!
SIC HER!

Queenie...?
Is that your little pink pussycat?
Because she's already *dead*, as are the two goons with machine guns you had outside.

You... you killed her?
You killed my Queenie?

Nah, I don't like to get my hands dirty.
I make ***The Help*** handle the messy stuff.
What are you --

Oh, that's just what I started calling him.
All I have to do is press a button, and The Help will do whatever sick shit I want.

So let me ask you one very final time, peewee.
Where are Upsher and Doff hiding?
Please.

Just tell her what she wants to know.

end chapter fifty

CHAPTER

FIFTY-ONE

Your daddy is a BAD man.

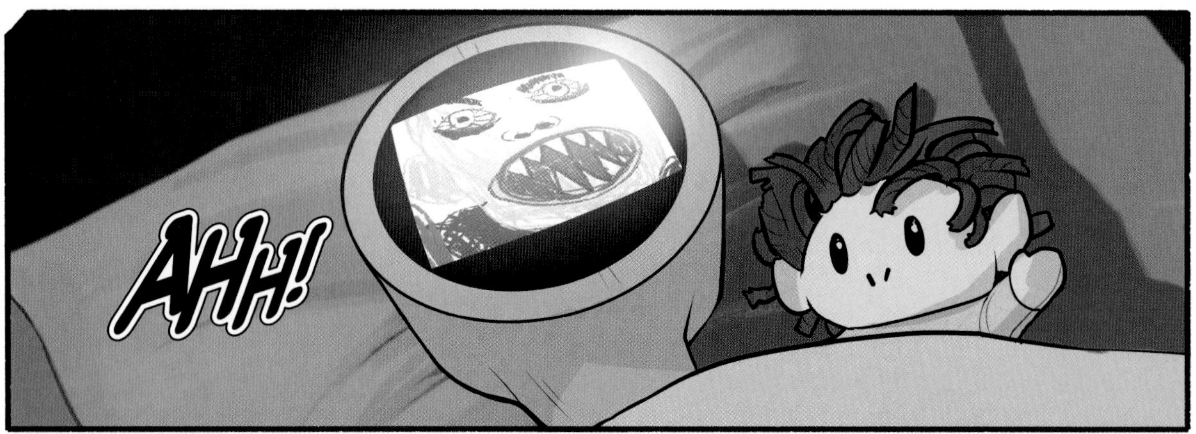
AHH!

AIEEEEEE!
Squire!
Squire, wake up this instant!

Nnh?
You were screaming like a castrated banshee... **again**.
Was it the same nightmare?

Father.
I would like to visit my mother.

Your...?
After the reporters give us our new bodies.
I would like to return home, to place a flower upon her **tomb**.

As would I, dear boy.
But she was laid to rest in the Robot Kingdom, which isn't exactly welcoming to foreigners, including the species you and I are about to join.

Is that what your dream was about?
The savage who took our sweet Princess?
It wasn't a dream, it was a **memory**.

The man with no hair told me that **you're** a savage... that you killed some woman.

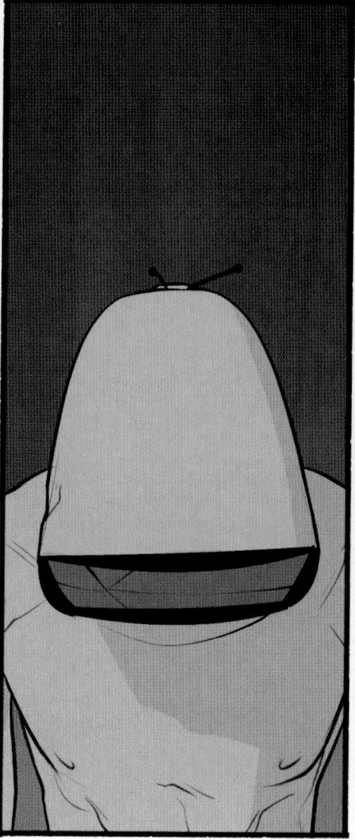

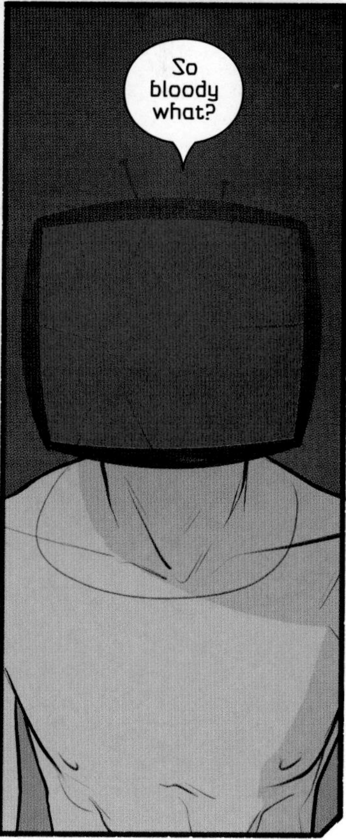
So bloody what?

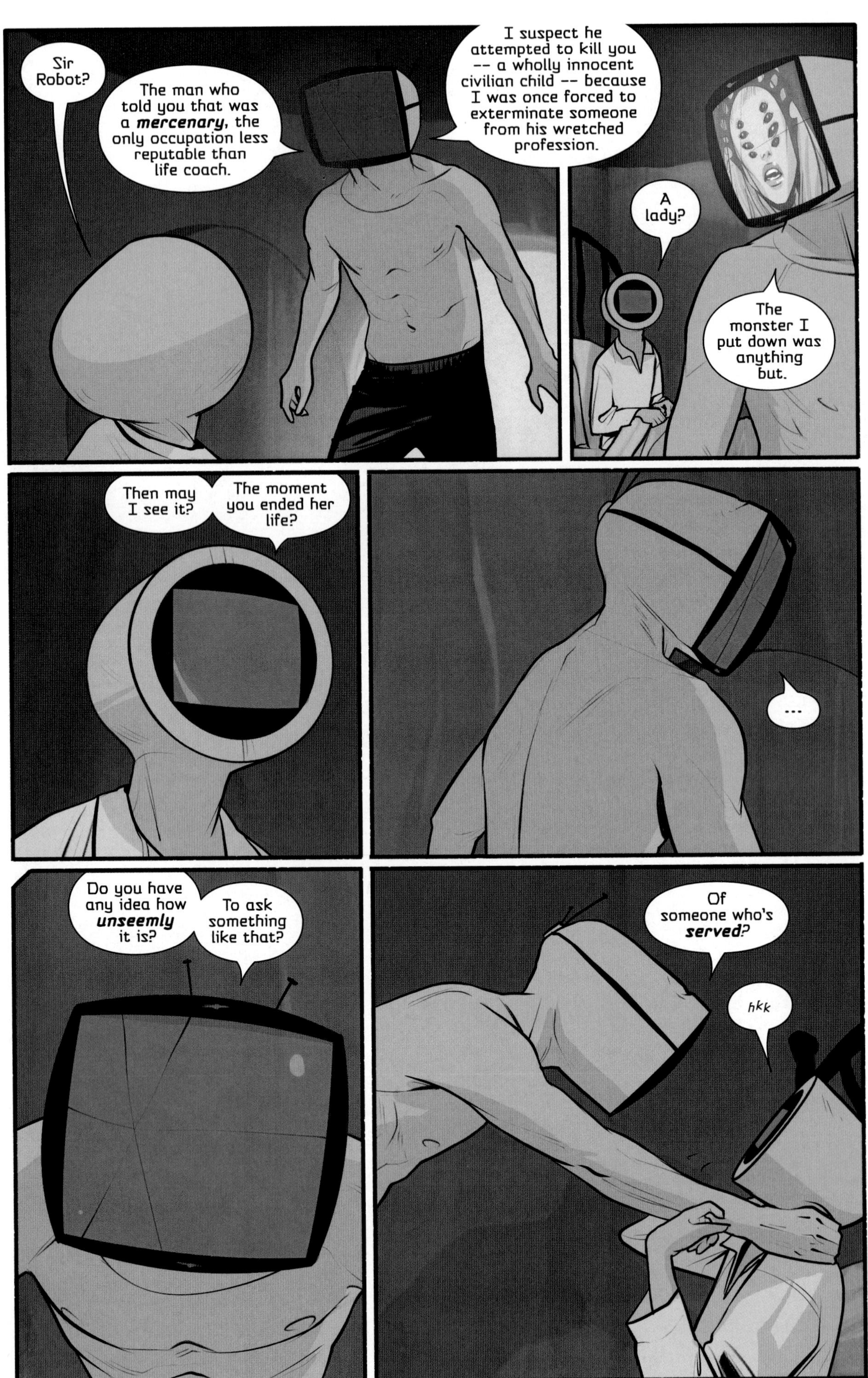
Sir Robot?
The man who told you that was a *mercenary*, the only occupation less reputable than life coach.
I suspect he attempted to kill you -- a wholly innocent civilian child -- because I was once forced to exterminate someone from his wretched profession.
A lady?
The monster I put down was anything but.
Then may I see it?
The moment you ended her life?
...
Do you have any idea how *unseemly* it is?
To ask something like that?
Of someone who's *served*?
hkk

...papa...
...you're...

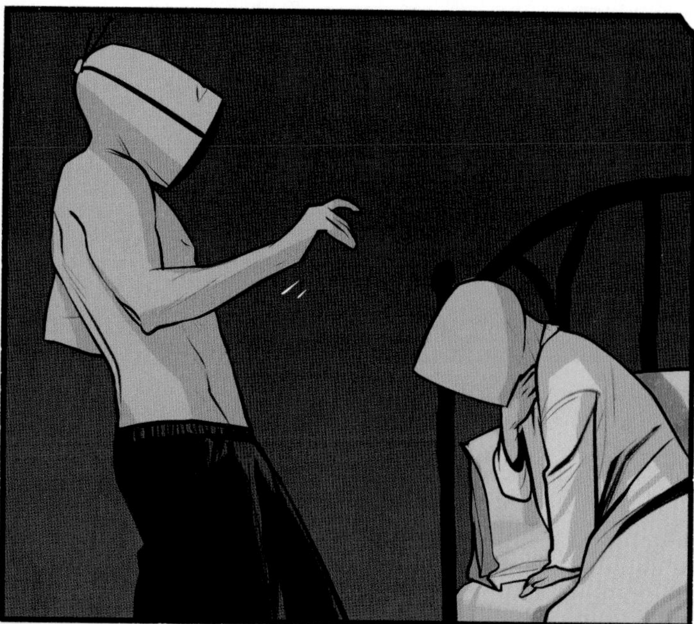

You must forgive me, Squire.
I swear, I... I would ***never*** harm you.

Your father is just terribly eager to ***start over*** with you.
I'm sorry it's taking so much longer than expected, but I give you my word our new lives here are going to be splendid.

Absolutely splendid.
Some people hate waiting, but not me.

Without anticipation, life can be comfortable, but it'll never be THRILLING.

Instant gratification is for boring assholes.
Help!
Why won't somebody help me?!

Careful, Hazel.
'Member what your folks said about crying wolf.
I'm not crying wolf, I'm crying **drowning**!

You're fine, silly!
Doff is right beneath you, holdin' on tight!

Actually, I got out a *while* ago.
Gah!

Gah!

Wait.
That means...

She's swimming!
All on her lonesome!
Well, she's mostly *not sinking*, but it's a start.

Tomorrow, we work on finally getting those horns wet, all right?

That was an awesome mean trick, Doff.

Told you those feathers wouldn't weigh you down.
Quack, quack.
Ghüs packed us three some mighty fine sammiches if you want to --

The holy heck **was** that?
Was it **under** me that whole time?
Mustached kingfish, mostly harmless...
...but I've been trying to get a shot of one since I was **your** age.

Are you going adventuring?!
Because I'm coming with!

Hazel, I promised your folks we'd never leave sight of their rocket.
But --
And what's number seven on this month's **challenge chart**?

"Take 'no' for an answer."
Which is bullcrap.
Number three!

CLOUD on a STICK

Umm, what am I looking at here?!

Are those *my* old glasses?
Oh, yeah, sorry to take these without asking, love.
Mm, I only seem to need them when I'm typing.
When you're...?

Marko, did you write a ***secret book?!***
THE CALLIGRAPHER
A Novel
by Anonymous
Chapter One

It'll probably be more of a secret *novella*, really.
If Upsher lets me take this wonderful machine with us.
What's it about?!
A lot of things, I hope.
The main character's a sign painter, and when a bunch of *demons* steal her enchanted stencils, she kills herself so she can go to Hell to get them back from --
Quiet, I'm reading!
Marko.
It is so, so...
...*so* many adverbs.

This is why I was trying to keep it a *secret*.
I mean, modifiers are fine in moderation.
Less fine every other sentence...
But, that's kind of the point I'm struggling to make, Alana: there's no such thing as "*good*" words or "*bad*" words.
It doesn't matter if it's Blue or Language or whatever, they're all just a bunch of meaningless symbols that we --
Are we gonna try to *publish* this?
God, no.
I've just been thinking a lot about *Yuma*, about *all* the people who've helped us get this far, and that story... it seemed to flow right out.
Hey, I like this part with the punching.
Really?
It's just a first draft. Obviously, I have no idea what I'm doing. Haven't written fiction since I was in *grade school*.
Baby, I have never been so proud.
Page three, and you've already sucked me in.

Deeply.

THE MISTOOK SUX BALLS

THE MISTOOK SUX BALLS
Staring won't make it ring.

You'd be surprised, Petrichor.
Most of my best work has come from long hours of sitting on my ass and watching shit.
Admit it, your editors are ***never*** going to get back to us.

Huh.
Is that your fear... or your secret wish?

Fuck off with your probing questions, Upsher.
Robot sold you *his* story, not mine.
I just want to make sure you understand *exactly* what you might be going through here... with this whole new identity thing?

"*Might*" being the operative word.
What, you think my bosses are going to *spike* a story that could change the course of the entire war?

I fought in some of the bloodiest "*course-changing*" battles of the last decade.
After each, I'd read newspaper reports from my comrades *and* the enemy, and *neither* side ever printed anything resembling the truth.

But *The Hebdomadal* is independent.
Other than making money, they don't *have* a side.
Every world out there has chosen between Landfall and Wreath, especially the ones that claim they haven't.

And Jetsam's government is as corrupt as any other, but my people actually believe in a *free press*, even if most of these illiterate dicks just look at the pictures.
BRIIING

Silence the thing already!
BRIIING
This is Upsher.
I see.
Understood.
Well?
It's going to be the front of next week's issue.
They're sending us ingredients for your guys' transformation **tonight**.
Anticipation and dread aren't opposites, just different versions of the same game.

Both involve knowing that something is going to happen, but not knowing when.

And whether you end up winning or losing, you at least get to reach a conclusion.

There's always some comfort in that.
Please.
Please just stay right --

Wow, this is like meeting an actual celebrity!

I'm star-struck, Doff.
I've been watching you in his flashbacks for months now.

The Will...?
Her name's *Ianthe*.
You make it out of this alive, tell whoever you can she's trying to --

Shhhhhhhhhhhhhhhhhhhhhhhhhhhhh.
RAHH!

Sorry about him.
Now tell me, where are you stashing Marko, Alana and their gross little angel?

I have no idea who you're --
Lying!
Lying Woman says you're lying!

...what do you want with them?

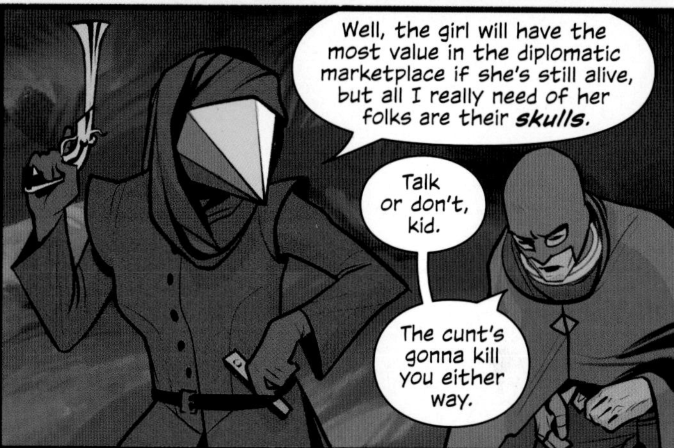
Well, the girl will have the most value in the diplomatic marketplace if she's still alive, but all I really need of her folks are their ***skulls***.
Talk or don't, kid.
The cunt's gonna kill you either way.

Then I might as well go down hard, *huh*?
That's how I'd play it.
Goddamn it you are a lousy sideki--

Uhn!

Stupid... fairy...
Everybody knows... how this scene... *ends*...

BRAM

Fucking phew!

That was a close one, *eh?*
Check his pockets for a trusty notebook or whatever these douches carry.

And smash that camera of his into...

...hold up.
What?

Oh, no.

end chapter fifty-one

CHAPTER

FIFTY-TWO

ATTACK!

Stop movin' around so much, Pedragor!
That is nowhere close to my name!
And why do *I* have to play with this fluff-goblin?

Because my son needed to relieve himself, and he still lacks the confidence to do so in public.
You make it sound like that's a bad thing.
Bodily functions bring me no shame. Should the need arise, I could happily drop mud in the middle of a congested thoroughfare.

Can we knock off the bathroom talk, please?
All's fair in the ancient art of the chicken fight, my dear Ghüs.
A worthy duo stays united through anything life throws at them, while lesser pairs --

Wahhh!

Are you all right, pet?
Nuh-uh, Sir Robot.
I'm *horrible.*

I really wish you two didn't have to leave tonight.
The feeling is quite mutual, Hazel.
But we've exploited your family's kindness long enough, and it's time for us to keep moving.

And who knows?
Perhaps Petrichor, Squire and I will cross paths with your lot again someday.
Like after the war ends?

Right.
After the war ends...
My father used to say that there's no such thing as "heroes" or "villains," that they only exist in storybooks.

Which is ironic, since pretty much all of his beliefs came from what he read in works of fiction.

So you've been on my family's trail ever since we fled *Cleave*?
Pretty much, yeah.
Doff and I heard rumors of a Wreath P.O.W. who escaped with one of his guards, but it was the Landfallian grunt whose *hand* you cut off that gave us our first real lead.

Which only confirms everything D. Oswald Heist warned us about.
Every violent action, no matter how seemingly insignificant, sends *ripples* throughout the cosmos, inevitably causing more of the same.

Then again, if you'd *murdered* that guy, instead of just lightly maiming him, maybe he never would have had the chance to rat out your family.

Spoken with the glibness of someone who's never been forced to take a life.
Well, I haven't offed anyone myself, but shit I've reported in the past has more than likely ended up getting people killed.
And that doesn't weigh on you, Upsher?
Look, my job is to uncover the truth.
Whatever other people do with it is way above my obscenely meager paygrade.
And a lack of proper compensation absolves you of any responsibility?
Of course not, Marko.
But if I worried how every evil son of a bitch out there would respond to what I typed, I'd never touch a keyboard again.
All the more reason that I'm going to stick to writing *novels.*
Why, because you think made-up stories have never resulted in actual casualties?
Putting new ideas into another person's head is an aggressive act, and aggressive acts have consequences.
Face it, you can be a writer or a pacifist, but you can't be both.
GUYS!

Has anyone seen Squire?

Isn't he back inside?
I thought he had to take a leak.
So did I, but the ship's bathrooms are all empty, and one of the ***drainage hatches*** was propped open.

Oh, dear lord.
You don't think he's done a runner, do you?

Let's not panic yet.
Marko and Alana's rocket is still the only way off this island.

How far could the kid have gone?

Fuck.
Oh, fuck me.

Where is he?
Where the fuck did he --

Ianthe —
I killed your stupid boyfriend, you skinned my sweet dog.
We're square.
Leave this place now, or I change my mind.
— The Will

I love that he writes in **cursive**...

deer Father -
Sorry, but I cannot joyn you. I haf to go HOME.
Pleas dont look for me.
~~Squire~~
PRINCELING

Hazel found it next to Friendo's water bowl.
If the child is hiding somewhere out there, we have to move quickly.
This place is nothing but condemned rides and vicious wildlife.

I appreciate your concern, but *I* should be the one responsible for retrieving Squire.
This... this is all my fault.

This is all your fault ***how*** exactly?

We'll cover more ground if he's still conscious for the search.

What's with the shrooms?
I figured we could use them as make-shift **signal flares.**
Pull the stem just beneath the cap and...

First person to find Squire fires theirs, and the rest of us will know to meet you.

I'm coming, too!
Honey, no.
You need to be Mommy's good soldier by keeping watch right here... in case Sir Robot's son gets scared and comes back while the grownups are gone.

You're leaving me alone?!

I can stay with her.
Afraid I don't know this terrain as well as Doff... who's probably headed home with Squire as we speak.

Let's hope.
You see or hear ***anything***, don't be afraid to call us all right back.
But you said it's dangerous out there, Daddy!

Don't fret about us, darlin'.
Ghüs raided the no-no closet to make sure we're all prepared for any creepy critters.

...
Pinky promise you'll be right back?

Baby, I pinky ***swear***.
It's tough for children to accept that their creators aren't gods, just regular people.

And regular people will always disappoint you.

Don't be frightened, Ponk Konk.
I... I think we're almost there.

Almost where, Squire?
I mean, ***Princeling***.

The news-paper is about to send over those magical ingredients for my father and Petrichor's new bodies, yes?
Well, I over-heard the reporter with the camera say that his bosses use some kind of ***tubes*** that run between their offices and this old park.

The pipes are apparently quite small... but thankfully, so are we.

Are you sure about this, Princeling?
It sounds quite perilous.

And it's only the first leg of our quest!
Next, we stow away aboard one of the paper's ***delivery ships***, and use it to finally reach the Robot Kingdom, where the royal family will welcome me back with open...

Oh!
You... you startled us, Mister Worm.

My friend and I were just on our way to --

Uhf!

AHHHH HHH!

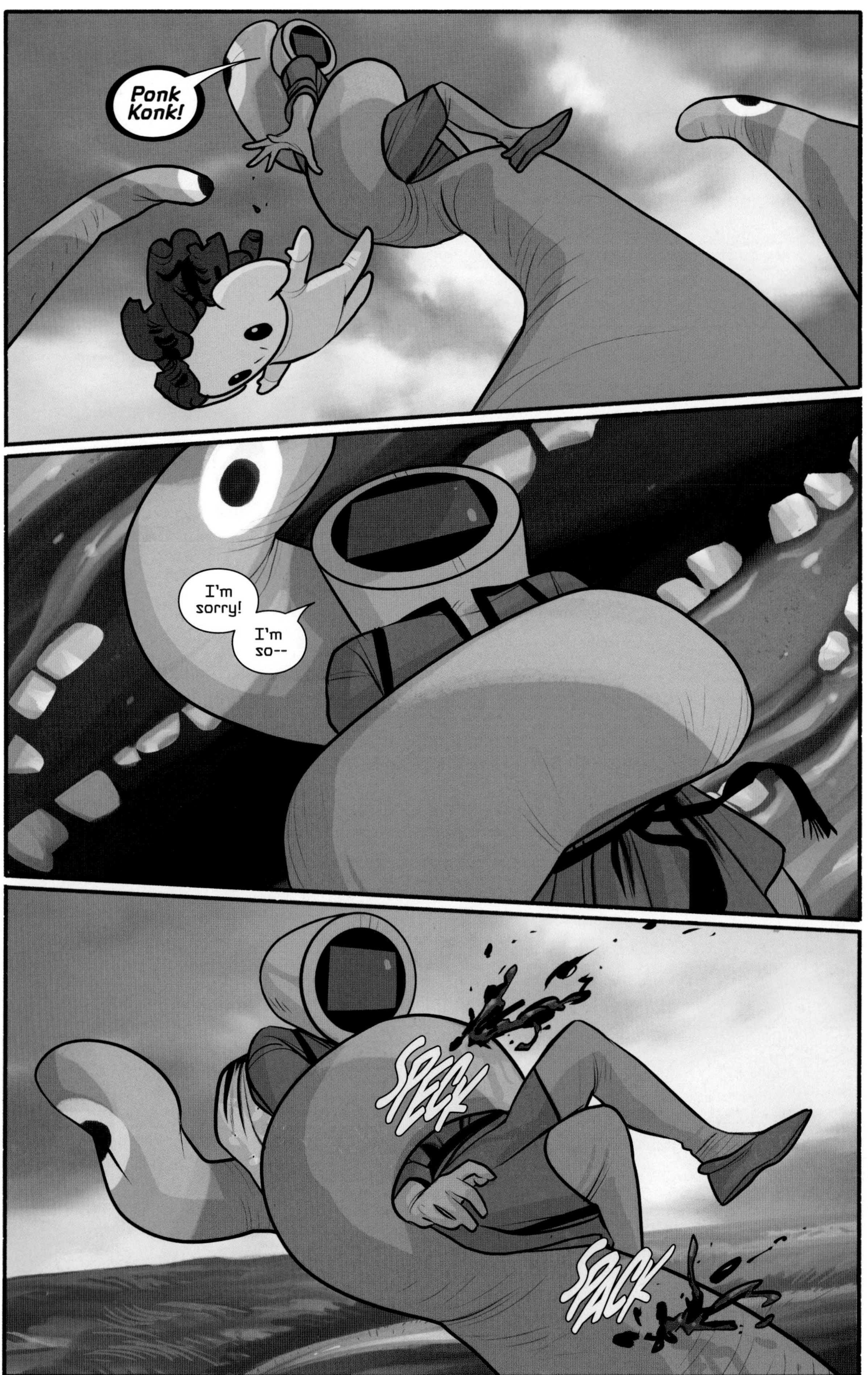
Ponk Konk!
I'm sorry!
I'm so--
SPECK
SPACK

Oof!

Who...?

You okay, little guy?

Goddamn, you're lucky I was here.

So fucking lucky.

SQUIRE!

Please, son!
If you can hear my voice, please just come...

...home?

The ruddy hell is that?

snf
snf

Forgive me.
I don't believe I've had the pleasure of --

NAHH!

Huh, didn't know if that was gonna work. Had to pry open my lance's regulator. Still getting back in my union's good graces.
Anyway, try to use that hand-cannon now, you'll blow your whole arm off.

Not now.
Not when we were so close...

Few years back, I ran with a girl called The Stalk.
You put a hole in her.
And I'm certain you intend to put one in me, but I'm not alone on this island.

Yeah, I know all about the fugitive assholes you been running with.
I'll take care of that job, too... but I ain't the business-before-pleasure type.
You clearly have no idea who you've been pursuing. If you kill me now, I give you my word you'll never get out of here alive.

I understand that you're hurt, truly I do.
But if... if you could just find some way to spare my life...

...I can see to it that no one will ever hurt either of us again.

end chapter fifty-two

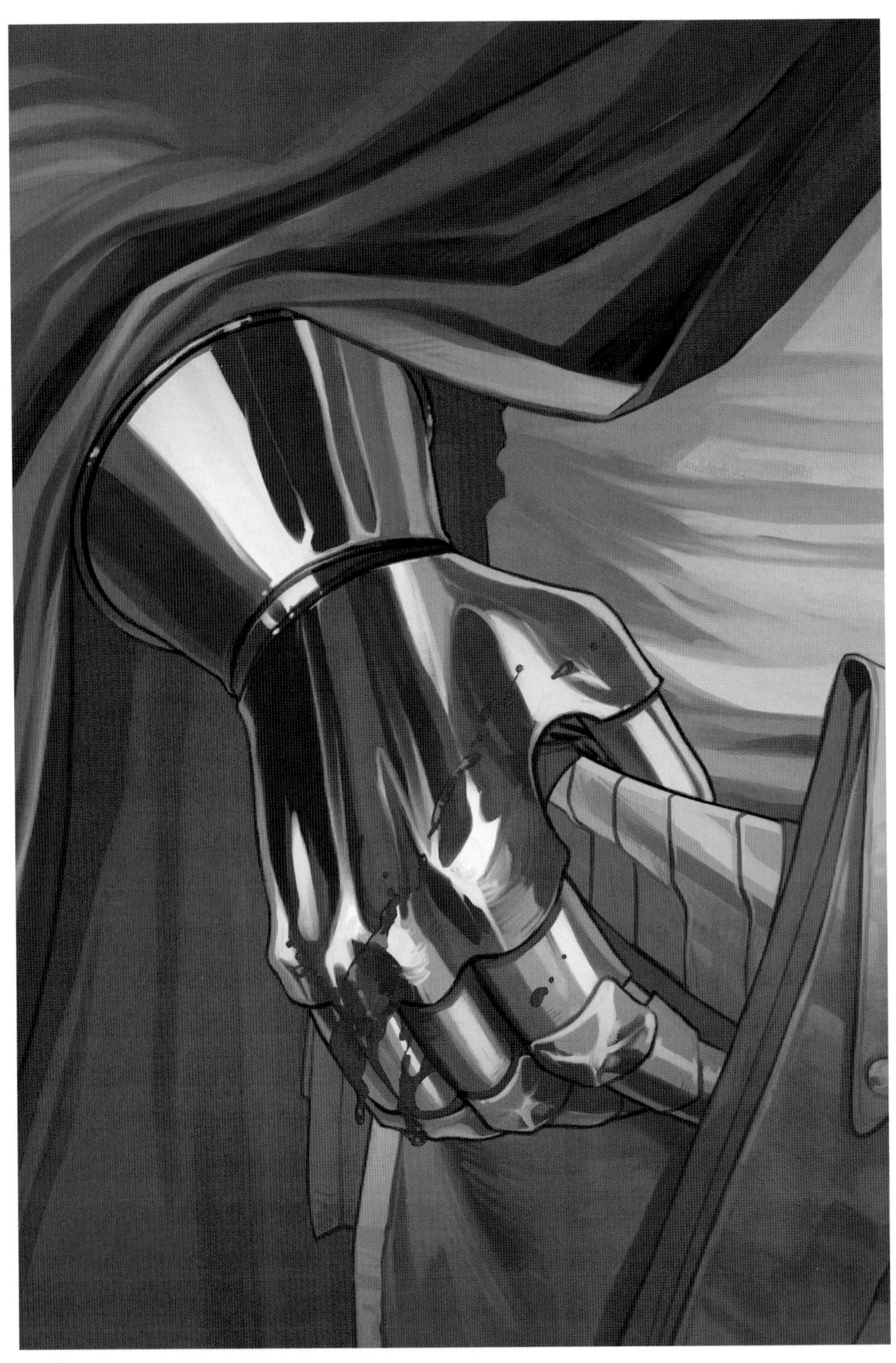

CHAPTER

FIFTY-THREE

This new phone accidentally takes a goddamn screenshot every time I touch it.
Fucking maddening.

Can I help you?

Special Agent Gale, I'm with Landfall Intelligence?
So listen, a friend of a friend told me you guys are planning to run some bullshit story about *collusion* between our side and --
If you needledicks try to block one word from being published, I'll take your entire *planet* to court.

Chill, Chief.
I'm not here to tell you what to print, just to give you some additional information.
And we'll quote whatever garbage denial your propaganda machine has cooked up, but I'm telling you now, I stand by my guys' reporting a thousand percent.

You mean these guys?
Mmm, yeah, drain my balls, you beautiful thing.

Looks like your star "journalists" are a bunch of extremist sex offenders.
Wonder how your **subscribers** would feel knowing *Heb* employees secretly engage in conduct that's still illegal out here in the sticks.

No way.
Videos like that... they can be **faked**.

And yet, it's my understanding that this entire hit-piece **you're** about to run is sourced from the screen of a single disgraced blueblood.

We **fact-checked** every last detail of Prince Robot's memory, and it all stands up.
Including that bit about the former *"Special Forces"* soldier who supposedly admitted to collaborating with the moonies?

Because he was actually nothing but a glorified line cook, one who never served anywhere **near** Phang.
Nice try, asshole, but we actually tracked that grunt down. Kid even offered to come out here and take a lie-detector test... with one of those **cats** and everything.
Yeah, that's not gonna happen.
And why the hell not?

Because the poor bastard hung himself last night.

Or is it *hanged*?
Grammar has never been my thing.
He...?

We got word that some nobody had been peddling a fairy tale to any stripper who'd listen about the Coalition fighting *along-side* Wreath.
Lunatic recanted as soon as we confronted him.
I just... I just wanted them to think I was **someone**, you know?

You did this.
You made him say all this, and you... you *killed* him.
A mentally ill veteran killed *himself* because a failing tabloid and its perverted staff was planning to exploit his ravings to sell papers.

Anyway, feel free to have everything on here authenticated before you decide to stop the presses or whatever.
And next time you want the truth, maybe use this thing to *call* me.

I'm always around.

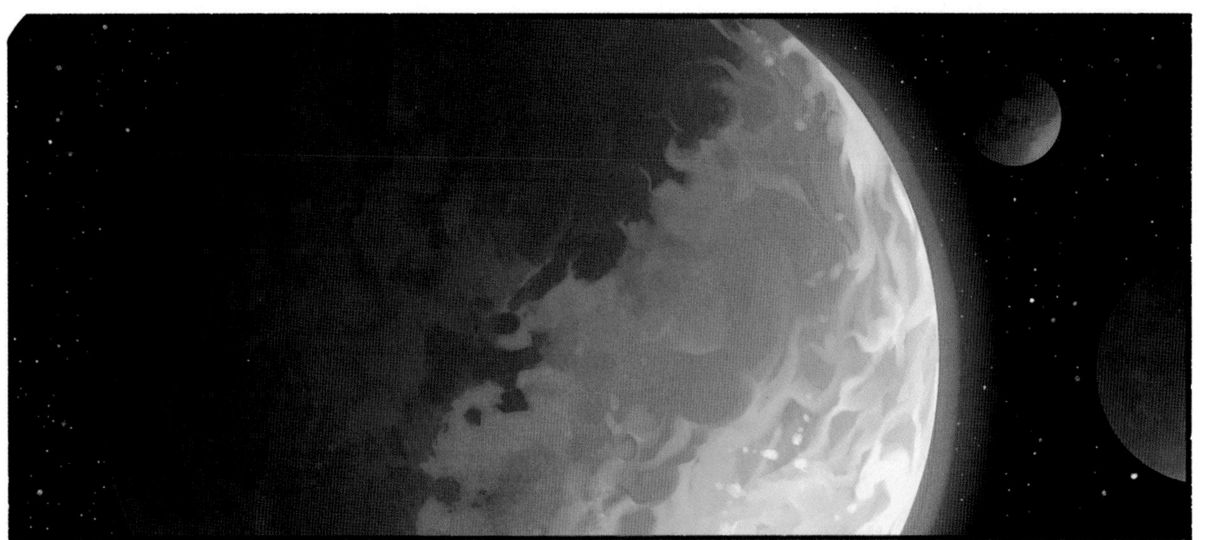

Squire?
Ghüs thought he heard something **movin'** out there. If it's you, holler before...

Aw, hell.

Shoo, ya awful beasts!

You okay?
I thought I heard --
It's Doff, the picture-maker. Somebody **shot** him.

What?!
You... you don't think it was the **boy**, do you?
Squire couldn't hurt a flea, Miss Petri.

Then we're not alone.

Revenigu, revenigu
Revenigu mian amikon al...

...mi?
Hazel!

Did you see it?
See it? I think I *did* it!
I, I, I made up a song, and when I sang it, it came true! They found Squire!

Well, somebody found something.
But maybe we should wait *inside* until we know more.
Good idea, Upsher.

Mind if we join you?

Huh.

And what makes you think I need **help** collecting a bounty?
Because it's not just the girl's parents you have to worry about.
Over the years, Marko and Alana have picked up a cadre of lethal associates, all of whom I can help you **defeat**... if you promise to let me live.

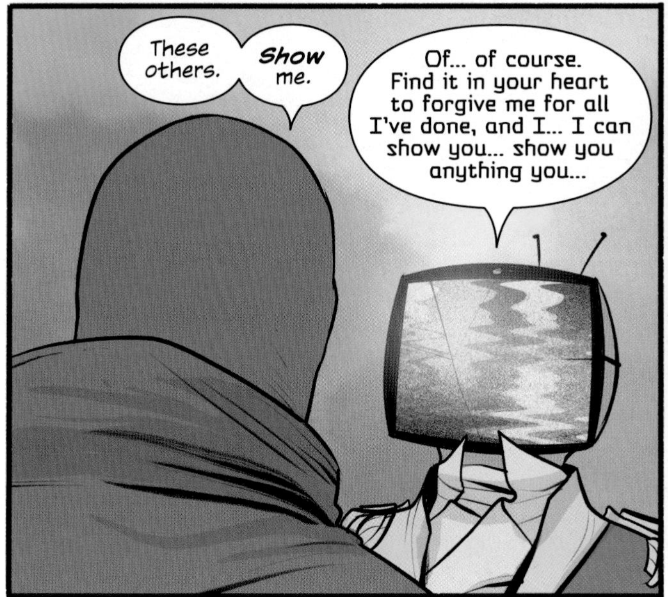
These others.
Show me.
Of... of course. Find it in your heart to forgive me for all I've done, and I... I can show you... show you anything you...

Damn it all.
I'm begging you, don't watch this part.

IV!
GET YOUR SCRAMBLED SKULL OVER HERE!

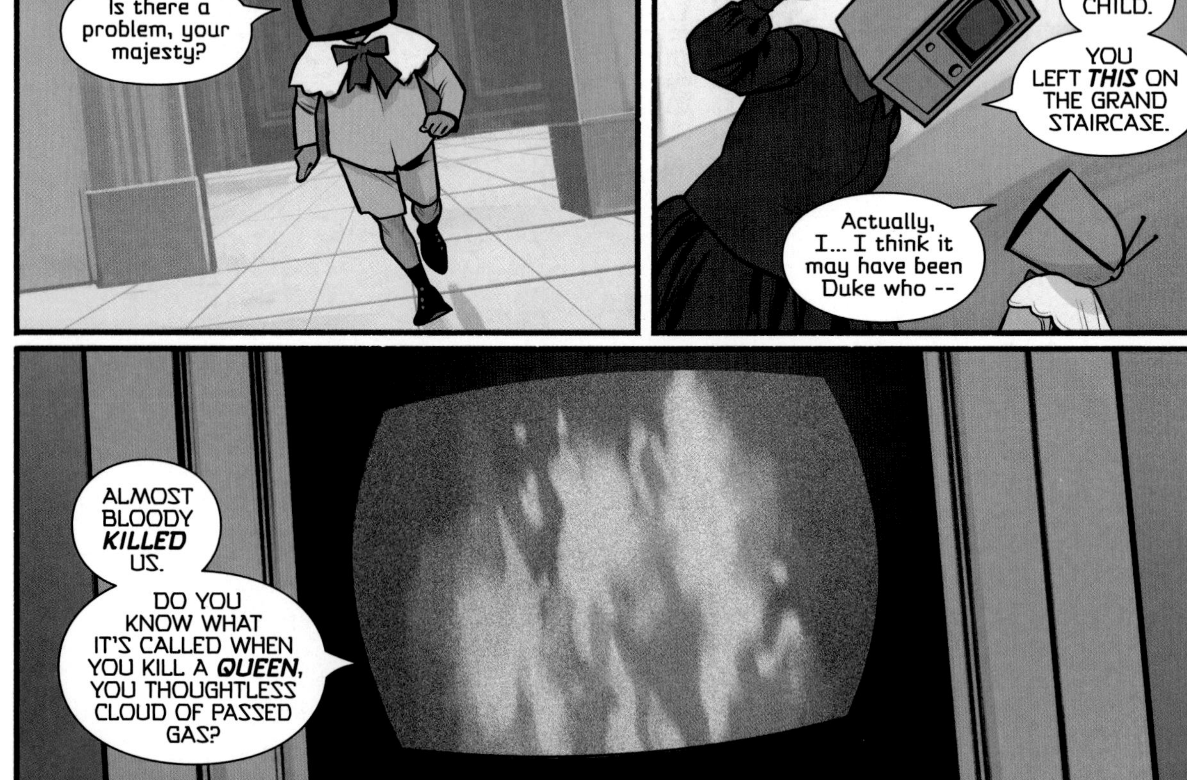

Ruh... regicide, I believe?
AYE.
EXACT SAME AS OFFING THE KING, AND DON'T YOU FORGET IT.

BUT WHAT DO THEY CALL KILLING A *PRINCE?*

Mummy, please.

NOTHING!
BECAUSE NO ONE GIVES A FUCKING *TOSS* ABOUT --
Enough.

This sad-sack shit supposed to make me feel **sorry** for you?
Forget that you ***murdered*** the love of my life?
I swear, I... I have no idea why that horrid drivel popped into my head.

I implore you.
Give me one last chance, and I'll show you exactly how to capture Hazel and --
Sorry.

What did you say?

Save me!

Use your acid spell or something, Hazel!
Don't!
You'll kill Squire, too!

Hold on, you're telling me that feathered bitch can do *magic*?
My boss is gonna make me an ***ambassador*** when he sees this.

Who *are* you?
Sure, let me spell my name so it'll be correct in print: It's I, A, *suck my hairy clit.*
Now open up that ship, or I end you like I did your boy toy.

What?
Uh-oh.

Is he all right?
I came as soon as I...
...shit.
Howdy.
Draw.

BRAM
Hnf!
AHN!

MOMMY!

Cockblocking little turd!

Thankfully, I brought enough ammo to kill every last --
Hey!

fzzzzzzzzzPOPP
FAHCKINGFAAHHHCK!
Careful!
She's still got a --
BRAM

Wow.

That... really... really... hurts.

Don't be scared.
Just check on Alana.

Hey, fruit.
Wasn't kidding about... offing Doff.

So be a... fucking man...
...and finish... what you started.

I fucking... dare you.
Kill me.

Kill me.

Kill me.

Wait your turn.

I'll deal with your wanted ass next, but me and this one got unfinished business.
I can imagine... but you should know that, by any objective measure, I'm ***way*** more valuable than Robot.
What are you ***doing***, you fucking simpleton? Didn't you hear? I was in the process of selling out your entire family!

Yeah, but I never believe ***anything*** you say.
Because you're a fucking simpleton!
Now get back to the others and --

They're long gone, including your son.
I made them all blast off the second I caught an unfamiliar ***stench*** on the island... no offense.

Oh, thank god.

It's just the three of us now.
So let's find a way to settle this like gentlemen, Mister...?
The.

Will.
Least I will be again after I bring *you* in.

And I'll surrender without a fight.
As long as you don't hurt *him.*

Pass.

end chapter fifty-three

CHAPTER

FIFTY-FOUR

Dad's folks used to hit him
when he was a kid.

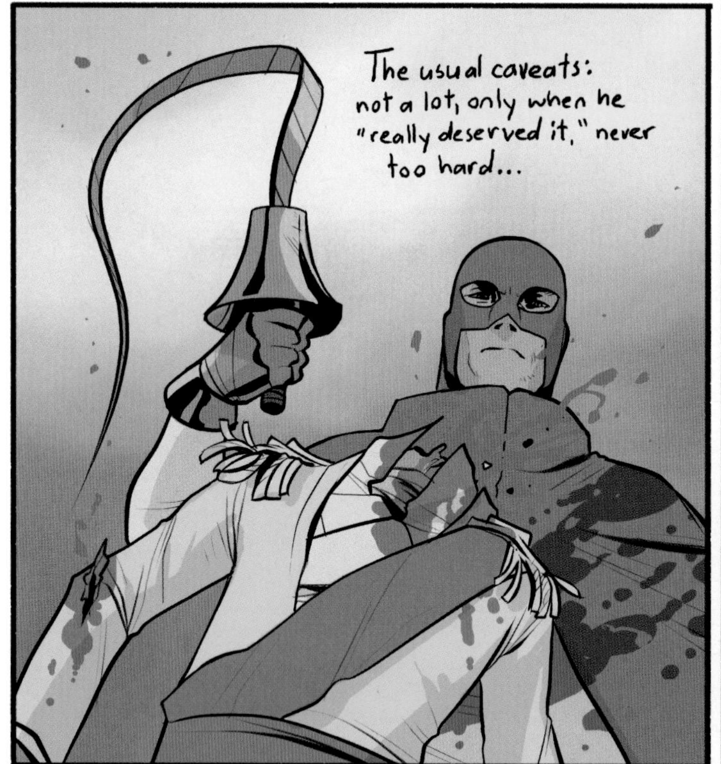
The usual caveats: not a lot, only when he "really deserved it," never too hard...

...they were just trying to raise a good boy, products of another time, you get the idea.

Still, my father always felt it had done a number on him.

KLICK

So before Mom and Dad had me, they promised each other they'd never resort to spankings or whatever, no matter how much I might misbehave.

And they never did.

Even though I was plenty bad.

Somehow, I managed to turn out all right.

Probably depends who you ask though.

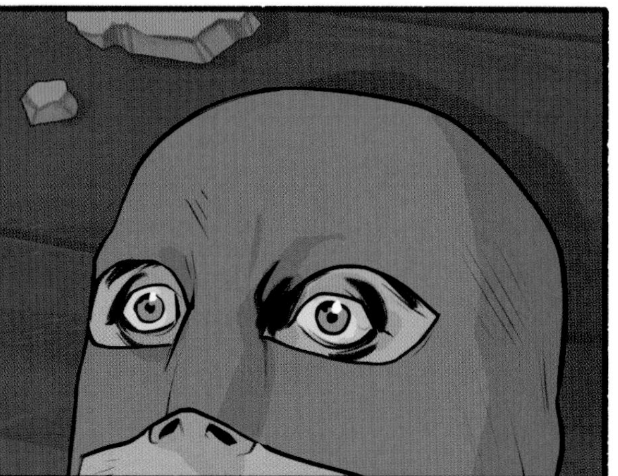

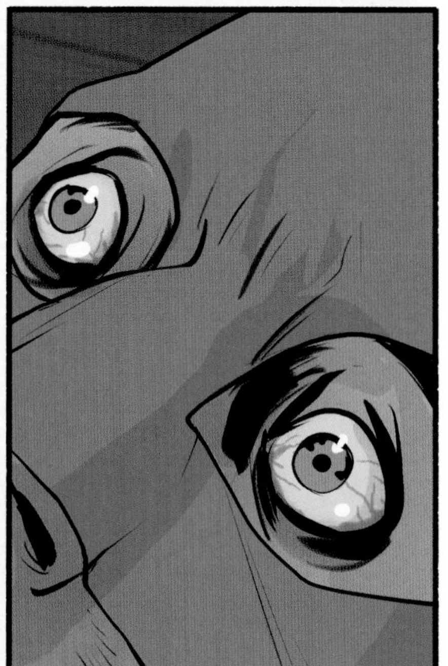

Don't you pass out on me, crybaby.
Dad, no!

Relax and enjoy it.
Makes the orgasm more intense, remember?
See you soon, kid.

You might as well let go, The Will.
Even if you haul my shitty ex back to Wreath, you'll never see *us* again.

LYING

KH

Fulmo.

The fuck?

Marko.

Set us down... or I hit you... **again...**
Yeah?
With what?

Ain't much weather out there.

And those thunder gags take a lot out of you people, don't they?
Bet you're feeling weak as piss.
You have no idea how I --

RAHH!

Gnnn

THOCK

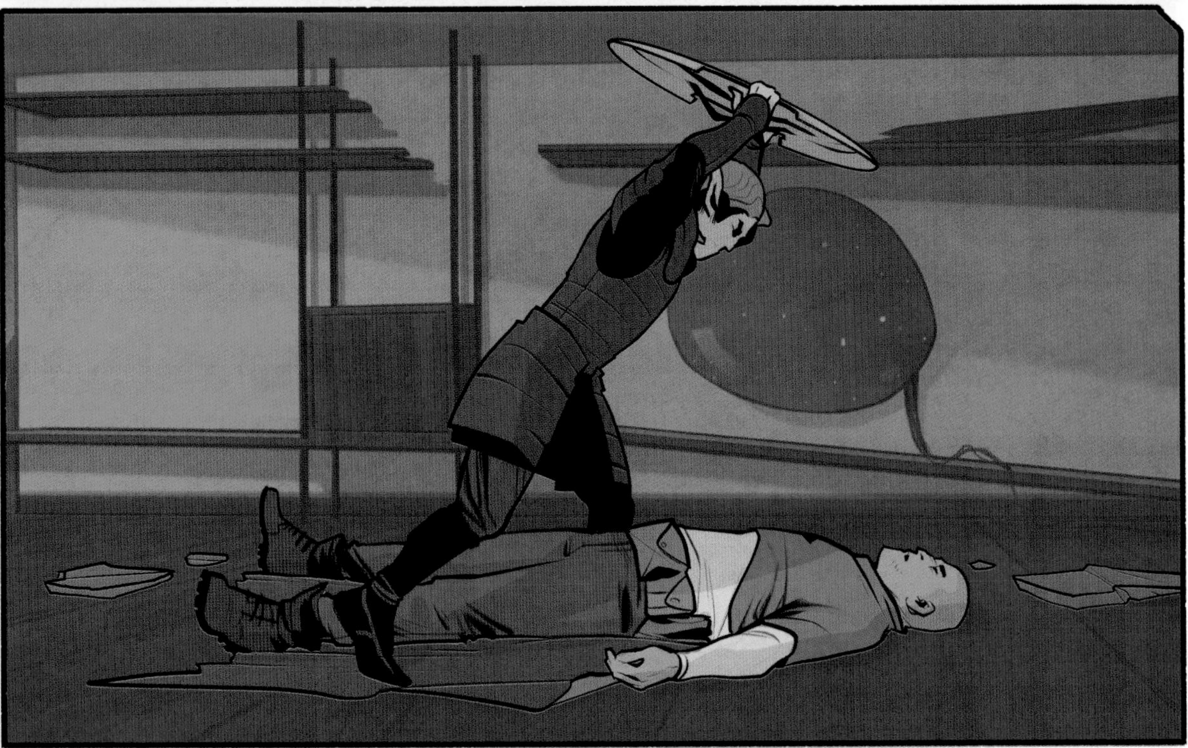

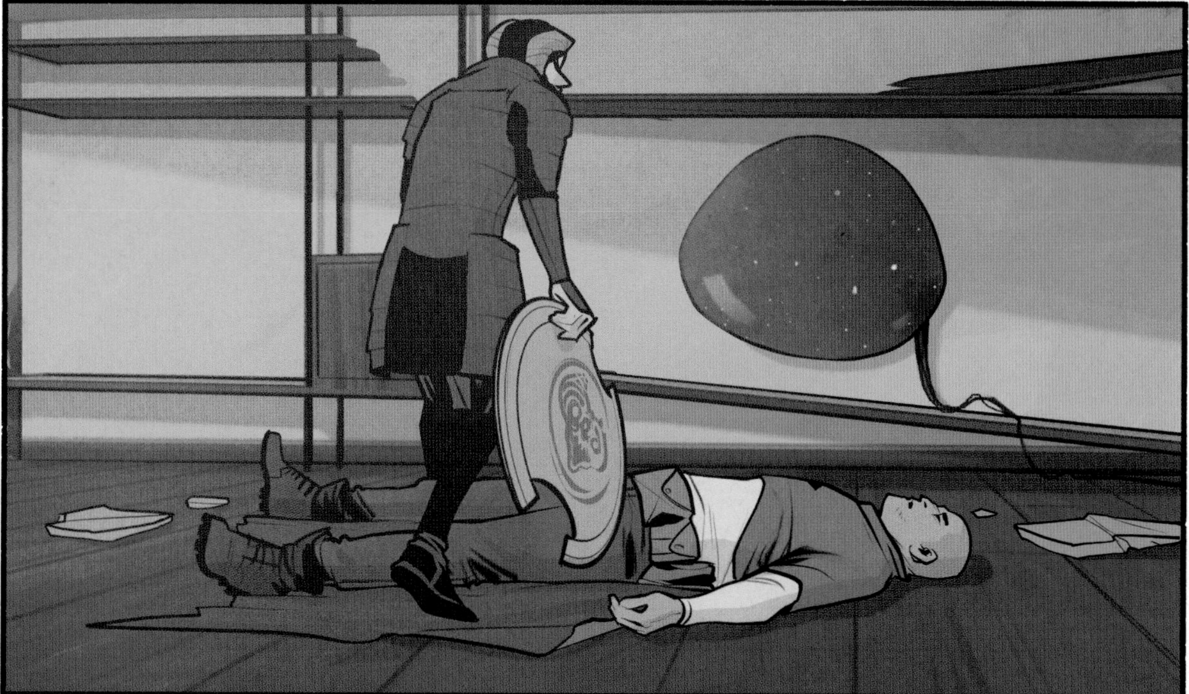

Daddy?

Mm-hm?

I love you super-duper-extra much.

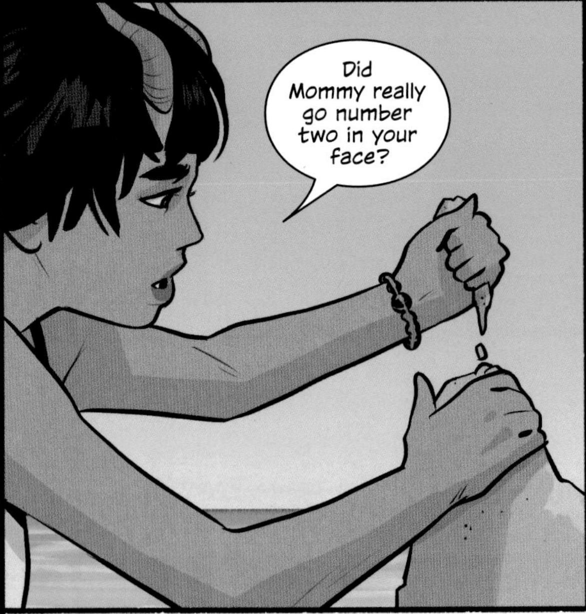

What?!
When I was born.
Mommy says she accidentally... went poo on you.

Oh, it wasn't just me.
She went poo on everything.
And that was the happiest day of your life?!

Every day with you has been.
But... does that mean *I'll* never be that happy?

You lost me.
Uh-oh.
Promise you won't get mad?

I don't want to have babies.
Not ever never.

Well, that's not something you have to decide right now.
I didn't decide.
I just kind of... know.
I'm so, so glad you guys made me.
But I maybe want to make other stuff.
Awesome.
For real? You won't be sad if you never have a kajillion grandbabies?
Honey girl, I don't care what you do, as long as you're kind to everyone you meet.
That's it?
My name is Hazel.
That is the hardest part of being alive.

Oh, man.
Here comes a big one.
I started out as an idea, but I ended up something more.

Can you help me with my moat?
Can I!
Not much more, to be honest.

It's not like I grow up to be some great war hero or any sort of all-important savior...
We're not gonna make it!
Not with that attitude!
Dig faster!

Faster!
...but thanks to my parents, at least I get to grow old.

Not everybody does.

to be continued

TO BE CONTINUED

4335 VAN NUYS BOULEVARD • SUITE 332 • SHERMAN OAKS • CA 91403

Dear Fiona and Brian,
When was Saga born?
Thanks,
Sam E.
Perth, Australia

Thanks for the postcard, Sam. Brian here, and since this third hardcover collection you hopefully already finished featured so much...

(spoiler warning, just in case)

...death, I figured we could use this space to discuss something slightly less depressing, like birth.

At the end Book One, our *To Be Continued* column explored the inside baseball of how we put together each issue for Image Comics, but we've never talked too much about how *Saga* came to be in the first place.

And I realize that's even insider-er baseball, so if this sounds like a drag to you, please skip ahead to the awesome sketches and stuff.

For me, the short answer to Sam's question is June 30, 2011, the day that Fiona emailed over this incredible "teaser" image we used to announce our series at that year's San Diego Comic-Con:

Fiona and I had already been discussing the characters and the story, but it wasn't until I saw her sweepingly romantic take on our fictional family, framed in the fashion of the best 1970s movie posters, that our series became "real," at least in my worryingly shiny head.

But because we have some pages to kill here, why not trace *Saga* all the way back to the seed of the original idea, and follow it from platonic, non-gross conception to delivery (of our first issue) on March 14, 2012?

A minor caveat: I culled some of the following details from emails and whatnot between the people involved, but a lot of it comes from my own gin-addled memory, so when in doubt, it's probably self-mythologizing balderdash.

1986

I was in fourth grade and I was miserable.

Not all the time, but definitely during any class involving math, when I would space out by imagining an ongoing battle between a sci-fi planet and its fantasy moon, a tale at least somewhat inspired by the kind of batshit magnificence I was exposed to as a Catholic school kid:

But it wasn't all highfalutin religious icons. I Hoovered up inspiration from everywhere, especially WGN's *Bozo Show* (home to the sacred buckets of the "Grand Prize Game"), which featured the cartoons of both *G.I. Joe* AND *Transformers*, two fictional wars that helped soothe at least one child perpetually worried about actual nuclear annihilation.

Obviously, I was also influenced by all things George Lucas, especially the PBS radio dramatization of *Star Wars*, some of which explored young, Tatooine-era Luke Skywalker's life in a way that felt as grounded as *American Graffiti*. I love that Lucas took inspiration from favorites like *Flash Gordon* and *The Hidden Fortress*, but made new stories in those genres that felt original and personal.

Over the years, I kept flunking math and thinking about my ill-advised land of make believe. There was never a Marko or Alana or Hazel, but my universe got more and more convoluted over the next decade, as I added talking animals and royal androids, somehow using them to work out whatever I was anxious about (everything).

And any distinctions between the heroes and villains of my disturbing one-person show began to blur as I discovered books like *To Kill a Mockingbird* and *Ender's Game*, movies from *Das Boot* to *Full Metal Jacket*, and the comics of a young Alan Moore and a younger Garth Ennis.

In the past, I've described this weird mental fantasyland as a "paracosm," mostly because I think it's a cool word, but these early versions of Wreath and Landfall were really just an elaborate daydream created to avoid a mundane adolescence.

By 1996, I was largely free of both math and Catholicism (sorry Mom, God), and I stopped escaping into my imaginary universe. That year, I was fortunate enough to sell my first script to Marvel, and while I was eager to break into the world of creator-owned comics, I never considered exploring my dopey childhood flights of fancy in my terribly sophisticated Stories for Mature Readers.

2010

My first child had just been born and I was terrified.

Not just about fatherhood, though that was certainly a large part of it. In anticipation of starting a family, my wife and I had purchased a house in 2008, just before the market collapsed, and we were suddenly what they call "underwater" on our first home. It definitely felt like drowning.

I had (probably foolishly) left the TV show *Lost* at the end of its fifth season, hoping to help create something new for film or television. But the modern Knights of the Roundtable comedy that I'd sold never escaped development hell, nor did a futuristic mockumentary series I'd written about blue-collar exterminators who make space travel safe for the wealthy. There were other scripts that never even made it close to the launchpad, and it felt like my brief Hollywood side-career was D.O.A.

On the comics front, I'd released the final issues of *Y: The Last Man* and *Ex Machina*, my long-running series with artists Pia Guerra and Tony Harris, and for the first time in over a decade, I didn't have plans for another new book. It was a particularly tough time for creator-owned comics (isn't it always?), and colleagues warned me of the serious financial risks of working on something that wasn't an established property.

But after a few months of watching me lose my mind over studio notes on rewrite jobs, my wife Ruth politely demanded that I at least take a stab at returning to comics, pointing out that helping to create an ongoing world that an artist and I had complete control over has always seemed to help keep me sane.

I didn't think I could afford to work on something that might be another misfire, especially a comic, but Ruth noted that I've never had luck trying to second-guess what will be "successful," so I should just write whatever I felt like writing.

It was kind and generous advice, but unfortunately, all I felt like talking about was our newly expanded family, a topic that seemed to universally bore the fuck out of everyone I spoke with, whether or not they had diaper bag-related adventures of their own.

I also didn't want to write a story for kids, even though I now had one. Lots of evenings back then were spent reading children's picture books aloud, and while those authors were definitely influencing the way I wanted to write, I missed the kind of messy, unsettling stories that are intended only for olds like me.

So with nothing more than the idea that I wanted to do a comic about a family (without it being family-friendly), I reached out to a handful of established artists. Understandably, nobody was interested, not just because this hypothetical project would contain filthy sex and graphic violence, but also because the market seemed too dependent on existing superhero franchises to support something new.

It reminded me a bit of the way some of my child-free friends had questioned why anyone would want to bring a new life into a chaotic and war-torn world that didn't seem to want or need more people.

And during a random shower one morning, I instantly knew I wanted to write something called *Saga*, a story about the perils of creation. Featuring robot penises.

I figured I could exploit my imaginary childhood universe by just shifting its focus. This longform epic would be about a newborn girl, one whose parents were Rosencrantz and Guildenstern-like bit players from opposite sides of a bloody, morally unclear, never-ending series of proxy wars.

We'd follow this baby as she grew up before our eyes more or less in real time, hopefully evolving along with my own children (at this point, my wife was improbably already pregnant with our second). I thought this could maybe be a non-boring outlet to explore my own fears and concerns about my offspring and whatever kind of future we might be leaving for them.

The story felt like it needed the spectacle of a blockbuster summer movie, but the emotional depth of a long-running TV drama... which meant it could only be a comic.

And that kind of comic would need a fearless artist who could make every aspect of these childishly absurd galaxies feel real and relatable, month after month, potentially for years.

Where the hell was I supposed to find someone like that?

2011

I was alone in a hotel room in NYC, far away from my family, secretly relieved that a small independent movie I had been trying to direct had "failed to secure funding." Now I could go back home... and work on the one story that was keeping me up at night.

At this point, I felt like I knew what the first and last pages of the entire *Saga* series would be, but I had no idea what the book should look like. The imaginary wars from my young brain had a complex narrative, but any visuals were stupidly simplistic at best. I didn't just need a collaborator, I needed an equal co-author to help me drag this half-formed universe out of the ether.

Since my past artistic partners on years-long series were understandably still taking time off from the monthly game, I emailed a few colleagues to ask if they knew anyone who might be able to tackle something of this scope. And I'm eternally indebted to writer Steve Niles for instantly responding that he'd had a blast working on *Mystery Society* with an artist named Fiona Staples.

Mystery Society, by the way, is an absolute must-read, as is Fiona's excellent Wildstorm miniseries *Secret History of the Authority: Hawksmoor* with criminally underrated writer Mike Costa. But I knew Staples was the one and only artist for this book when I Googled her artwork and these were the first two images that popped up:

That variant cover to *Vampirella Quarterly* #6... well, what more needs to be said?

But it's the Boba Fett one that really got me, a deep-cut reference to the ill-fated *Star Wars Holiday Special*, executed with sly humor, badass style and an absurdly perfect palette.

I wrote Fiona that second, introducing myself and asking if she might have interest in working on a creator-owned ongoing series and...

You know what, I should just email Fiona now and let her speak for herself.

BKV Hey, Fiona! I think this is the longest I've gone in nearly eight years without seeing new artwork from you, and it makes my stomach hurt. Do you have a doodle from the back of a shopping list or anything to share?

FS Hmm... I needle-felted this doll of my cat.

BKV Well, that's amazing.

Before we start blabbing about the past, can you tell us about any future projects readers might be able to expect from you during our book's extended "Intermission"?

FS I've contributed a short story to *Sex Machine*, the latest Smut Peddler anthology! It's a collection of robot/AI themed erotica. My nerdy story is about video games.

BKV I'm fortunate enough to have read it, and I loved your story because *a)* you are as magnificent a writer as you are an artist and *b)* it's proof that you're the filthier half of *Saga*.

Seriously, what does your family think of the perverted shit you're occasionally forced to draw?

FS We don't talk about it. I think my parents and I have a tacit agreement to never mention the adult content, but it's also possible they don't read the book...

BKV Let's hope. Anyway, do you remember what you were up to when I first wrote to bother you on March 5, 2011?

FS Not a whole lot! I had recently finished *Mystery Society* and I had the intention of doing more creator-owned stuff (Robert Kirkman's infamous 2008 rallying cry may have lit a fire under me) so I was working on a couple of pitches with different writers. But your email was one of the most exciting surprises I've ever gotten. There was no reason for you to know who I was!

BKV The fact that you weren't already a household name is ridiculous. You didn't just draw great pages, you seemed to be the most professional artist I'd ever met, right from jump. I am constantly a frazzled mess, but you're always so unflappable about deadlines and stuff. What's your secret?

FS The secret is that I'm not like that at all, and when we're working I'm 100% consumed with worry about deadlines. I feel like every single issue has almost been late, and has only reached the printer on time thanks to Steven Finch and the lightning-fast Image production staff. I'm glad to hear you're frazzled too, though.

BKV When we first spoke on the phone, I most remember you mentioning that you loved Kubrick's *2001* and that you weren't a huge fan of drawing tech stuff (a conversation that inspired our Rocketship Treehouse, along with many other best parts of our series). Any recollections about that development process?

FS Well, I remember thinking that I should try to sound smart so I said my favorite sci-fi movie was *2001* instead of *Starship Troopers*. Weird how *Saga* has way more in common with the latter. I guess the truth has a way of coming out?

***

There's a reason I hear Fiona's voice in my head when Lying Cat speaks.

Yeah, I'm ashamed that I hated Paul Verhoeven's *Starship Troopers* when I first saw it, because I thought it was a too-broad comedy, and not the horrific prediction of our present it later proved to be. Over the years, it's become one of my all-time favorite movies, and Fiona said maybe one of the truest things ever about *Saga* when she rightly pegged our book as "a cross between *Starship Troopers* and the Lynn Johnston comic strip *For Better or For Worse*."

Anyway, around this time, we reached out to only one publisher, Image Comics. My friends and longtime Image creators Jay Faerber and Robert Kirkman had both been raving about them to me for years, and Fiona and I were excited about the prospect of truly owning and controlling our creations, with zero content restrictions or creative interference.

Publisher/Chief Creative Officer Eric Stephenson was immediately enthusiastic about our short pitch, and he couldn't have been more generous with his time and wisdom as he helped us navigate the world of creator-owned comics.

Image generously agreed to advance Fiona her page rate, and in return, I happily agreed to write the first six issues "on spec." In success, I'd get paid if and when Image made back its small fee and recouped its initial investments, and in the (hugely unlikely) event there was ever any additional income beyond that, Fiona and I would split it evenly.

This gamble was more than a little scary, especially with a mortgage, a second child on the way and no other steady income, but it's a chance I could afford to take thanks not to my fleeting Hollywood work, but to the steady royalties from my past creator-owned comics. I'd been privileged enough to learn that co-owning 100% of something read by even thousands of people will always be more profitable than working as an employee on something watched by millions.

Of course, there was a good chance 0% of anyone would want our twisted romance, but I felt increasingly confident about hitching myself to Fiona's rocket.

Based on my early discussions with her, I went away and hammered out this quick "mini bible," a document that was only ever supposed to be for Fiona's eyes. Against my better judgment, I'm reprinting it here (with some parts redacted to prevent major future spoilers and/or personal embarrassment), if only to help illustrate how much depth and sophistication Fiona brought to my shallow character descriptions...

SAGA

A brief summary by BKV for Fiona Staples
March 20, 2011

The Theme

This is a story about creation and why people create new things—whether that's children or artwork or *whatever*—in a world that doesn't always want something new.

The Story

Set in an epic fantasy/sci-fi universe, this is the tale of a young romantic couple forced to fight as soldiers on opposite sides of a meaningless, never-ending galactic war. They're kind of like Romeo and Juliet... but instead of killing themselves at the end of the story, our heroes end up *getting pregnant* at the start, and deserting their respective armies as they search for a more peaceful existence. But as these two AWOL deserters try to raise the daughter they've risked everything to bring into this universe, mom and dad are pursued by a whole mess of assassins, bounty hunters, and other outer-space baddies concerned about this new family threatening the status quo.

The Tone

Romantic, in every sense of the word. There's a reason great love stories like *Casablanca*, *Doctor Zhivago*, and *Gone With the Wind* all had epic, bloody wars as their backdrops. When the stakes are constantly life and death, everything becomes more vibrant. Our war may be hell, but the universe where it takes place is often bright, clean and poppy. Still, this is (hopefully) a complex story for discerning adults, so even though our settings will often be crazily imaginative, characters' emotions should always feel grounded and real.

Thankfully, this is everything I already love about your artwork, Fiona, so please just be yourself! I'll make some detailed suggestions in this document, but they're just suggestions. I sought you out because of your unique voice, so feel free to make this world and these characters your own.

The Universe

SAGA is set in an original universe that's hopefully unlike anything we've ever seen. Most of our story will take place in

█████████.

For as long as everyone can remember, there's been an epic war waged between an Earth-like planet in this solar system called **LANDFALL**, and its one large moon, which everybody calls **WREATH**. Like the ongoing conflict between █████████, this war has far-reaching consequences, and is now fought across multiple societies on all planets. Basically, it's a huge clusterfuck that's never ever going to end.

Landfall is a futuristic, technological wonderland, and while there are many different species native to this world, everything born here has **wings**. Some people have huge beautiful condor wings, others might have leathery wings like a bat's or even smaller vestigial wings like a penguin's, but if we see a character with some kind of wings, we automatically know where they were born.

Wreath, on the other hand, is a more medieval world of sword-and-sorcery style magic. Again, there are lots of different species on this planet, but everything born on Wreath has **horns**, whether that's one little unicorn horn or giant caribou antlers.

I guess I'm using the old "angels vs. demons" iconography as a visual shorthand for two different sides of an unwinnable war, but the story should never feel overtly religious. Our goal should always be to make everything in this universe feel new, even when it's sometimes comprised of familiar elements.

There are plenty of other non-winged/non-horned aliens, monsters and robots in our universe, but this war between one planet and its moon impacts absolutely everyone, and it's what our heroes will constantly be trying to escape.

The Heroes

ALANA: Our female lead, I'm picturing Alana being about 19 years old, petite and attractive. A bit of a reckless wild child who was raised in a fast-paced consumerist society, Alana is forced to grow up fast when she gets pregnant young. Alana was born on the planet Landfall, so she has wings, which I'm envisioning looking like those of a dragonfly, equal parts beautiful and icky. Maybe she also has some cute pointy ears or something, but other than that, I think she should look fairly human.

There's kind of a glut of redheaded female heroes in comics at the moment, so maybe she has short brown hair? Or some kinda highlights? Whatever looks cool to you, Fiona. Alana used to wear either hi-tech battlefield armor or retro sci-fi pin-up style outfits, but now that she's a mom on the run, she mostly wears more low-key "civilian attire" (she can hide her wings under a jacket when she needs to). However you decide to design her, if we don't meet people dressed as Alana at conventions, we haven't done our job!

Alana is brilliant and cunning and hilarious, but she's not much of a fighter. Drafted to become a soldier at a young age, Alana was trained to use a variety of hi-tech weapons (including an old **raygun** she still carries, █████████ █████████), but she never had the stomach for combat. Working as a guard at a Guantanamo Bay-style prison camp, Alana meets a dashing young enemy soldier who ends up changing her life...

MARKO: Our male lead, Marko is also about 19 years old, but mature beyond his years. A native of Wreath, he was trained to be a magical soldier, but soon grew disenchanted with the hypocrisy of his moon world's organized religion and its bullshit "prophecies." A conscientious objector, Marko surrendered on the battlefield to his winged enemies, only to have them torture him as a suspected spy. Marko is strong, confident, and principled... but he's more trusting and naive than the street-smart Alana.

Marko is a humanoid alien, but I think he can look more animalistic than Alana. I'm picturing him with two horns that closely hug the sides of his head, and he should also have some kind of fangs. Maybe he has a coating of short fur or a lion-like snout? Regardless, Marko should seem equal parts monstrous and attractive.

Like his new bride Alana, Marko wears civilian attire these days, including something like a hoodie so he'll be able to hide his horns when he needs to. He and Alana both wear special **decoder rings** as their wedding bands, mystical artifacts that allow them to communicate with any species. While Alana carries her hi-tech raygun, Marko never goes anywhere without his **enchanted broadsword**, one that the idealistic pacifist refuses to ever remove from its **ornate scabbard**. Marko isn't the fiercest warrior around, but he's a hell of a dad.

HAZEL: And this little brat is the star of our show. She's named after her eye color, a combination of Alana's green eyes and Marko's brown eyes. At the opening of our series, she should look like a normal dark-haired infant girl, but she has two little bumps on her forehead where her horns are starting to appear, and █████████ █████████ █████████? Beyond that, she's an ordinary humanoid baby, one who will primarily just eat, shit and cause problems for our heroes in their first year as parents. But a grown-up version of Hazel will be the **narrator** of our story, and █████████ █████████ █████████ █████████.

The Hunters

THE WILL: In our universe, bounty hunters are called "freelancers," an unsavory group of mercenaries loyal only to themselves. One of the best freelancers is a guy known as The Will, an older, seemingly ordinary human man who looks kind of like Bruce Willis or Jason Statham (tough-guy bald, not comic-book writer creepy bald). The Will wears the tattered cloak of an unnamed masked hero he █████████, a two-tone cape that I'm picturing being blue on the outside, red on the inside. Anyway, this old cape also has a masked cowl attached, but The Will always leaves that flopped back behind his head. The rest of his attire is more casual, maybe blue jeans and black boots. He's got the hilt of a lance-like weapon attached to his belt, but he rarely uses it.

The Will's sidekick is a spotted alien panther called **Lying Cat**, so named because it has the ability to detect when people are lying. Together, The Will and his talking animal fly around in a badass space helicopter called the **Starwhacker**.

Because the political leaders of the Wreath moon are

opposed to directly killing their own kind, they've outsourced the job of executing the deserter Marko and the enemy combatant he impregnated. The Will is happy to take the gig, but ████.

PRINCE ROBOT III: In the Saga universe, robots are all part of an extended royal family. This "Robot Kingdom" long ago allied itself with the technological planet Landfall in the war against their enemy moon. Prince Robot III is an android soldier who's survived multiple violent battles against Wreath that have left him badly traumatized. The shell-shocked veteran just wants to settle down and "replicate" with his new bride, but for political reasons, Prince Robot is ordered to complete one more mission before he's allowed to reproduce: find and kill the traitorous Alana before she and the dirty "moony" she escaped with can do any lasting harm.

As always, these are just suggestions, but I picture Prince Robot III having a humanoid body but a head shaped a little bit like a vintage "flying saucer" television set (I even like the old-school rabbit ear antennas). But because his television screen's "face" is usually blank and dark, Prince Robot should be tall and lanky, so we can use his body language to convey emotion. Both of his hands are clearly robotic, and can transform to become various technological weapons. Prince Robot is a somber, tragic figure who's normally dressed in royal military attire with sashes and meaningless medals.

Other Players

The five characters named above will be the central players of this ongoing drama, but along the way, our heroes will reconnect with lots of ████, as well as make several new allies/enemies, including the ghost of a teenage alien girl who will act as Hazel's first of many babysitters, and ████.

But Fiona, if there are any creatures or character types you love that I haven't mentioned yet, just let me know. This is a big universe, so there's room for anything from astronaut nuns to underwater werewolves and everything in between. I just want to write things you'll be excited to draw!

A Brief Overview of Our First Arc

Our first six-issue arc will open with the birth of Hazel, as we learn about how the very different Marko and Alana first fell in love, and introduce the men who will be pursuing this newly formed family for potentially years to come.

Much of this first arc will take place on **CLEAVE**, a rainy planet closest to this solar system's artificial sun (which looks kinda like a giant disco ball, but more on that later). Marko and Alana have deserted the muddy battlefields where they met, and escaped into the native population of Cleave's capital, which looks like an alien version of a poor but densely populated city in someplace like Morocco.

When the safehouse where they've been hiding is compromised, Marko and Alana are forced to run with their newborn. But in order to escape Cleave, the new parents will first have to cross old battlefields and new challenges to reach the mythical **ROCKETSHIP FOREST**, where they'll find the living wooden spaceship that will serve as their "mobile home" for the rest of our series.

But because this unique craft can only travel between planets ████.

So while getting their ship will be the basic plot of our first six issues, this is really a story about those first six thrilling, terrifying, sleepless months that most new parents experience with a new child (or that some creators experience with new monthly books).

Here's hoping the kids can pull it off.

***

And these are the unforgettable first sketches Fiona sent back, along with a photo of the desk in the 500 sq. ft. apartment where she brought our first issues to life:

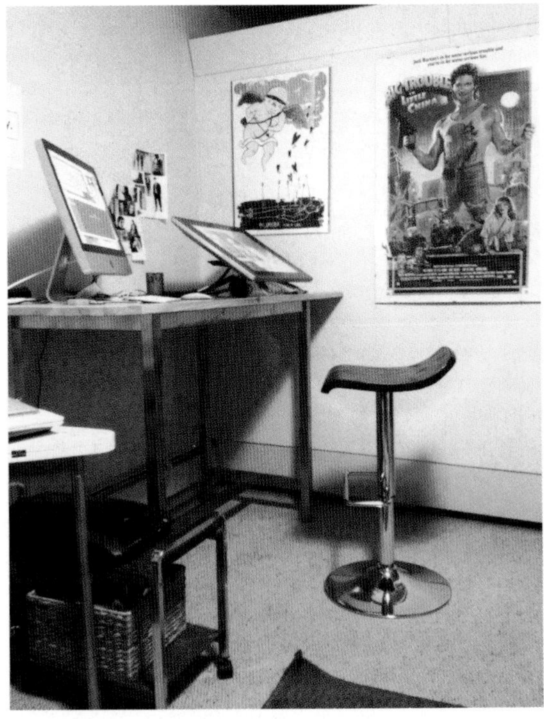

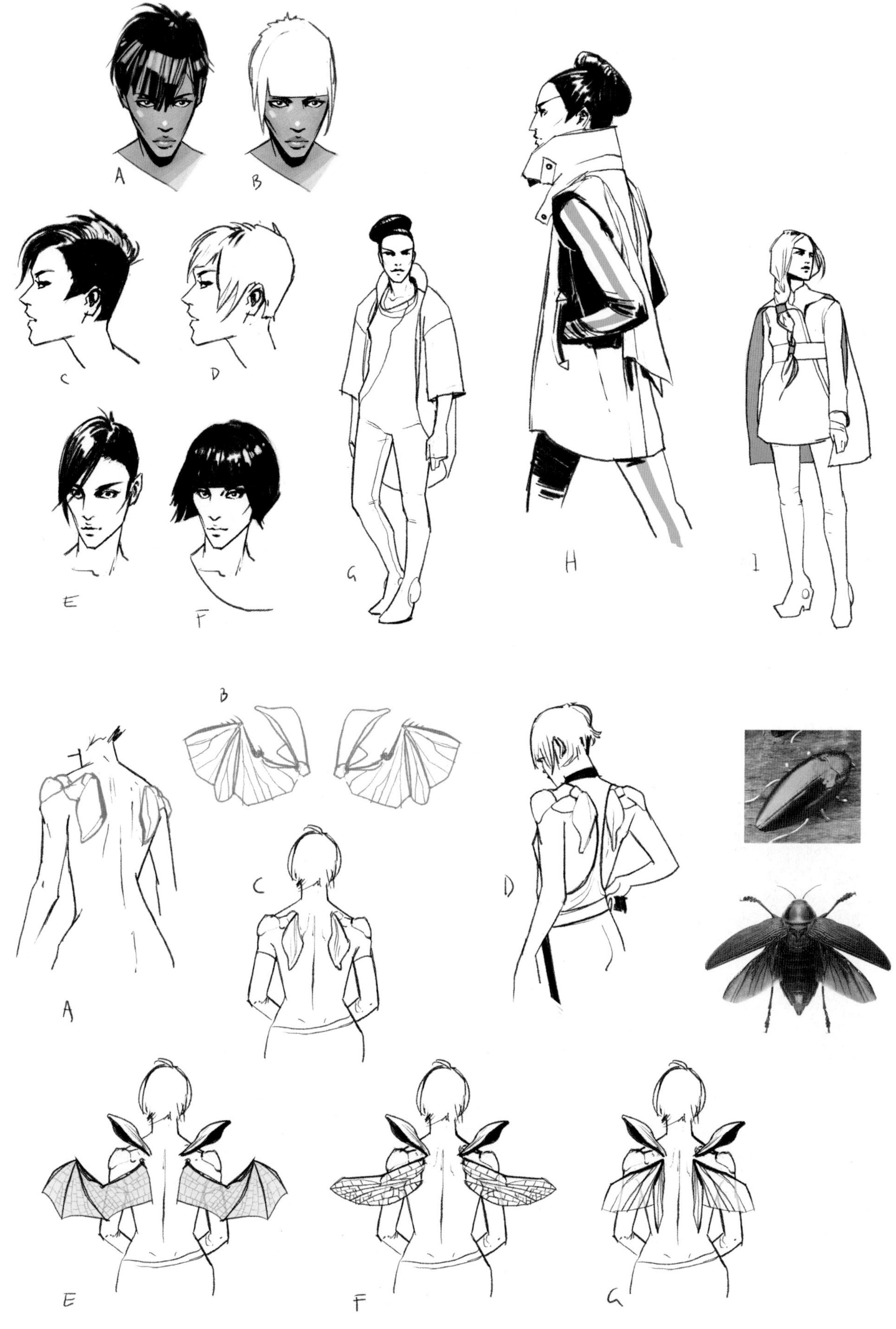
A
B
C
D
E
F
G
H
I
B
A
C
D
E
F
G

braid
mohawk
Antelope

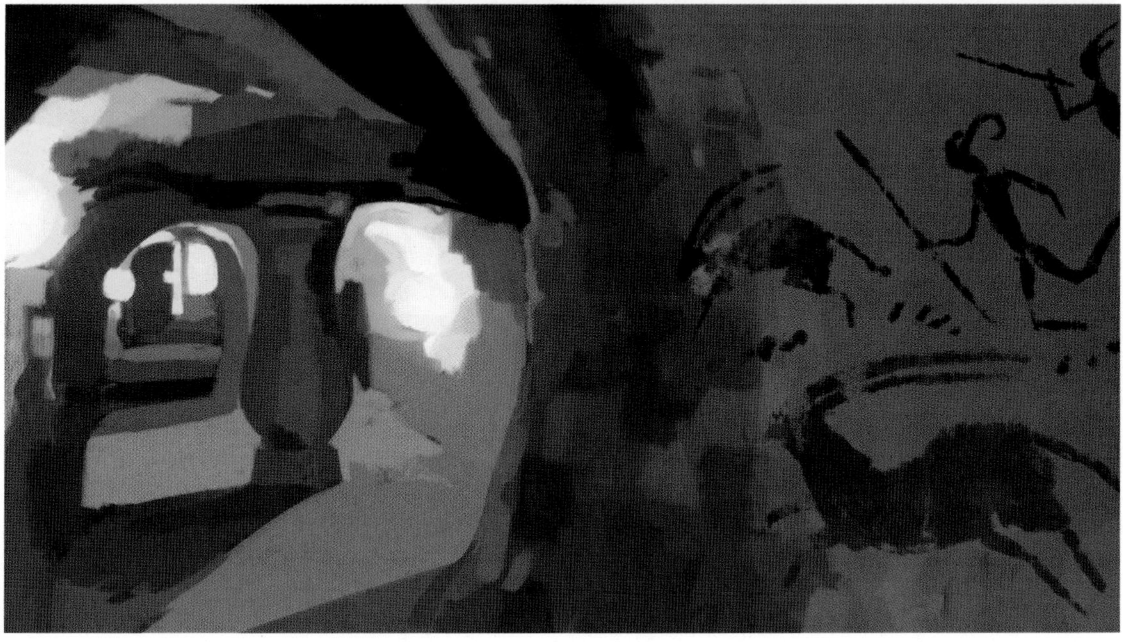

LANDFALL
FLYING
SOLDIER
opens
to land

BKV Fiona, I've admitted before that I had myopically presumed our sci-fi/fantasy leads would be white, and I'm forever grateful that you opted to go in a different direction. What can you tell us about your inspiration for Marko?

FS Just that there was a dearth of Asian male romantic leads, it was something that I personally wanted to see more of, and I was finally in a position to design characters that looked more like the people I knew. I think as more issues went by and I tightened up my art a bit, Marko's look got closer to what I had always envisioned. Sometimes it takes a while to get there!

BKV In the original document I sent you, I obnoxiously say that if "we don't meet people dressed as Alana at conventions, we haven't done our job." But now we really DO meet people dressed up as Alana all the time, which is obviously a testament to your take on the character, who was more complex and interesting than my description from the very first sketch. Where did she and her nutty beetle wings come from?

FS The mini bible stated that Alana had insect wings, not like fairy wings but actually "slightly gross," and it was important that she was able to hide them under clothing. So I decided on a batwing-like structure that could fold up and be tucked into shell things. I have no idea what you were picturing originally but I'd sure like to see it!

BKV The word "iconic" gets tossed around a lot, but your take on Lying Cat (who I had somewhat unimaginatively described as a "spotted panther") definitely is. Did her breed and coloring come to you instantly?

FS You wanted The Will to be bald and I cheated you by actually giving him a shaved head. But his sidekick is legitimately hairless! I just thought it would be funny and distinctive, and blue was more space-like. I don't have any sketches of other iterations of Lying Cat so it must have come to me instantly.

BKV Every character in your first issue is designed with such love and care. Are there any you hated and/or still hate to draw?

FS No, back then I was designing characters with the assumption that I'd be drawing them for hundreds of years, so I made it easy on myself. There's no one I hate to draw!

BKV Sorry again about The Stalk. And everybody else I murdered.

***

Shortly after I sent Fiona that mini bible, my second child was born and everything changed.

At least for me. I felt like I grew up a lot, as did the characters I was starting to write and Fiona was continuing to draw. Marko and Alana were no longer lovestruck teens, but actual adults… or as "adult" as any new parent can seem.

Image and Fiona let me enjoy a luxurious paternity leave before I got back to work on our double-sized first script, which I finally finished on June 6, 2011. Here's how it opened:

Brian K. Vaughan Fiona Staples

chapter one

Fiona – So cool to be working with you! I love your style and your energy and your pacing, and I can't wait to see what you do with this story. As you'll see, my panel descriptions are sometime pretty detailed (and I'll occasionally throw in annoying web links if there's some specific visual that I'm too lazy to describe), but these are all just SUGGESTIONS. If you ever see a better way to layout a page or frame a shot or whatever, please go to town. And feel free to write or call anytime with questions/concerns/complaints. Maybe we can talk again after you've had some time to read through this beast. Have fun! – BKV

PAGE ONE

Page One, SPLASH

We open tight on a PROFILE SHOT of the right side of a panicked young woman's face. We're so close that her head fills almost the entire page.

This is ALANA, our heroine. She's probably only in her early 20s, but her face is world-weary. She's seen a hell of a lot in her years. Right now, Alana is SWEATING profusely; her face is slick. Her short-cropped, multi-colored hair is even more of a mess than usual. At the moment, Alana is a little heavier than she normally likes to be, but it lends a friendly softness to her face.

At first glance, Alana might appear to be an attractive human woman… but eventually, you notice the STRANGE THINGS jutting out from between her shoulder blades, strange things we can see only a glimpse of in this close-up. More on them shortly.

For now, all that matters is the fact that Alana seems terribly WORRIED about something. Her expression should be a mixture of horror and embarrassment.

1) Handwritten Narration*: This is how an idea becomes real.

2) Alana**: Am I shitting?
3) Alana: It feels like I'm shitting!

**A note for Fiona and/or our letterer: I'd really like to do something different with our Narrator's "voiceover," since it will run throughout the series. Rather than putting it in an old-school square caption box, I hope we could leave room in the artwork for it to appear like this narration was hand-lettered directly and organically onto the artwork, maybe in legible script instead of cursive? The handwriting should look adult, but it's okay if it's got some character to it, and it can occasionally playfully "interact" with the artwork. For example, here, maybe* *the narration can ARC in a semi-circle above Alana's head? I know most artists hate their own handwriting, but because this narration is so native to the art, you may want to handle it yourself, Fiona. There won't be too much of it in each issue, I promise...*

***As for the regular dialogue, I'd love it if we could go with a readable mixed-case font instead of traditional ALL CAPS, which younger readers all tell me still looks like YELLING to them. I try not to over-emphasize words too often, so dialogue should only be bolded as indicated, please.*

PAGE TWO

Page Two, Panel One

This half-SPLASH should be a wide establishing shot, as we pull out to reveal that Alana is EXTREMELY PREGNANT. We can also see that she has insect-like WINGS coming out of shell-like PROTRUSIONS on her back. Everything is popping out as Alana uses her elbows to prop herself up a bit while attempting to GIVE BIRTH on a grease-stained MECHANIC'S TABLE.

Alana should be barefoot, wearing some kind of breezy, SUNDRESS-like outfit. The dress is being hiked up by a MYSTERY MAN, who currently has his head between Alana's legs to get a better look at the action. This should probably be framed from the characters' sides, so that we can hide this man's identity (as well as Alana's naughty parts).

Anyway, Alana and the figure helping to deliver her baby should be the focus of this panel, but we can also see background details that begin to suggest that this dimly lit, windowless room is some kind of GARAGE. It's futuristic, but not glistening clean. There are mechanical parts for FLYING CARS stored next to BUBBLING CAULDRONS and other, more mystical artifacts. We're not in Kansas anymore, etc.

1) Man Under Alana's Dress: Just keep pushing. We're so close.

2) Alana: Seriously, you'll never have sex with me again if I defecate all over you.
3) Alana: Unless you're secretly into that.
4) Alana (smaller font, whispered): Please don't be into that.

5) Handwritten Narration: But ideas are fragile things.

Page Two, Panel Two

This next large panel can be from Alana's point of view, as the figure looks up from between her legs to smile proudly at her (and us). This is MARKO, our hero, a dashingly handsome man with piercing eyes and Asian features. Oh, and he's also got POINTY EARS and two massive RAM HORNS growing out of his short black hair and curving down along his high cheekbones. I loved the swashbuckling Blade Runner attire you gave him, Fiona, and he can be dressed in that for this scene. But right now, all that matters is seeing this handsome monster's beaming face as he stares at the mother of his child.

6) Marko: You have never been as beautiful as you are right now.

7) Handwritten Narration: Most don't live long outside of the ether from which they were pulled, kicking and screaming.

PAGE THREE

Page Three, Panel One

Reverse angles for this shot of an exhausted Alana, as seen from Marko's P.O.V.

1) Handwritten Narration: That's why people create with someone else.

2) Alana: Right, because nothing's more lovely than a fat woman spread-eagle in the back of an old body shop. It's like something out of a fairy tale or...

Page Three, Panel Two

Pull out to the largest panel of the page for a shot of both characters, as Alana rears her head back and SCREAMS. Marko chivalrously rushes to her side, grabbing her hand. We can see that he has a BROADSWORD whose hilt is CHAINED to the ornate SCABBARD at his belt, so it can't ever be unsheathed. Remember that both characters wear matching silver RINGS.

3) Alana: AHHHN, HOLY FUCK!

4) Marko: Do you need a healing spell? We agreed, Alana! No shame in managing pain!

5) Handwritten Narration: Two minds can sometimes improve the odds of an idea's survival...

Page Three, Panel Three

Push in close on Alana. She has her eyes closed, but she doesn't look like she's in pain, more like she's about to climax.

6) Alana: It -ehn- doesn't hurt at all. It... it feels **good**.
7) Alana: Is it sick that it -ehn- feels so good?

Page Three, Panel Four

Cut back to Marko, who's silently reaching between Alana's legs. We can't see what he's looking at, but we can see that the serious young man is starting to CRY. Uh-oh.

8) Handwritten Narration: ...but there are no guarantees.

Page Three, Panel Five

Cut back to Alana, as she suddenly grows CONCERNED.

9) Alana: You're crying. You never cry.

10) Alana: What's wrong? Marko, what is it...?

BKV Sorry about my long-winded first script, Fiona. Do you remember having any artistic (or moral) concerns after reading it?

FS My only concern was that I wouldn't finish it on time, and I didn't really. So that ate up any lead time we might have had and ultimately led to our first Vacationanza.

BKV Before you started work on this issue, you offered to do a promo piece for San Diego, and it instantly crystalized what I thought the tone/direction/plot of our entire series could be. I don't know how to ask this any other way, so: where did it come from?

FS I was going for that '70s adventure movie poster feel, without really knowing what the story was going to be about. I think that was the first time I drew The Will's funny seedpod helicopter.

BKV Dammit, Staples, it's called a Starwhacker!

***

We were making great progress, but we still needed a logo, and Eric Stephenson strongly suggested we go with Fonografiks, who inevitably also became our indispensable letterer/credits designer/backmatter maestro/etc.

Steven had already done excellent work at Image, but I was sold the second I saw this extraordinary "dime store" cover treatment he had done on his own for *Ex Machina.*

Having never before had a say in the logos for my past comics, I had some frustratingly specific thoughts about *Saga*, which I included in my first script:

SOME PRETENTIOUS
THOUGHTS ABOUT OUR LOGO, ETC.

Instead of a big, bombastic, old-fashioned superhero-style logo, I think we should just use that simple, clean, Futura font I used on the cover page of this script, with our names above the title and the centered, lowercase "chapter one" somewhere beneath it.

Futura was a favorite of both NASA and Stanley Kubrick, and it still looks adventurous and exploratory to me. And I like how the mixed-case futura "Saga" makes three perfect little circles, like our trio of heroes. Kinda, right? Ugh, I'm losing my mind. Anyway, we can also talk about the design for our credits (which will go on the INSIDE COVER, I think?). They should be equally stark and simple, probably.

Same goes for our old-school LETTERS PAGE, which I think I'll write for the BACK INSIDE COVER of every issue, if that's cool? I think that's the only extra space we'll have for this ad-free first issue, but if it's all right with Eric and Image, Fiona, you're welcome to use the BACK COVER of this first issue (and extra pages of future issues) if you ever want to share sketches/plug other work/whatever. Hopefully, this is going to be our book for a long time, so I just want to make it a nice place for everyone to visit each month.

To be continued!

BKV Steven/Fonografiks, thank you so much for putting up with me, and for gently pushing for something more unique than good ol' Futura! I'd forgotten just how many spectacular potential logos you created...

FG I think I produced around thirty comps in all for the teaser poster, with various layouts and type treatments. There was a lot of back-and-forth discussion as we tried to balance aesthetics with more practical considerations. My concern with Futura was how the tall S and long descender on the lowercase G meant the logo as a whole would take up a lot of cover real estate and limit Fiona's composition options, so I was looking to steer towards something more compact and proportional while giving you that same clean, simple feel.

I'd used Gotham on a couple of prose book covers earlier that year and enjoyed working with it, so gave it a run out hoping you'd take to it too.

BKV Do you think we ultimately made the right choice, or is there one of these orphans you'd still like to find a home for?

FG Absolutely the right choice (though we did eventually settle on a heavier weighted version for the book itself that would be easier to read against a fully illustrated background). There's a subtle warmth and humanity in the curves of those letterforms that contrasts nicely with the angularity of the uppercase Futura elsewhere, and plays to the themes of the book.

BKV Well, as Fiona already said, we could never make this series without you and your patient midwifery at every stage. What do you remember about those nutty early days of the series?

FG The demand for new printings. Once we were underway, seemed like I was having to come up with new trade dress variants each week. Over the first eight issues, we had something like twenty-five different designs. Certainly kept me busy.

BRIAN K. VAUGHAN
FIONA STAPLES
SAGA
Ongoing from Image Comics in 2012

brian k. vaughan
fiona staples
SAGA
ONGOING FROM IMAGE COMICS IN 2012

Brian K. Vaughan
Fiona Staples
SAGA
Ongoing from Image Comics in 2012

BRIAN K. VAUGHAN
FIONA STAPLES
SAGA
ONGOING FROM IMAGE COMICS IN 2012

BRIAN K. VAUGHAN
FIONA STAPLES
Saga
ONGOING FROM IMAGE COMICS IN 2012

Brian K. Vaughan
Fiona Staples
Saga
Ongoing from Image Comics in 2012

BRIAN K. VAUGHAN
FIONA STAPLES
Saga
ONGOING FROM IMAGE COMICS IN 2012

BRIAN K. VAUGHAN
FIONA STAPLES
Saga
ONGOING FROM IMAGE COMICS IN 2012

BRIAN K. VAUGHAN
FIONA STAPLES
Saga
ONGOING FROM IMAGE COMICS IN 2012

BRIAN K. VAUGHAN

FIONA STAPLES

Saga™

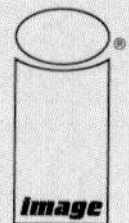

ONGOING FROM IMAGE COMICS IN 2012

BKV We unveiled Steven's logo (and Fiona's image!) at the 2011 San Diego Comic-Con, where I'd once been a guest of honor, but now had to quickly dig up an old issue of something I'd written to prove that I was really allowed to have a "professional" badge. It was a properly humbling reminder that, no longer how long you've been making them, every new comic is as hard as your first. Harder, sometimes. None of us is lucky enough to have a "built-in" audience or a "brand." Readers are earned, one issue at a time.

Photo: Pat Loika

BKV Fiona, we met in person for the first time in San Diego, and five minutes before we walked on stage to announce our epic ongoing series, you calmly mentioned that you had never drawn something past issue #6.

FS Yep, every issue since *Saga* #7 has been a personal record for me. I remember announcing our upcoming series at the Image panel and getting a sense of curiosity and general goodwill from the audience. It was heartening. I think I also took that moment to confess to you that I'd struggled with deadlines on my last book because there was nowhere for you to go.

***

With the positive reaction from San Diego filling our sails, Fiona got to work on the script (a process detailed in our first hardcover, True Believers!), which ended with this note about our cover:

CHAPTER ONE COVER SUGGESTION

You made it! Congratulations for reading to the end of this monster (or at least skimming to the last pages). Don't worry, Fiona, as we work out our shorthand, my scripts should get less detailed, and hopefully better tailored to your ever-expanding strengths.

Anyway, now that our first issue is done, let's talk about your first cover. Especially because this is the debut of a new series, I think the goal should be an iconic image that's as striking, beautiful and unexpected as that naked Demi Moore *Vanity Fair* magazine cover from years ago. Only completely different.

Here's what I'm thinking: it's a shot of MARKO & ALANA, framed with them standing side by side. On our right, Marko is sort of heroically staring off into the distance, maybe with his hand on the hilt of his sword.

But on our left is Alana, who is holding her Heartbreaker raygun at her side with one arm, and casually BREASTFEEDING a swaddled Hazel with the other. Alana's wearing her little minicape slung over one shoulder, while maybe her other shoulder is bare, her top having been pulled aside to feed. Again, this should feel intimate, but not sexy. Alana is maybe looking RIGHT AT US, with a very slight smile that says: *"Hey, my kid's hungry, the fuck you want?"*

I don't know if white backgrounds are overdone on covers, but I do think ours should be stark, minimalist. Maybe a light sprinkling of stars in the night sky behind Marko and Alana, something to suggest the space element of our story? I'm rambling.

Anyway, I think a badass breastfeeding cover played straight (not for laughs) would definitely jump out on the stands and quickly convey that we're the kind of mature big-budget fantasy/sci-fi story you'd never be able to get in movies or television, only in comics.

***

Fiona spun that straw into gold, and included a few proof-of-concept examples of possible future background colors, some of which later became actual covers:

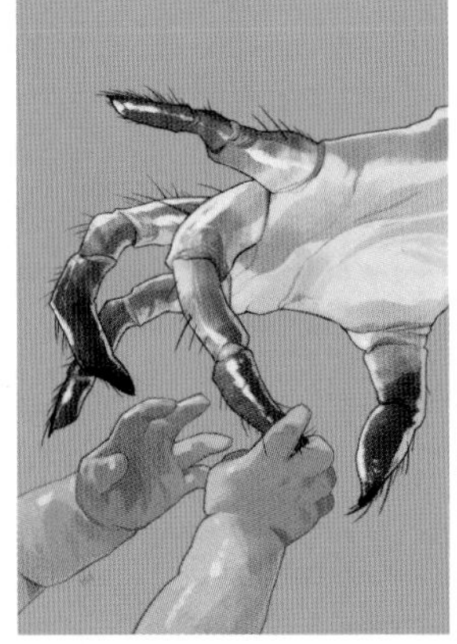

BRIAN K. VAUGHAN
& FIONA STAPLES
Saga
CHAPTER
ONE
image

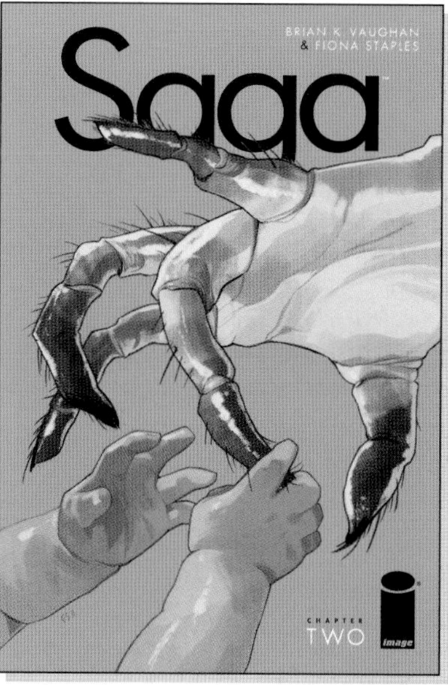
BRIAN K. VAUGHAN
& FIONA STAPLES
Saga
CHAPTER
TWO
image

image
BRIAN K. VAUGHAN
FIONA STAPLES
CHAPTER
THREE
Saga

BRIAN K. VAUGHAN FIONA STAPLES
Saga
CHAPTER ONE
$2.99
20
1992-2012
image

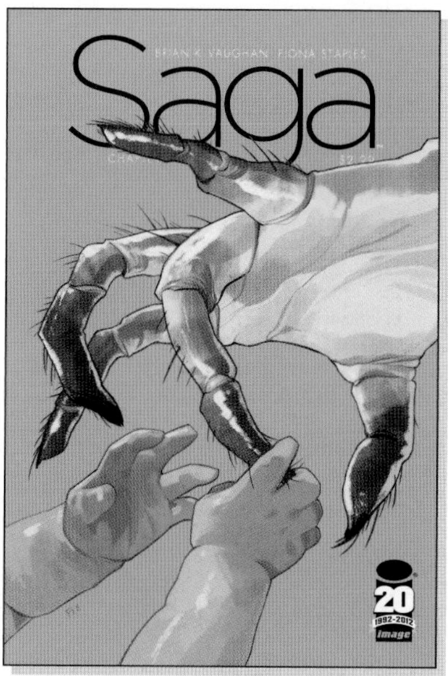
BRIAN K. VAUGHAN FIONA STAPLES
Saga
$2.99
20
1992-2012
image

20
1992-2012
image
BRIAN K. VAUGHAN FIONA STAPLES
Saga
CHAPTER THREE
$2.99

BRIAN K. VAUGHAN FIONA STAPLES
Saga
CHAPTER
ONE
20
1992-2012
image
$2.99

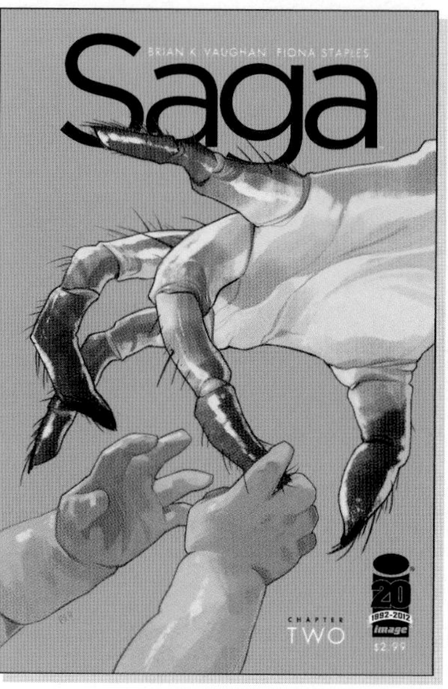
BRIAN K. VAUGHAN FIONA STAPLES
Saga
CHAPTER
TWO
20
1992-2012
image
$2.99

20
1992-2012
image
$2.99
BRIAN K. VAUGHAN
FIONA STAPLES
CHAPTER
THREE
Saga

China

Poland

Croatia

South Korea

Italy

Czech Republic

Greece

Germany

Japan

Serbia

Finland

Russia

France

Mexico

Brazil

Spain

BKV Fiona, did you anticipate the minor controversy that eventually erupted over your fairly innocuous first cover?

FS As a childless 27-year-old I spent zero time thinking about breastfeeding and had no idea there was a dialogue around it. I thought, "no visible nipple; we're all good" and sent in the cover. Maybe a few people objected to it, but the support we got from mothers was pretty awesome.

BKV It was genuinely unbelievable, as is the fact that your image has now been reproduced almost a million times across multiple printings and over twenty different international editions.

Thanks to our friend Amber Garza, Director of International Licensing at Sequential Rights, for assembling these examples (not to mention negotiating the deals with our global partners!).

As someone who worried we'd likely be cancelled before our second arc, I'll never forget the first time I saw a political protester at a rally holding a banner with your image of Lying Cat on it. When did you first have a sense that *Saga* was connecting with readers?

FS The instant I saw any kind of fanart for it.

BKV Indeed. Hey, you happen to be married to a fellow extraordinary artist/writer. What impact has my best friend Ben Rankel had on *Saga*?

FS Aside from keeping me alive by taking on a disproportionate chunk of household/life responsibilities when I'm on deadline, Ben is my test audience. He reads my comps as soon as they arrive while I sit and creepily observe his reactions.

He is also a talented reference model.

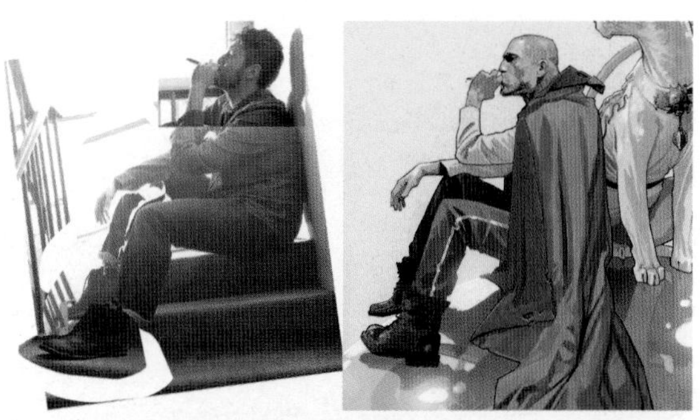

BKV Do you have other favorite memories from the book's first year, or were you too busy working?

FS I had time for signings at some excellent stores—Another Dimension in Calgary, Happy Harbor in Edmonton, and Strange Adventures in Halifax. That kind of support when we only had one or two issues out was huge, because it seemed like the book's momentum snowballed from there.

BKV Any advice for creators considering embarking on their own long-form serialized comic series?

FS Take breaks if you need them. I don't think twelve issues a year, every year, forever is sustainable for most people. So grateful that Image was on board with our breaks between arcs, because Vacationanza is a life-changing gift.

BKV Amen. Speaking of life-changing breaks, have you been playing any good video games during ours?

FS So the best game I played this year is a 1-bit mystery called *Return of the Obra Dinn*. It's the year 1807 and you are an insurance adjuster investigating a ghost ship that's reappeared after being lost at sea. It's incredibly satisfying to gradually uncover the fates of the fifty people who died gruesomely aboard the *Obra Dinn*.

BKV Finally, and most importantly, what kind of candy do you guys give out at Halloween?

FS A wide variety last year, because Ben kept going out and picking up more in case we ran out. We got over 100 kids! Best dressed was the girl in a homemade "box of one dozen donuts" costume.

***

We salute you, Box of One Dozen Donuts Girl, and all of you who dare to bring something new into the world.

Like anything I've ever been a part of that turned out to be life-changing for me, *Saga* emerged from a lot of failure, fear and frustration. So for any creators out there who might feel lost or stuck at the moment, I'd encourage you to just keep making stuff you care about, especially when it's with people you love.

Which is exactly what we intend to do... eventually.

Despite all the endings in this collection, *Saga* isn't over yet. Fiona, Fonografiks, and I look forward to returning with Chapter Fifty-five, as Hazel embarks on a strange new leg of the journey she began way back in that first family portrait.

To be continued,
BKV

BRIAN K. VAUGHAN Along with *Saga*, BKV is the writer and co-creator of *Paper Girls, Y: The Last Man, Runaways, Ex Machina, Pride of Baghdad, We Stand On Guard, The Private Eye,* and most recently *Barrier*, a digital comic about immigration at *PanelSyndicate.com*. His work has been recognized at the Eisner, Harvey, Hugo, Shuster, Eagle, and British Fantasy Awards. Brian sometimes works in film and television in Los Angeles, where he lives with his family and their dogs Hamburger and Milkshake.

FIONA STAPLES *Saga* artist Fiona Staples has been drawing and colouring comics since 2006 and her work has been recognized with multiple Eisner and Harvey awards. She has produced covers, interiors, character designs, and illustrations for clients including Marvel, DC, Archie, Prada, Starz, and Wizards of the Coast. Fiona lives in Calgary, Alberta.

FONOGRAFIKS The banner name for the comics work of designer Steven Finch, 'Fonografiks' has lettered and/or designed a number of Image Comics titles, including the Eisner-nominated *Nowhere Men* and the multi-award-winning anthology series *Popgun*. In addition to his award-winning work on *Saga*, he currently also letters and designs the Image series *Injection, Maestros,* and *Trees*. He lives and works, surrounded by far too many books, in the north east of England.